DANGER
INSIDE THE
BELTWAY

A THRILLER

TERRI GREENING

This is a work of fiction. Names, characters, places, and incidents are products of the author's imagination or are used fictitiously and are not to be construed as real. Any resemblance to actual events, locations, organizations, or persons, living or dead, is entirely coincidental.

World Castle Publishing, LLC
Pensacola, Florida
Copyright © 2024 Terri Greening
Paperback ISBN: 9798891262522
eBook ISBN: 9798891262539
First Edition World Castle Publishing, LLC, August 13, 2024
http://www.worldcastlepublishing.com

Licensing Notes

Cover: Cover Designs by Karen
Cover-designs-by-karen.com
Editor: Karen Fuller

For those who dream.
For those who hope.
And for those who persevere.

CHAPTER 1

Tarryn Blue gazed out the white-gridded windows of the White House Press Briefing Room as she waited for the news conference to begin. It was another brilliant, blue-skied day in Washington, DC, and she was glad to be one of the journalists invited to a reception later in the Rose Garden. She enjoyed being outside on nice days, something she wasn't used to since starting her new job at the *U. S. News Chronicle* a few months ago. Her busy schedule kept her on the move and indoors much of the time. But she didn't mind. She was thrilled to be doing the people's work, covering important stories and keeping the public informed. It was what she'd studied to do at Georgetown, and now she was doing it in this exciting venue. She couldn't believe her luck at securing her dream job right after she graduated with her master's in journalism. That way, she didn't have to return home to Michigan and the family that had broken apart after her parents' divorce. It still saddened her to think about it.

She turned when she heard a familiar voice.

"Hey, Tarryn. Great story last week. Very well-researched. And a byline already? They must think you're a real up-and-comer over there."

Grady Pellington of the Pellington Review sat down next to her in one of the padded, theater-like seats. He reminded her of a sidekick movie actor from the fifties with his slick, dark hair and sleazy grin. She didn't want to talk to him because she preferred to keep to herself, but her editor had told her it was important for her to network and keep her eyes and ears open for future stories.

"Yes, thank you. They put me on an international banking and finance story because I majored in finance as an undergrad," she said, mentioning just enough to impart her background. "I got interviews and quotes, and it all came together."

"Good deal," he said, smiling widely.

She looked away as she tucked a recalcitrant lock of brown hair into the low ponytail she'd tied back with a flowered silk scarf and tried to look professional. It was flattering to receive a compliment from such a well-known reporter, but she didn't want him to get the wrong idea. She had a boyfriend, her wonderful college sweetheart, Todd, although much to his chagrin, she hadn't seen a lot of him lately. Her new job had kept her busy, but luckily, it seemed to be slowing down a bit. She'd finished her article and was only occasionally sharing the political beat with another reporter. Hopefully, she could spend more time with Todd before she got started on another article. They were going to be married as soon as he bought the ring she'd picked out a few months ago.

She pulled a pen out of her purse and sat back with her notebook poised to record answers to the questions she'd written in it and to the ones others asked. Just in time, too. The press secretary stepped in on her high heels, followed by a very good-looking, sandy-haired man in sunglasses. He stopped near the door and put his hands behind his back as she walked over and stood behind the podium. For a moment, it seemed to Tarryn that he was looking straight at her, but then he turned his head. She wondered why he was wearing shades inside and dressed in khakis, but maybe he was undercover for some reason or didn't want to be recognized if a camera panned over to him. That wasn't unusual in DC.

"Not too many questions today, please. There's an unfolding situation that requires my attention," the press secretary said, shaking her red hair back. "Yes, Grady," she continued, pointing at him.

Grady stood. "What are the president's thoughts on the rumors of an economic downturn and possible recession? Is this partisan politics talking, or is this the real deal?"

"Glad you asked that. This is something the White House takes very seriously, and we're working on a solution with our economic advisors. There's nothing to be concerned about at the moment, and we'll keep you posted." She pointed to someone else.

"But..." Grady said.

Before he could continue, another reporter shouted a question, and Grady dropped into his seat and slapped his notebook on his knee.

"Were you referring to my story?" Tarryn leaned over and whispered when it seemed he'd calmed down a bit. She caught a hint of cardamom and supposed he'd slapped on some cheesy aftershave over his slight shadow of a beard.

"Yeah. I'll get more out of her later," he said, "whenever that *World Reporter* guy shuts up. What a loudmouth."

Tarryn nodded. It was cutthroat in the Briefing Room, with everyone vying to ask questions. She wasn't as aggressive as some because she was new and didn't want to ruffle too many feathers. And this was only her second press conference. It seemed to her, though, that the press secretary was avoiding answering questions about the international economy, and she wondered why that would be. Could the article she'd written have something to do with it? She made a note to herself to talk about it with some economic and financial researchers she knew. She was about to try to ask a question herself, but the press secretary suddenly held up her hand and walked over to the man with the sunglasses who seemed to have signaled to her. He cupped his ear with his other hand and appeared to be listening to something through an earpiece. After quickly conferring with him, she returned to the podium.

"No more questions for now. An urgent situation demands my attention. Those of you who are staying for the reception can head out to the rose garden now." She turned and followed the man out of the room amidst a clamor of questions from reporters.

It seemed like an odd thing to do, and Tarryn wondered if there was more to the press secretary's leaving than what she'd said. Maybe it was actually due to a security issue about the information she was relaying, given that the security guard had signaled to her. Or was he from the Secret Service? Anyway, she made a note to herself to check on the reason.

"I wonder what that was all about," Grady said, stuffing his notebook in his pocket. "Hey, do you want to go get something to eat with me? They usually put out quite a spread here."

Tarryn stood and picked up her purse. She didn't want to be rude, but, on the other hand, she didn't want to spend much time with Grady. She had a pretty good idea he wasn't just interested in her professionally with the way he was leaning toward her, and people that tried to get too close to her made her uncomfortable. Sometimes it even brought out a slight stutter she was embarrassed about and tried to avoid. She often wondered if that was why she had turned to writing as her main form of communication.

"Maybe I'll see you out there. I want to talk to somebody first," she said, heading for the ladies' room. She could ditch him there. It wasn't that he was so bad. She was just a very private person and careful about who she shared her thoughts with. And she didn't want to share her thoughts with him. He was too pushy, and she didn't want him using or possibly publishing anything she might say about the international banking scene or the stock market.

She freshened up in the ladies' room, making sure to smooth the wrinkles out of her pale pink sheath dress and adjusting her neutral, kitten-heeled pumps. When she returned, the Briefing Room was nearly empty. She headed outside into the warm, early afternoon sunshine and walked down the white-pillared colonnade to the rose garden, where a number of people were talking and eating delectable-looking scones and pastries. The flowers were beautiful, and the sweet, musky scent of roses wafted through the air.

"Tarryn, you made it," Grady called out, walking toward her.

She cursed her luck. But it was too late to hide. What was she going to do now? He obviously wasn't going to leave her alone. She glanced around. The man with the sunglasses who had been in the press conference was standing by himself near the punch bowl. He appeared very professional and somewhat menacing with his shaded eyes. He looked like he worked out, too. And there was obviously a concealed weapon under a bulging vest. She still got the feeling from the way he glanced at her before scanning the crowd that he was singling her out, but she didn't know why, given that she hardly knew anyone there. Maybe if she squelched her misgivings and stood near him, Grady would stay away. And maybe, if she was discreet, she could find out why the press secretary had left in such a hurry. After all, she was a reporter, and she was supposed to ask questions. She flashed Grady an apologetic smile and hurried over.

"Excuse me," she said. "You're a security guard, aren't you?"

He looked over at her and paused before he answered.

"In a way," he answered and took a sip from his cup.

She wasn't sure what to make of the amusement in his voice, but she didn't have time to figure it out.

"Could I stand next to you for a minute? There's a guy I want to get away from, and I really need your help," she said breathlessly, hoping he would agree, even though she was mortified at having to ask him. He was so handsome he probably had women coming on to him all the time. She hoped he wouldn't get the wrong idea. But that's what a security guard was for, wasn't it? He was supposed to protect people.

He appeared to stare at her from behind his mirrored glasses.

"I wouldn't ask, except my boyfriend isn't here, and I don't know what else to do," she added quickly to fill the awkward silence.

"Sure," he said after a moment. "What's his name?"

"Who?"

"Your boyfriend."

"Oh," she said, feeling even more awkward. "His name's Todd."

Grady came over, and before she could say anymore, she felt a strong arm encircle her waist.

"Let's get out of here, babe," the security guard whispered loudly just as Grady walked up. "There are all sorts of unsavory characters around." He held her to his side in a proprietary embrace.

"Is this man bothering you?" Grady asked, and Tarryn nearly rolled her eyes at the irony. She was even more surprised that the security guard had called her 'babe.'

"Who are you, anyway?" Grady asked.

"Name's Todd. I'm her boyfriend."

Tarryn tried not to blink at what he said. He was really playing along.

"Is that right? What's her name?" Grady asked, sounding suspicious. "I thought I saw you at the press conference."

"Fiancé," Tarryn said quickly before he could answer.

"This is my fiancé, Todd. He works here. Todd, Grady."

Grady stared at him for a moment.

The arm tightened around her waist, and despite herself, she leaned into him, nearly swooning as she felt his muscular chest.

"Yeah, all right. Email me at the Pellington Review if you need any notes from the press conference. I'm in a pool with a few other reporters, and I'd be happy to pass some along," Grady said brusquely. He gave a casual wave and backed away.

Tarryn looked after him before turning back to the security guard, who hadn't let go of her yet.

"Thanks," she said, looking up at him, glad that he'd rescued her. She'd figure out how to explain the situation to others later if it came up. For now, she breathed a sigh of relief as she contemplated him. He had quite a chiseled chin with a little cleft in it, along with a tiny, white scar. She wondered what it was from, but she didn't want to ask him a personal question and risk having him think she was interested in him. He was already holding her pretty close. He was very attractive, but she had Todd to think about. He was attractive, too, in his lawyerly way. "You really saved me," she added, feeling a rush of gratitude and maybe, to her dismay, something more. Perhaps she should ask him a question about the press conference and steer her feelings in another direction. But he started talking to her before she could do that.

"That's what I do," he said, grinning through a very slight shadow of whiskers. She briefly closed her eyes so he wouldn't guess that she wondered if it was smooth or scratchy.

"If you need anything else, call me. He reached into his pocket, still keeping a firm grip on her."

She opened her eyes just as he handed her a business card with an insignia on it. As she took a step back to take the card from him, he released her.

"FBI?" she asked, surprised to see the address on the card. "Special Agent? I thought you were a security guard."

"I'll keep you secure," he said, grinning again.

"Oh. Really," she huffed, turning away from him. She wasn't in the mood to deal with another pass, even though the hard muscles she'd felt while he held her gave her shivers. But he had gotten her out of a tough situation, and she didn't want to get on his bad side in case she needed information from him in the future. She still wanted to find out if the press secretary was in danger for some reason, although she didn't know if he would tell her given that he was FBI and not a security guard. But it might be worth a try some other time. "Thank you for your help," she said over her shoulder.

"Keep in touch," he called after her as she walked away.

"Hey Tarryn, over here," a reporter she'd met at the last press conference called out.

She picked up a cup of punch from the other end of the table and headed over to mingle with the crowd. A few people complimented her on her financial story, and she thanked them, glad she'd made an impact. But something about the press reaction to the story bothered her. She didn't know what it was, and thinking about it tired her out. She sipped her drink. It was a warm day, and the delightfully fizzy pineapple juice punch revived her. She contemplated some more. The questions about the economy that the press secretary had dodged in the Briefing Room also concerned her.

Something was wrong. She liked to keep on top of the economic situation, which was why she was still part of the secret research group she'd belonged to while she was doing her graduate program in journalism at Georgetown. She thought it was funded by a government grant, but she didn't know for sure its specific origin. All she knew was that she could research to her heart's content as long as she shared her findings with the research group, and that was fine with her. She trusted them, and they trusted her. They helped each other out. And they used their findings to better the world and increase economic and financial knowledge in whatever way they could. At least, that was her understanding.

Her interest in the economy started when she was an undergraduate in a business program back home in Michigan and continued when she came to DC. Maybe she'd stop by the research office on her way home. She could say "hi" and see if anyone knew of something unusual going on. She looked up to see Grady standing near some perfectly manicured bushes off to the side, staring at her. He might be even more interested in her than she realized. It seemed like a good time to leave. She said 'goodbye' to the people she was talking to and headed in the other direction. She glanced around, but she didn't see the FBI agent, whose name was Brock Spencer according to his business card, anywhere. Maybe that was for the best, too. She didn't want to end up in another awkward situation with him. She set her punch cup down on the table and made a quick exit.

She took the bus to DuPont Circle and caught the Metro where she slumped in her seat and scrolled through her emails as the train headed toward Foggy Bottom. She noted one from Todd asking her to meet him at one of their college hangouts later. She couldn't wait to see him again. It had been a while, and she missed him. But she had her job, and he had to study for the bar. Despite promising herself she'd let it happen when it happened, she couldn't help wondering if tonight would be the night he popped the question. It could be anytime. It could be this time. Sure, Todd was more of a fancy-dinner, get-on-his-knee traditionalist — a true gentleman, which was one of the things she loved about him — but that didn't mean he was entirely incapable of spontaneity. She smiled to herself.

Her parents liked Todd, and she was sure they would

approve of the marriage. He fit in with the Georgetown crowd, and his parents, who had also graduated from Georgetown, knew people her parents had known. Her father had held a diplomatic post for several years when she was a child, and they had visited Washington often during that time. She hoped it wouldn't be as awkward at the wedding with her parents as it had been at graduation when they didn't sit together. She was pretty sure they wouldn't want to be around each other at the wedding either, although she still wasn't clear about what had caused their marriage to fracture. It probably wasn't any of her business, anyway.

She got off the Metro and took the escalator up to the street. The economic research "lab," as they called it, even though it was just a few floors with a small kitchen and no "lab" at all, was in a nearby brick townhouse. It was where she and other students, various professors, outside advisors, and professionals gathered with their laptops and iPads using an extra-secure server. It was like their own secret society of brain power, accessed by invitation only, that wasn't directly affiliated with any universities or institutions. And yet they did fascinating research. They shared extremely sensitive information, and Tarryn was continuously amazed at the things they found out and came up with together.

Today, she walked past the petunias planted in the small plot of land between the sidewalk and the street and turned down a short path that led to stairs and the front door. A small pot of red geraniums struggled to survive on the landing. She walked in and was immediately greeted with the cool silence of the townhouse. It smelled like dusty wood and coffee.

"Hello? Carla? Paul?"

There was no answer, which was somewhat odd because there was usually someone in the kitchen or in the living area at one of the tables they had set up to play chess, but maybe they were all in the research room on the second floor. She continued up the wooden stairs to find that she was right. Carla, a friend and colleague from another newspaper, was typing furiously at a desk and bobbing her head in time with some tune on her headphones. A few people were reading books in shabby, overstuffed armchairs or lounging on the sofa.

"Hi, guys," she said.

"Tarryn," a few people said, waving and smiling.

Professor Hall, their resident international banking expert and chess club leader, came over to her. He'd answered a difficult question for her about the economy one time for school and saved her hours of studying in the library. And she'd picked up a few killer chess moves from him, too, over the years. A lot of students went to him for help and advice, and he always made time to see them. He'd helped many students navigate the difficult curricula of their respective universities and achieve their degrees. And they'd won more than a few chess tournaments against other clubs because of his excellent instruction. As a result, he'd built up a great deal of goodwill in the research lab, the chess club, and elsewhere.

"Great article," he said, removing his thick, black-framed glasses to look at her. "I'd like to discuss it more in-depth with you. Could we get together and talk when you have the time? I know you're busy with your new job, but there are some points I'd like to go over. How's your stint covering the White House going, by the way? I know a few economic advisors over there. I'd like to talk to them, too. Very interesting analysis."

"Thank you, Professor Hall," Tarryn said, pleased that someone so well-versed in the economy felt that way about her writing. "The job's going fine. I just covered another press conference. I'd certainly enjoy talking one-on-one sometime, and I appreciate your input and the input of everyone here on the research for the article. That's what I came here to talk about." She looked around.

Carla waved and went back to her typing.

"Have you heard any reactions to the article that I might not know about? I'm getting a funny feeling about it, and I don't know where it's coming from."

The professor nodded and put his glasses back on. "I can understand why you feel that way. Upon reading the entire article and your previous analysis of the information, I came to my own conclusion. That's what I'd like to discuss with you. Perhaps we can set up a time later this week. I have a class soon that I need to prepare for."

"Okay, sure," Tarryn said, suddenly wary that she'd made some sort of grave error in her reporting. Visions of having to publish a retraction swam through her mind, and she felt herself flushing in anticipation of the embarrassment. Would the paper fire her? Or was she going to have to spend the next few years rebuilding her credibility with sources when her career had only just gotten started?

Professor Hall went over to a shelf of books near the window where he picked one out and began reading it. She was about to join him and ask him what previous analysis of hers he was referring to but decided to talk to Carla instead. She walked over. Carla stopped typing and took her headphones off when she saw her.

"Hi, Tarryn, what's up?" she said, brightly.

"I just wondered if you wanted to play chess sometime. I haven't played in a while, and I'm looking for a game."

"Sure. I'll text you later this week." Carla said. "I have to finish this paper first. Nice article, by the way," she added, tucking her thick, blond hair behind her ears and putting her headphones back on.

"Thanks," Tarryn said. She looked forward to a game with Carla, the resident chess master. She was really good and made a worthy opponent. Tarryn was known to be a pretty good player herself, but she didn't publicize it. She walked over to Paul and Jamie who were playing chess by the window. They had been in the international finance class she'd fit in last semester amongst her writing classes. Jamie looked up at her when she got there.

"I didn't know our research was going to get put together that way in your article," Jamie said, dimples depending as she grinned. "What a coup. Bet you'll be hobnobbing with the big guys now."

"What do you mean?" Tarryn asked, keeping her voice low so as not to interrupt Paul's concentration on the game.

"Only that people are going to want to find out more about you now that you've been published. You didn't tell anyone about the research lab, did you?" Her eyebrows furrowed slightly.

"What? Well, no," Tarryn stammered. "Of course, I kept it a secret. Why?" Was there a hint of fear in Jamie's expression?

"No reason. I just wondered," Jamie said. The dimples returned.

"Yeah, great writing," Paul added after placing his knight in front of a pawn. "I'm looking forward to reading what you write next. Great stuff, especially about the fluctuations of the rates of return in the stock market over time. Let me know if I can help in any way."

"Thanks," Tarryn said. "I'll let you know." But she wasn't sure if she would. He was smart, but he was better at chess than finance.

She was glad Paul and Jamie didn't seem to think anything was upsetting about the article, but the conversation had left her more unsettled than Professor Hall's suggestion that they have a "discussion." Of course, she'd kept the lab a secret, but why was Jamie worried about it? Did it have to do with fear that political pundits commenting on the article might express agreement or disagreement with their economic work based on their political leanings? Or was she more likely afraid that the source of funding for the lab could be leaked? There were rumors that it was funded by the National Security Agency (NSA) who didn't want the research or its backing known, and that's why secrecy was so important. If it was and that fact was exposed to the public, the lab could be scrapped, and they'd no longer be able to do research together. It didn't bother Tarryn where the money came from. She just wanted to do research. But maybe it would bother other people, and maybe the NSA would shut down the lab if there was a risk of it being exposed. She made a note to try to find out more at another time. For now, she needed to get back to the off-campus apartment she had rented for the summer and prepare for her date with Todd. She scheduled a chess game later in the week with Paul before saying goodbye and heading down the staircase. As she reached the last step, she decided she was worrying for no reason. Her article had gotten people talking, and that was what she wanted, wasn't it? To influence the public conversation?

Feeling surer of herself, she exited onto the sidewalk and waited for a taxi to pass before crossing the street. Maybe the article's positive reception among her colleagues at the lab was a sign that she should be bold in other areas of her life, too. Maybe instead of waiting for Todd to propose, she'd...

Without warning, a black Mercedes screeched past her, reached the intersection, and whipped through the turn. Where did it come from, out of nowhere? Had the driver been waiting for her? Watching her? It suddenly hit her that someone could have recognized her because of all the hype about her article. If it hadn't been well-received by everyone, maybe Jamie's concerns about secrecy were even more appropriate. She glanced behind her at the second-floor windows. The white curtains gave the appearance of a residence with no hint of the presence of the lab. She glanced back down the street and saw no indication of the car. How silly of her. It was probably just someone late for class.

She shook her head and started for home.

CHAPTER 2

Brock Spencer strolled down Pennsylvania Avenue, heading for his favorite restaurant after a long day at the White House. A number of very urgent situations had arisen recently, including one involving a potential banking crisis that had everyone on edge. Because of that, he'd been bombarded with a great deal of detailed information about the economy, much of which he didn't fully comprehend, and he needed to relax and take it all in.

From what he'd gathered in a meeting he'd sat in on with the press secretary and members of the Cabinet, a recent article had hinted at financial instability, which had frightened the public and led to fears of a panic and a run on the banks. There were even fears of a stock market crash due to the discovery of possible shell firms with dubious origins being used to obscure trades and financial transactions. These transactions could all be on paper and not a reflection of actual cash flow which meant people could be being led astray as to where their money was, if it was anywhere. Unauthorized investment firms catering to wealthy clients and promising attractive rates of return had also been uncovered. All of these companies seemed to lead back to the same source. If the source ever took these shady companies out of business or they simply ceased to exist, the resulting adjustments could send ripples through the US economy as consumers and the government realized they were unable to access their money. The question many of those in the Cabinet asked was who was doing this and why and how dangerous would they be if they feared discovery because of the article. It was possible that someone was making a lot of money at the expense of a lot of people. But they didn't know how.

In the meantime, Brock had been assigned to shadow the press secretary, who had to comment on the controversial article, and to dig into the story's background and find the sources of the journalist who'd written it. It seemed it had made some very powerful people very upset. He wasn't thrilled with the assignment, which, for one thing, he'd been pegged with at the last minute, leaving him unable to dash home from the field office and dress the part. He was winging it in his khaki chinos instead. Shadowing the White House press secretary was fine, but getting stuck with the grunt work of pulling up information on a story by a newbie journalist, no one had ever heard of was ego-shattering. But he swallowed his pride and agreed to do what he'd been asked to do.

He'd imagined Tarryn Blue, the journalist who'd written the story, to be some stuffy economic wizard who kept her head buried in a book. However, the attractive thumbnail image of her on the Internet had made him wonder if he was wrong. He'd planned to find her and come up with a story that gave him a valid reason to be around her without revealing his identity. The news conference had started before he had a chance to do that, but he'd glimpsed her scribbling notes in the crowd.

As it turned out, the deception wasn't necessary anyway after she ran to him for help at the reception in the Rose Garden. Now she knew who he was, although she didn't know he was assigned to find out who her sources were. But that didn't matter. He could keep that a secret. It didn't seem like that was something she'd be happy about.

He smiled when he thought of the light scent she wore that he'd caught a whiff of when he pulled her to his chest in the

Rose Garden. Was it gardenia or maybe jasmine? He wouldn't mind experiencing that heady feeling again. He wondered if she really had a boyfriend or had just been using that as a ruse to get away from the jerk at the reception. He hoped she didn't, for some reason. He wasn't sure why. Or maybe he did know why and didn't want to admit it. She hadn't turned out to be the stuffy bookworm he'd imagined at all. She was very alluring. But he needed to keep things professional if he was going to do his job right. Even though he wasn't officially investigating her personally, socializing with her was still a gray area, given that she'd written the story. And he wanted to do his job right, even if the menial tasks were beneath his pay scale.

He reached the restaurant and stepped into the cool, dim atmosphere of the bar, where he ordered a scotch straight up. He needed it after the day he'd had. He thought he'd have a drink and maybe a burger before heading back to his apartment near Capitol Hill. Mickey, the usual bartender, pulled a couple drafts and sent them down the counter before setting the scotch in front of him.

"So, what's happening in the high echelons?" Mickey asked, good-naturedly, grinning through his short, brown beard and wiping his hands on his apron.

That was how he typically referred to Brock's government job.

"Couple of senators came in earlier, but they kept to themselves in a corner booth. I didn't get much of a lowdown yet today," Mickey continued.

In Brock's experience, bartenders often witnessed people — even seasoned politicians who should know better — at their most loose-tongued, and Brock had learned quite a few secrets swirling around Washington from him.

"Same old, same old," he said, answering Mickey's original question and leaning his elbows on the polished wood counter.

He took a sip of scotch.

The enticing smell of french fries and beer reminded him that he was hungry. He hadn't had much to eat since the reception earlier that day. He'd have to remedy that soon. But first, he savored the scotch for a moment, enjoying its smoky warmth and contemplating whether to say more. Mickey was good at giving advice, but he didn't always keep confidences, so he was careful about what he told him. Much of Mickey's charm was in his storytelling nature, which kept Brock and seemingly others coming back to the bar to find out what was happening. But Brock preferred to be on the receiving end of the stories and not part of them. Mickey didn't even know he was FBI. He thought Brock had a desk job. But today, Brock needed to tell someone about the girl he'd met.

"Hey, Mickey, what would you do if a beautiful woman threw herself at you, but she already had a boyfriend?" he asked. "Would you go after her anyway or back off?"

Maybe Tarryn hadn't *thrown herself* at him, but it didn't hurt to embellish the facts a little bit. He didn't have a whole lot of experience dealing with women, and he didn't want to be obvious about it. He supposed the reason had to do with keeping people at a distance. He'd learned to do that as a kid to protect himself from being emotionally hurt by his erratic father, who he'd loved desperately. His father had loved him, too. Brock knew that. But he'd been so caught up in his own problems he didn't really understand other people's feelings. Brock suffered because of it. He had wanted his father's understanding. And when he didn't get it, he put up a wall. His girlfriend in college thought he didn't like her because he was so distant and broke up with him even though he'd tried to explain that it wasn't her. He didn't want that to happen again. It had hurt him a lot. Being misunderstood made him feel like an emotionally abandoned child again, and the only way to keep that from happening was to maintain a suitable distance from people, especially women.

"Just a second," Mickey said, turning and pulling a draft for someone.

Brock sipped his scotch and thought about Tarryn as he watched Mickey wait on a few customers at the other end of the counter. He wondered what she was like outside of work. But he didn't have the nerve to ask her out. He'd stick to investigating the background of the story and keeping things professional. That seemed like the safest way to go.

A well-dressed woman sitting a few chairs down from him at the counter smiled at him, and he smiled back but looked away quickly. He didn't often talk to women at the bar, even though people usually assumed he got around for some reason. He'd been told in jest by a colleague that it was because of his dreamy blue eyes and chiseled chin, although she'd made no mention of the small scar on it. That was fine with him because he preferred not to talk about it or its grim origin. But the truth was, he was by himself most of the time and not just because of his painful past. Due to the nature of his job, it was easier and safer to keep to himself and not trust too many people. He had a bit of a reputation as a hardnose at work because of it, although he really wasn't. At least, he didn't think so.

"Oh, man, not a bad problem to have," Mickey said, returning to his spot in front of Brock. He dried a glass mug with a towel and set it on the counter. "Is she someone from work?"

"Yeah," he answered. "You could say that. She's radiant. I've never met anyone like her."

"Well," Mickey said, dropping the towel and combing his fingers through his beard. "Here's what you want to do. You probably already know, but let me reinforce it." He put his hands on the counter and leaned forward. "You go after her."

"What? Really?" Brock asked, surprised that Mickey was so adamant.

"Yeah, really. Otherwise, you'll never know if things could have worked out, and not knowing is worse than finding out one way or the other."

"You sure?"

"I'm sure," Mickey said. "I let my angel, Marlene, go, and she married someone else. She used to wait tables here. I never found out if I would have had a chance with her. Here I am now, just me and the bar, wondering if I could have had her with me. I'll always wonder. You gotta find out, man."

Brock took in his sorrowful expression. "Thanks," he said. "Sorry, that happened to you. You could be right." His stomach growled. "You got any beer nuts or anything?"

"Yeah, just a second," Mickey said, turning to wait on someone else.

Brock took another sip of scotch and glanced around, taking in the maroon cushioned bar stools and the stained-glass hanging lights that cast a dim glow over the polished wood tables and booths of the bar. It was still relatively early for the dinner crowd, but a few people straggled in. One of them looked over his head and pointed. Brock turned back around and sucked in a breath when he saw the featured story on the news channel streaming behind the bar. Mickey set the beer nuts down in front of him.

"Mind turning it up?" Brock asked.

"Sure," Mickey said, reaching for the remote.

A news anchor reported the story.

"Billionaire Leo Harrington was spotted at a New York auction yesterday walking away with a contemporary piece of art for which he reportedly bid $500,000," he said, while a video played of a tall, dark-haired man in an Armani suit leaving a skyscraper with two other men. "This could quell rumors about the financial health of the Harrington hedge fund, which is known for its wealthy, often famous investors. The hedge fund was mentioned in a bleak financial analysis in the U. S. News Chronicle last week along with several other investment instruments and institutions."

"You can mute it again if you want," Brock said, when the reporter went on to talk about other things. "That's all I wanted to see."

"Do you know him?" Mickey asked, muting the TV. "I don't know what kind of guy would drop a half mil on a painting."

"Yeah, really," Brock said, agreeably. He did know of people who spent that kind of money — and far more — on art. His degree in art history had opened the world of art and art commerce to him. But he didn't mention that now. He wanted to stay low-key about his background. "I don't know him, but I've heard he's pretty flush and has homes in France and Italy as well as the U.S."

"That's not all," Mickey said, dropping his voice. "He may have recently plunked down some cash for a mansion in Georgetown. Rumor is he's bankrolling a relative running for Congress soon."

"No kidding?" Brock asked. "Who told you that?"

"Oh, I can't tell you that. I have to keep my sources close to the vest, you know, or no one will tell me anything."

"Right, right," Brock said, smiling. He'd wait it out. Mickey would probably let it slip sooner or later.

Harrington was obviously rolling in it if he paid cash for a mansion in Georgetown. The ones he'd been in for political fundraising parties with his grandmother, who lived across the Potomac River in Virginia, were nice — nicer than the apartment he crashed in any way. But most places were. They were homier anyway. He didn't like to be there because he hadn't decorated it much although it did have a nice view of the district from his balcony, but it was lonely. He didn't know many people. Most of his fellow renters were government staff who worked all day or newly minted congressmen and women who headed back to their districts when Congress was no longer in session. Some of them had little kids they pushed on the swings in the small playground area set up in back. He smiled when he thought of it. Maybe someday he'd have children if he found the right woman. He liked kids, and if he had a chance to have a happy family, he'd give it a try.

"And I know about the article he was mentioned in," Brock added after a moment.

"Doesn't everybody?" Mickey asked. "I'm a little queasy about my 401K after hearing all the hype lately about a financial collapse."

"Did you read the article the anchor mentioned in the Chronicle?" Brock asked.

"Yeah, I keep up on things," Mickey said. "I have to know what's going on in the world with the clientele we get in here."

"I suppose that's true," Brock said. He turned when he felt a tap on his shoulder.

"What'd you think of the press conference?" A man with curly blond hair and a neatly trimmed mustache stood behind him, a pint glass in one hand. "I saw you walk in there when I left to go to the Hill."

Riley Keagan was an economic advisor to the President. Brock knew him from when they went to college together out east. Most people were surprised to find out he himself was Ivy League, so he usually kept that part of his background quiet even though a lot of people in DC had prestigious degrees. He'd had to go through a lot to get there, and he didn't like being put on the defensive about it by people who thought he was putting on airs. There were also those who thought he got in because of his grandfather's endowment to the university. He didn't think that was true, although his last name probably hadn't hurt anything.

"Hey, Riley. It was good but short," he said. Riley was the

kind of guy who *would* keep a confidence — and who very well might have insight into what was causing the economic fears. "Can we get together sometime and talk about it?"

"Sure," Riley said. "I'm here for dinner with the economic club, but I'm up for another time if you want."

"I'll call you," Brock said, raising his glass as Riley walked away.

He gulped the last of his drink and stood up.

"Leaving already?" Mickey asked. "Happy hour isn't even over yet."

"Yeah. Put it on my tab. You got me thinking. I have to go see a girl," he answered, grinning.

Mickey smiled. "You do that," he said, lifting the glass and polishing the counter. "Let me know how it goes."

Brock gave a backwards wave and left. He put on his sunglasses as he stepped outside into the warm, late afternoon air and walked across the street to catch the bus toward Georgetown. He preferred the convenience of DC's mass transit system over driving and usually kept his car parked at his apartment in the Capitol Hill district. He knew Tarryn's address, and it might be a good idea to check on her, even if that wasn't officially part of his job. If the TV news was picking up the story, it was probably all over the Internet by now, too. There could be people who didn't have her best interests at heart looking for her. It wouldn't bother him to see her again, either. He was glad it wasn't a long ride because he was still hungry. There were a few good places in Georgetown where he could grab a quick bite after he made sure she was safe.

As the bus headed through town, his phone pinged. It was a text from his brother, Stu, in Detroit asking him to call him when he got out of work. He would. It was always good to hear from family back home. He and his brother had been through a lot together, and Brock trusted him as he did few other people.

They'd had each other's backs at the rough, local school they'd attended until their father died, and their grandfather stepped in to pay for a private prep school for them both. Their loyalty to each other had stuck with them into adulthood.

Not many people knew that he'd grown up in the inner city. Those that did attributed his street smarts and the toughness that he seldom showed to it. He could be tough when it came to criminals, criminals like the ones who had beaten his father dead over a stupid gambling debt. He often wondered if the reason he'd gone into law enforcement was so he could arrest guys like that and put them away. It probably was.

It was also probably why he shied away from advertising his roots. His wealthy grandfather had disinherited his father for a similar reason to gambling but on a much larger scale. His father had lost all his money in the stock market in a shady deal, and his grandfather refused to give him any more despite his grandmother's objections. That was why his father turned to a life of petty crime and gambling that had devastated their mother and their family and eventually gotten him killed.

Brock's father hadn't been perfect. Brock had learned that early on. But the true lesson Brock learned from his father was that family legacy was a trap — something that made you think you were immune to life's hardships, but only left you to drown when the safety net used to control you was yanked away. Ever since, he'd determined that whether he succeeded or failed in life, he'd rely on himself.

When he got to the stop, he headed to Tarryn's place. It was a typical off-campus townhouse, three-floors, red-brick. He didn't notice anything out of the ordinary when he neared it. But he stopped and ducked behind a tree when he saw her come out of the door and turn to lock it. She looked completely different than she had earlier. Her hair was down and pleasantly tousled, and she wore jeans and a sleeveless top. She looked young and fresh and surprisingly casual, not at all like the cool professional beauty he'd seen earlier. There were obviously more sides to her, and he wondered what they were. He watched to see where she was going while pretending to scroll through his phone in case anyone was watching him.

She headed down the stairs and walked toward the far corner where her street met the one lined with shops and eateries for the college students. When she turned left, he slid his phone back into his pocket and followed her. He reached the corner in time to see her disappear into "The Purple Pen," a local hangout. He crossed diagonal to the crosswalk and headed for a pizza joint where he could manage surveillance and wait for her to come out. Just before he walked in, a man nearby ran across the street, yanked open the door to "The Purple Pen," and pulled Tarryn into his arms. The door slammed shut behind him.

Brock did a quick pivot. Who could that be? One of her sources? It was possible, although his actions seemed overly familiar if he was. It might be a good idea to check it out. He zigzagged through the slow-moving cars to cross the street and jerked open the door of the restaurant. She was laughing and walking toward a booth in the back with the man he'd seen. She obviously knew him and wasn't afraid. It could be a source or the boyfriend she mentioned. He looked around quickly and made a plan. If he sat at a table by the antique jukebox, he could stay out of sight and watch them. He ambled over and sat down, ordering a burger and a coke when the waitress came by.

From his vantage point, he noted their movements. Plainly, from the way Tarryn was giggling and leaning toward him, they were an item. He must be the boyfriend she mentioned, but he wondered what she saw in him. He looked kind of weaselly. And Brock thought he was better looking than the guy was, too, which wasn't saying much, but still.

By the time the burger arrived, Brock was starving. He

dug in, thankful for the respite from his semi-stake-out. All she was doing was making googly eyes at her probable boyfriend, and it was bugging him. He stuffed some fries in his mouth and scrolled through the emails on his phone, checking a few interesting ones. Nothing that couldn't wait until morning. But he did text his brother, Stu, back and tell him he was fine but to keep an eye on the stock market if he had any heavy investments. He took another bite of his burger and sipped his coke. He'd wait it out here until they left.

CHAPTER 3

Tarryn sat across from Todd in the booth at the Purple Pen and giggled again at the punch line of the lawyer joke he'd told her. He was so silly sometimes. But that was one of the reasons she loved him, that and his easygoing personality and adorable dimples. No matter what was bothering her, even her new, as yet unexpressed fears about possible fallout from the article and about the car that had peeled out at the research lab, he always made her feel better.

"Thanks. I needed that," she said. "I haven't laughed for a while because of all the work I've been doing. It feels good."

She glanced around at the mostly empty wood tables and chairs, glad that the restaurant was sparsely populated. That way, they could concentrate on each other without interruptions. Most of the students had left for the summer and wouldn't return until classes began again in the fall. She tapped her foot in time to the low beat of a familiar love song.

"Yeah, I can imagine," Todd said when she looked back at him.

She lost herself in the deep green pools of his eyes. She'd missed those eyes and the way they drew her to him. She had been so looking forward to seeing him again after finishing the article. And now she could. Their reunion was everything she'd hoped for. She hoped Todd felt the same way and would propose because of it. The children they eventually had would surely have his beautiful eyes. She couldn't wait to start her new life with him.

Todd's voice was as smooth and comforting as it had always been, although a little more hesitant than usual. He was good at talking, especially at persuading people, which he'd shown when he insisted she pick out a ring a few months ago. He wouldn't let her say "no" to him, not that she'd wanted to. They were a perfect pair, really. He told jokes, and she laughed at them. It wouldn't be a bad way to start a marriage. Maybe he actually would ask her to marry him tonight. It sounded like it. He'd been so adamant in his text about getting together and had told her again how much he'd missed her. And he'd hugged her as though he'd never see her again when he came in the door. Maybe he'd picked up the ring. Maybe it was in his pocket right now. She smiled. It was nice to be with him again after their weeks apart. Her article had taken up so much time, and now that it was done and published, she could spend more time with him, something he'd been asking for a lot lately.

"I'm so glad to see you," she said.

"I'm glad to see you, too," he said. "It's been so hard being away from you." He frowned. "The fern dried out. I forgot to water it. You're the only one that ever did." He looked down and rubbed his face with his hands.

Tarryn didn't know what to say for a moment. This was an emotional side to him she hadn't seen before. Maybe she should have. He was usually cool in a way that made it seem like he was ready to walk into a courtroom, but he didn't look cool now. Had he kept his emotions from her? She searched his face, taking in the haggard lines and sallow cheeks she hadn't noticed before. She suddenly wondered if she hadn't been paying enough attention to their relationship. She had just assumed they were in a good place because she'd picked out the ring. And she thought he understood her work issues because he was busy, too. He'd even told her he was happy for her when she got the job.

"I'm sorry, Todd. I really am. It's not just the fern, is it? I didn't know our distance from each other affected you so much. I had to finish the article. If things keep going the way they are, the stock market could crash soon, and a lot of people could lose a lot of money."

He nodded slowly. "I know. I read your article." He paused before continuing. "You didn't say you missed me," he said, quietly.

"I missed you. I did. But I had to finish my story. You understand, don't you, how important the article was?"

"I do," he said. "I really do, and I'm glad you wrote it. But that doesn't change how difficult it was being away from you and not hearing from you very often. I don't know why you couldn't fit me into your busy schedule somewhere."

He brushed his cheek. Did she see a tear? That was so unlike him. He was usually so logical and matter of fact. She hurried to explain.

"You're right, of course. It's just that my new job is so important to me. I can finally tell the people the things they need to know. I have a voice now because I'm being published. I'm being listened to. It's something I've wanted all my life."

He looked away, and she hurried to continue.

"I didn't mean to hurt your feelings. Really, I didn't. I'm sorry. But to be completely fair, every time I called you, you were busy. You only wanted to see me when you had time, and that didn't work on my schedule. I felt bad a lot of times, too." She paused for a moment, remembering the last she'd called. He'd been in a hurry and said he'd call her back but didn't. "It's all behind us now, anyway," she said, trying to forget how devastated she'd been.

He didn't answer.

"Isn't it?" she asked.

For some reason, she felt wary. What happened to the happy-go-lucky guy she knew him to be? A slow, country song wailed from the antique jukebox, and Tarryn listened for a moment as she tried to think of what to say.

"Why don't you come over and see my new place tonight? We could be alone and…" She was going to say "celebrate" or something more intimate, but he hadn't asked her to marry him yet, so she said something else. "I mean, how's studying for the bar exam going?" she asked instead, trying to put a lilt in her voice as she quickly changed the subject.

"Good," he answered. "But boring. I do a little at a time when I can."

"I suppose it would be. That's a good way to do it," she said, keeping her eyes on him. Something wasn't right. "You know, the reason I called last time was to tell you I reserved a ballroom at the hotel downtown for the reception. If you hadn't been in such a hurry, I would have told you."

He paused. "Again? You did something like that all by yourself again that we should have done together?" He shook his head. "That's sort of what I wanted to talk to you about," he said, combing his fingers through his dark bangs and smoothing them back.

"What is?" she asked, tilting her head.

She didn't really want to talk about the bar exam. She wanted to steer the conversation toward their impending marriage. But it seemed he had other ideas.

"Nothing." He took his hand down and looked at her. "I have an opportunity to be a law clerk for a Circuit Court judge out east while I try to pass the bar."

"Really? That's great. But don't you mean after you pass the bar?" she asked, wondering why he sounded upset.

She sat back when the waiter brought over the frosty mugs of root beer they'd ordered. He set them on the table and left.

"No. I mean before. The job's open now. I'm taking it, Tarryn," Todd said.

"What?" she asked. Her cheeks numbed as she tried to hold onto some semblance of a smile. "Taking what?"

"The job," he said, leaning forward and ignoring the root beer. "I would have told you sooner, but you haven't been around. I start in a few weeks."

Her heart dropped, literally dropped. It sank into her stomach and punched her in the gut.

"I don't understand," she stammered. "You can't. We're getting married. You can't leave. You can't leave me now."

It didn't seem real. How could they make wedding plans if he left? His face blurred in front of her.

"I have to leave. Things haven't worked out the way I thought they would here. I need a new start, and this job is it." He looked down at the table. "I'm sorry."

"Wait. Okay. Maybe we can make plans long distance. Other people do it. Then, when you come back, I'll have everything set. That would work," she said, making new plans in her head. "Plus, if we wait, we can get the church that wasn't available this summer." She nodded and tapped her lips. She could see this happening.

"No, Tarryn," he said.

"Why?" she asked, suddenly hoping he wouldn't tell her. "Or I could come with you," she added. She kicked herself. Who was she kidding? She wasn't going to leave Washington and her new job. But she was desperate. She looked into his eyes and knew it was too late.

"I don't want to get married anymore," he said quietly. "It's over."

"No. It can't be. You bought the ring. You told me you wanted to propose. That's w-why we're here," she said, startled to hear the light stutter she thought she'd lost as a child. She'd worked her whole life to overcome it and to communicate effectively through speech and writing.

"No, it isn't. We're here because I wanted to tell you in person," he said.

"This can't be happening," she said, looking down at the table. She looked back up at him. "Why? Is it because of the story? The story's done."

"It's not just the story. It's the whole thing. I love your passion for your work. It makes you who you are, and I love that about you. But I can't deal with that anymore. You're too...moral. I need more from a relationship than you're willing to give me."

"Too *moral*? How can someone be too moral?" She spoke slowly to counteract the stutter even though her thoughts were racing. She tilted her head as she tried to understand. "Is there some reason you don't want me to have morals?" she asked, wondering if he felt guilty about something.

"I don't know. Maybe. It's just that you don't have to save the world with your writing. It's not up to you to do that. I need someone who puts me first. I'm sorry," he said.

He sounded cold and distant. It was so unlike him. He wasn't overly emotional, but he wasn't aloof either. He was just Todd. But he didn't seem like Todd anymore.

"Okay, I won't be moral anymore," she said, cringing at the desperation in her voice. "Please don't leave me. I'll do something else," she said, even though she knew she wasn't going to do "something else." Writing was her life. And it was the one true way she could express herself effectively. But she'd say anything at the moment to stop what was happening. She couldn't bear to think of losing Todd and the marriage she'd been so looking forward to.

"No. It's not just that. You think you're so smart and that you can do everything by yourself, and you can't," he said. "You didn't even ask me about the ballroom for the reception. You went ahead and did it without even checking with me first. Don't I have a say in anything you do that involves both of us?"

The derogatory words sideswiped her ego and bruised her soul. "What? Of course, you do. What do you mean?" she asked. "You never called me back, so I went ahead and reserved it. What's wrong with that? I thought you'd be happy I found a place that was still available." There must be something more that he wasn't telling her. He hadn't berated her before for being smart and ambitious, and independent. He used to admire those things about her. What could have changed?

"Everyone needs people, Tarryn. You can't do everything on your own all the time and expect things to work out with people."

"Work out with people? Like whom? You?" She looked at his set chin and squinted as she raised her eyes and focused on his face. "I said I was sorry I hadn't spent more time with you lately. Can't you forgive me?" she asked, heartbroken at his words. She paused at the thought of something. "Is there someone else?" she asked.

He flinched and stood up. "I'd better go," he said, tossing a twenty on the table next to the untouched drinks.

"Wait. I love you. You can't just go," she said, choking through a sob.

"Yeah, I can," he said. "I mean." He paused and looked at her for a moment as she put her hand to her mouth to stifle her cries. His face softened. She reached for him, but he didn't reach back. "I have to, Tarryn. For me. It's too hard to be without you so much. I can't deal with it happening over and over again, which it will if I don't just end things now." He turned. "See ya," he said quietly. And he walked through the restaurant and out the door.

She sat still, staring after him until the door closed behind him. He was gone. It wasn't possible. Everything she'd planned for with him had ended, and she hadn't even seen it coming. She grabbed her stomach and groaned. The pain was unbearable. She slid out of the booth and stumbled toward the bathroom, barely making it inside and locking the door before she gave in to the paroxysms of grief that racked her body with nausea. When it was over, she sat back on the cold floor and leaned her head against the wall. It felt like the end of the world. And she had thought the evening would be the best one of her life.

After a while, she grabbed the purple-themed sink that mirrored the deep bruise in her soul and pulled herself to her feet. She stood up slowly and rinsed out her mouth before shuffling out the bathroom door. Somehow, she made it through the restaurant and out onto the street. It was warm still, not having cooled off yet for the evening. A black car idled near the corner, windows up.

Tarryn wandered, at first not sure where she was going. Gradually, she realized she had meandered near the park, where she often went to think and relax. She'd come here often after her mom called and told her her dad had moved out of the house, and they were getting divorced. It had calmed her. She needed that now more than ever.

She sat in her favorite spot on the wide, slabbed steps next to the water and gazed out over the Potomac. The pale blue and purple reflections of early twilight shimmered on the surface, and the lights on the Key Bridge glowed in the distance. Something about the history and the beauty of the place grounded her. This was a place and time of great importance. It made her feel real and worthwhile to be there, something she especially needed after hearing Todd's hurtful words.

What was she going to do now? He wouldn't be around anymore to make plans for the future with. What had happened to the funny, warm, and smart man she'd fallen in love with? And what about the family they were going to have and the home?

How could that all be gone? And all because she was pursuing her dreams? It didn't make sense. How could he love her but not accept her for the writer she was? It was too much to take in. She dropped her head into her hands.

"Hello, little lady," a deep voice said.

She jerked her head up to see a man with a pockmarked face in a dark trench coat standing next to her on the step above the one she was sitting on. It struck her that the coat was an odd thing to wear on a warm evening. And she didn't know where he came from, either. She almost stood and ran, but the vibrating tenor of his voice mesmerized her. And she stayed still.

"Who are you?" she asked. The hairs on the back of her neck stood up. He smelled like sweat and chewing gum.

"That doesn't matter," he said.

She caught the hint of an accent, but she didn't know where from. His left hand moved inside his pocket. He had a gun, or at least seemed to. She pulled back.

He chuckled.

"You're not scared, are you?" he asked. "No need to be. I'm only here to relay a message. If you listen to it, you will be fine. I suggest that you do that. Stay away from the investment story. Do not write about it. Do not talk about it. It does not exist for you. Do you understand?"

She nodded, biting her lip nervously. He obviously knew who she was, and that terrified her.

"Good. Then we're done here," he said.

He turned and walked down a path heading away from the river. She followed him with her eyes and swallowed hard. Her body stiffened. She wondered if this was what 'shock' felt like. Before she could catch her breath, a man darted by and ran after the man in the trench coat. He looked familiar, but she couldn't tell who he was in the dim light. The man in the trench coat looked back and took off running. She jumped up in spite of herself and watched with her hand over her mouth until they disappeared in the distance. What was going on? Who were these people? It was time to leave. She hurried up the steps and down the path but stopped when she saw the man who'd run by her nearing her from the other direction. He was tall and muscular and strode with the gait of someone who was used to being in charge. As he stepped out from the shadows into the glow of a streetlamp, she gasped. It was Brock Spencer.

"What are you doing here?" she asked, almost as frightened of him as she had been of the man in the trench coat. "Were you following me?"

"Relax. It's okay," he said, stopping abruptly and raising his hands, palms out.

She looked at him across the gap between them.

"He threatened you," he said. "I heard him. If he'd tried anything else, he'd be in bad shape now."

"Bad shape? What do you mean? What are you doing here?" she asked again, her voice rising.

He paused as though considering his answer. "I, um, see a girl who goes to Georgetown for the summer session. I walked her to her door this evening and came here afterwards. I was walking down the path when you sat on the steps, and I heard that guy threaten you when I walked by. So, I went after him, that's all. It was a fortunate coincidence that I was here. I'd hate to think what could have happened otherwise."

She wondered why it seemed he changed the subject away from his date so quickly. "I see," she said, frowning. "What's her name?"

"Who's name?"

"The name of the girl you're seeing," she replied. "Maybe I know her."

"Oh. Her name's Buffy."

"Buffy Cameron?"

"No. She's just a girl taking a class here for the summer," he said, staring directly at her.

"You said that," Tarryn said, staring back at him. His unwavering gaze seemed sincere. "Oh, well, a lot of people go here," she said, brushing it off. He was right that it was fortunate he'd been around. "Anyway, I wonder why that guy threatened me. I don't even know him."

"You're a public figure now, Tarryn," Brock said. "People you don't want to talk to may want to talk to you even if you don't want them to like that guy. He gestured toward the far trees where the man who threatened her had gone. "It's time you realized that."

She paused and took in what he said. How could her whole world change so drastically because of one story? Todd left, and now her life was in danger? At least it sounded like that. It was mind-boggling.

"Okay, well, thank you," she said, thinking that was the appropriate thing to say to someone who had probably just saved her life. "I had no idea. It's nice to know there are knights in shining armor around when you need them," she continued, smiling slightly.

"Well, I don't know about that," he said. "But I am glad I was here."

She swallowed hard. Was it gratitude she felt or something more. He *had* just rescued her, and that made her feel like she mattered to someone even though she no longer mattered to Todd. The delicious shivers she'd gotten while in his embrace at the reception returned.

"Come with me," he said, motioning to her. "We need to get out of here."

She hesitated. She wanted to, but should she trust him?

"Please," he continued. "We need to get out of here now in case he comes back."

She decided not to put up an argument. She was too scared, and it was getting dark. She moved toward him, then walked with him down the path and out of the park.

"I'll walk you home," he said. "Do you have a roommate?"

She glanced at him quickly before deciding to answer. "No. I just moved into a furnished apartment for the summer," she said, pulling away a bit. "Why?"

"Hmm. I don't think you should be alone tonight," he said. "Not with a guy like that around. I want to keep an eye on you until all this dies down, whenever that is."

She shivered again.

"Are you cold?" he asked, sounding surprised. "It's still pretty warm out."

He put his arm around her as they walked. His body was hard and taut. She leaned into him and felt the distinct outline of a gun. He must have a holster under the vest he wore over his shirt.

"Who do you think it was?" she asked, looking up at him.

"The man in the park?" he asked.

"Yes."

"Hard to say, but it was probably someone that read your article," Brock answered. "You'll need to be more careful."

She glanced up quickly, surprised at his brisk tone of voice.

"Sorry. I didn't mean that to sound condescending," he said, in a softer voice, "but you've obviously uncovered something upsetting with your article, and it's more than just the revelation of an economic downturn. I don't know what it is."

"Yeah. Professor Hall said something like that," she said to herself.

"Who?" he asked.

She'd obviously said it out loud.

"Oh, just someone I studied with," she answered. "He was helpful with some basic economic research I based a financial thesis on."

"Well, he's right. You do need to be careful," Brock said.

They walked past bustling restaurants and bars and turned the corner onto the quiet residential street she lived on. As they neared her apartment, the tension grew between them. She could feel it, and it wasn't just her own fear of what was happening around her after the story was published. It was something kinetic, something rising and real.

"I don't know what to do," she said when they got there, feeling awkward as they stood silently together. She wanted Brock to stay around, if only to lessen the loneliness she felt after the break-up with Todd. She needed someone, and Brock was there. The silence continued, and the heat rose between them. It wasn't just her. She was sure of that. But she wasn't sure she was ready to do anything about it now. Then again, maybe. His sand-colored hair blew in the slight breeze that was picking up, and he looked casual and free. "I feel like I should ask you up for coffee or something, but I don't really know you, and my landlady probably wouldn't like it. She's pretty gossipy. She'd probably tell someone you'd been here," she said, softly.

"Your landlady?" he asked.

His voice cracked, and her body tingled pleasantly. It was nice to think someone could find her attractive when Todd so obviously didn't.

"Yes. Mrs. Griffith. She's an older woman who keeps an eye on things. I guess I remind her of her daughter in Boston, too, so she's kind of protective of me. There she is right now," she said, pointing at a gray-haired woman in a fuzzy bathrobe standing on the stoop and shaking out a rug.

"I won't come in then," he said. "I'll stay out here and keep an eye on things from across the street if you want."

"Across the street. Outside? All night?"

"Yes."

"No. That won't do," she said. "You saved my life. You can come in. We'll find a way to make the sleeping arrangements work. Mrs. Griffith," she called out as she made her way to the front of the building and climbed the steps. "Can you hold up for a minute?"

"Tarryn. I didn't see you. I was just going to lock up for the night after sweeping the steps. I can't leave all this pollen on them," she said. "There's even more than there was earlier when I came in after gardening in the backyard. I must have stepped in it, too. It's all squashed." She held a broom in one hand and the rug in another. She looked behind Tarryn at Brock. "Who's this?" she asked, sounding suspicious.

"This is my boyfriend," she said. The ruse had worked when Brock started it before. She'd try it again. If only Todd could see her now, he wouldn't think she was "too moral."

"The lawyer? He doesn't look like a lawyer," she said, eyeing Brock up and down, seemingly unimpressed with his creased chinos and vested, blue, button-down oxford.

"I work in contracts, mostly," Brock said, sounding dry.

Tarryn glanced sideways, amused that he was such a good actor. Maybe he did this often with women.

"He's my fiancé, actually," she said, upping the game and enjoying the way she felt him stiffen beside her. "He asked me to marry him tonight," she said, embellishing the truth even more."

"Really?" Mrs. Griffith said, glancing at Tarryn's hands.

"The ring's a little too big. I'm having it sized," Brock added smoothly.

Tarryn glanced sideways at Brock again. He seemed to be enjoying himself.

"Well, congratulations. I guess it's okay to let him in," Mrs. Griffith said.

"Of course it is," Tarryn said. "Shall we go up?" she asked Brock.

They walked in, and Tarryn closed the door behind them, leaving Mrs. Griffith outside to sweep the steps. She headed up the stairs with Brock behind her. He was the first man she'd had in her new place. Todd had never been there. But for some reason, it felt right, especially after the way they'd had each other's backs when talking to Mrs. Griffith. When she got to the top, she started to unlock the door to her apartment but pulled the key out and looked at it instead. She turned to look at him.

"What's wrong?" he asked.

"Nothing. It turned easily for some reason, that's all. It's not much here, but it's a good place to sleep," she said. "I hope you like it."

She opened the door, stepped inside, and screamed.

CHAPTER 4

Brock pulled Tarryn out of the apartment and pushed her into the hallway behind him. The door hit the wall hard and bounced back. He pulled his gun out, kicked the door back open, and edged forward, keeping two hands on the gun. He saw what she had seen. The room was trashed, dumped upside down from ceiling to floor. He scanned the room, but he didn't see anyone.

"One bedroom or two?" he asked, keeping her behind him. Whoever trashed the place could still be there, and he didn't want her to get hurt.

"One," she said. Her voice was thin and scratchy.

"Stay behind me. Don't come in," he said.

He edged toward the back and kicked open the bedroom door before throwing open the door of the closet. The bedroom and closet were ransacked, but no one was there. He checked the bathroom and the shower. All clear. He slowly lowered his gun and walked back into the living room.

"You can come in now," he said. "It's safe."

She inched in while looking around with her mouth open. "What happened?" she asked. "Who would do this?"

"Probably the same guy that threatened you in the park. But not necessarily. I'm not sure what we're up against yet."

"We're?" Tarryn asked.

"Yeah. You and me. I'm in this with you all the way now. There's crazy stuff going on around you, and I'm here to stop it," he said. It upset him that these things were happening to her. She was a classy lady, and she didn't deserve it.

"Well, thank you," she said. "I'm not sure what I would do if you weren't here. I've never dealt with anything like this before." Her arms shook.

He holstered his gun before walking to her and touching her arm. "Take deep breaths, and stay here. I'm going to check the stairs and see if whoever did this is still around. Hopefully, no one heard you scream. This isn't something we want to make public yet, if at all." He walked past her and stepped stealthily down the stairs to check before walking back in. She was still standing where he left her. "Looks okay. Your landlady's still outside sweeping the stoop. Must be that no one else is home."

"No one else is here during the summer," she said.

"Good," he said. Come over here and sit down." He picked up cushions and dropped them on a small sofa. "You've had enough to deal with today. You need to rest. I'll fix this place up a little."

"Thanks," she said, plopping down and leaning back on the cushion. "Should we call anyone about this?" she asked.

"No. I'm it," he said. "Law enforcement is on the scene. I'll take care of things. He walked to the door and locked it, then walked back over to her. "The lock doesn't look jimmied. I wonder how they got in. Did you lock the door when you left?" If she hadn't, it could explain why the key turned easily earlier.

"I don't know. I thought so," she said, rubbing her forehead with her hand. "But I don't always because Mrs. Griffith is usually here, and I don't worry about it. I usually lock the outside door to the house when I leave, though."

"Make sure you lock this door from now on," he said firmly, determined to keep her safe. He didn't want someone breaking in again when Mrs. Griffith's back was turned. This could have been done by the same man he'd seen casing The Purple Pen.

He didn't tell her he'd seen a black Mercedes coupe, driven by the man he'd chased away in the park, leaving the restaurant earlier after she did. Or that it had pulled out of a parking space down the street and idled past him when he stepped outside to follow her. He didn't want her to know he'd been there and had seen her arguing with her boyfriend or whoever he was. She was already upset that he'd been in the park, although it seemed she'd bought the white lie he told her about being there because he was dating a girl at Georgetown. He understood why she'd gone there. He sometimes walked through the National Mall and Memorial Parks near the Capitol at night when he needed solace. The glow of the lighting of the memorials and the smooth calm of the reflecting pool brought him peace and a sense of being a part of something larger than himself. It seemed she felt a similar way about the park on the Potomac.

"Okay, I will," she said, nodding.

He looked around. The room was a mess. It was a good thing she wasn't home when whoever did this showed up. It could have been the man he'd chased who had looked oddly familiar to him for some reason and not just because he'd seen him earlier driving the car. He couldn't place him. But he'd seen him before somewhere. He could have possibly been staking out her place and maybe her boyfriend's place, too, if that's who it was in the restaurant. Or maybe he'd been out of sight down the street from Tarryn's apartment, watching her leave at the same time Brock did. Somehow, he'd known she was going to be at The Purple Pen. He'd probably driven back and trashed the place after making sure she was at the restaurant and then returned to wait for her afterwards.

"Any idea what someone could be looking for?" He turned over an end table and placed a lamp on it. It must have been something important.

"Not really, unless they wanted my research. Oh, my

gosh. That must have been it. Where's my laptop? What if they hack into it? It has my finance thesis on it and a list of sources I used for the article." She jumped up and scanned the room, grasping her arms. After a moment, she exhaled. "That's right. I left it at work. I was going to return to the Chronicle after the Rose Garden reception, but I never did." She sat back down on the sofa and leaned forward over her knees, keeping her arms folded. "That's a relief."

"Yeah. Whoever it was probably would have taken it. Anything else?" he asked, trying not to look interested in the fact she had a list of sources on her computer. That was one of the things he was assigned to find out about. He made a note of it.

She looked up at him. "I don't know unless they were after me," she said. Her eyes widened. "Do you think they were?"

"Hard to say. They were after something," he answered. "Probably your research. Someone wants to know what you know or, maybe, who you know. Your article touched on something, that's for sure. We can only guess what it is at this point."

He picked up a cracked frame with a photo in it and set it on the table. "I guess you'll have to get a new frame for this," he said. "The photo looks okay, though. Who's the guy with you?" he asked. It was the guy who'd been sitting across from her in the restaurant.

"Todd," she said, softly, rocking back and forth. "That's us at the National Mall with the cherry blossoms in the spring."

"So there really is a boyfriend?" Brock asked.

"No. There really was a boyfriend," Tarryn replied, seeming to falter on the words. "He broke it off tonight."

"I'm sorry," he said, struggling to think of something more to say.

It made sense that that's what had happened, given what he'd observed in the restaurant when he looked up from eating his burger. He had nearly choked when he'd seen her red face and the drastic change in her expression to abject misery from the happiness he'd seen before. The joker across from her had been talking adamantly and had obviously upset her. Brock had set his coke down just before the guy stood up, tossed some money on the table, and stalked past him out the door. He'd looked back just in time to see Tarryn run into the bathroom. Now he knew what had happened. When she came out later and left, he'd made sure to stay behind the jukebox and keep his head down so she wouldn't see him. He'd tossed some bills on the table himself and followed her to make sure she was okay. The black Mercedes had passed by him then.

But now, here in the apartment, she looked so devastated that he wasn't sure where to take the conversation. He didn't want to say the wrong thing and risk being pushed away. His gruff tone had made his girlfriend in college, and other women do that, and he didn't want that to happen with her.

"It's okay. I just need time to process it. I picked out the ring a while ago, and I thought he was going to propose. So, it's kind of hard to deal with," she said in response to his sympathy. Her eyebrows furrowed into a deep crease.

"Wow. That's rough," Brock said. He folded a crocheted afghan that was on the floor and laid it on the back of the sofa. He picked up another frame, but this one held a print of a Monet.

"Water Lilies? Are you an Impressionist fan?" he asked.

Her eyes brightened, and the crease on her forehead disappeared as she looked over at the painting. "Yes, actually I am. Why?" she responded.

"Oh, no reason. I like Monet, too, that's all," he said, surprised to find in her a kindred spirit. He didn't know many people who shared his love of art. He was too busy going after bad guys to search out art history friends. He set the picture near the wall so she could hang it up later. And then he thought of something else. "Is it possible your boyfriend did this?" he asked.

"What, trashed the apartment? No, it wasn't Todd. He's not that kind of person. Besides, it wasn't the kind of break-up that could lead to something like this."

"Hmm. What was the reason, if you don't mind my asking?" Brock asked, not convinced that her boyfriend didn't do this. He could have invited her to the restaurant so that someone could search her apartment while she was gone.

Tarryn looked down, and when she looked back up at him, her eyes were glistening. "He broke it off because I spent too much time writing the article and not enough time with him. It was my fault, not his," she said. Her voice trailed into a whisper.

He was going to say something, but before he could, she dropped her head into her hands and sobbed. *Now, what should he do?* She'd had a terrible day, and it appeared that this break-in was only the beginning of something far more sinister than he had originally thought, given that she'd been followed and threatened in the park. He was going to need to stay and make sure she was okay, especially since her boyfriend had bailed. He patted his pocket, looking for a tissue, but he didn't find one.

"I'll be right back. Hold on," he said. He maneuvered through the mess and headed to the small kitchen, where he grabbed a box of Kleenex. He returned and set it down next to her.

"Here," he said, sitting down next to her. "You've had a bad day. You'll feel better after a good night's sleep."

He patted her arm, feeling awkward, and when she looked up at him, he handed her a tissue. Her face was red and blotchy.

"Thank you," she said, sniffling before blowing her nose.

"I'll stay until you feel better," he said.

She nodded and grabbed another tissue, looking up at him with her wide, brown doe-eyes.

He was overwhelmed with a need to keep her safe. She was so young and vulnerable, and yet so smart and determined, and she had unknowingly gotten herself trapped in a dangerous situation with a lot of powerful people. But nothing would happen to her while he was around. He would see to that.

"I wish Todd had given me a chance to explain," she said. "I thought I did, but it didn't go over too well. I mean, I know I wasn't perfect. I didn't always text him right back when he texted me. And I missed a lunch appointment with him one time because I forgot. But I had trouble getting a hold of him, too. And now, all of a sudden, he's leaving town, and he doesn't want to get married anymore. I wish I could do things over." She hiccuped.

"Why?" he asked. "It's an important story. It needed to be told. It's his problem that he didn't understand that." He shook his head. It seemed a lame reason to break up with someone. He knew what it was like to get caught up in work. He'd done that plenty of times, although it could have been one of the reasons he'd had trouble getting dates. Anyway, there must be more to it than that, and her boyfriend's sudden departure from their relationship and imminent departure from DC seemed suspicious.

"Maybe," she continued, "but I should have spent more time with him. Now here I am with a trashed apartment and no boyfriend and no ring and just, well, everything," she wailed, covering her face with her hands and sobbing again.

"It's okay," he said, patting her knee.

He didn't know what else to do. He wasn't used to women crying in front of him, and he wasn't sure how to handle it. But he did want to find out one more thing.

"Was your writing a problem for Todd before tonight?" he asked.

"What? Well, I didn't know it was, but it must have been if that's the reason he doesn't want to get married."

"Hmm," Brock mumbled.

"What do you mean, "hmm?" Tarryn said. "Do you think

he was right to break up with me or something?" Her voice rose.

"No, not at all. I'm just thinking of things, that's all," Brock said, softening his voice and hoping to soothe her. "I'll tell you what. It's getting late. Why don't you get some sleep?"

"I don't know if I can sleep," she said.

"Well, why don't you try," he said.

"What are you going to do?" she asked.

"I'll stay out here on the sofa if you'd like. No one will hurt you while I'm around. I'll see to that," he said, to make her feel better.

"All right," she said, sniffling.

She got up and walked away slowly. After she disappeared into the bedroom, he checked his phone. There was a White House meeting in the morning, and he made a note of it before setting the phone and his holster and gun on the coffee table. She came back out after a moment in her same clothes but wearing fuzzy, pink slippers and carrying a stuffed animal. She'd pulled her hair back in a loose ponytail, and tiny tendrils curled prettily about her face.

"What's this?" he asked when she set the stuffed animal on the back of the sofa.

"He's my teddy bear, Theodore Bearimore," she said. "He was on the floor in the bedroom. At least he's okay."

"You named your teddy bear?" Brock asked.

"Yes, of course. My mom gave him to me for my birthday when I was five, and that's always been his name. I'll probably give him to my kids someday if I ever have any. I'm not sure about that yet. It helps me sleep to have him around."

"Right," he said, shrugging and thinking that was a unique thing to do, especially for someone who seemed as sophisticated as she was. *But she was definitely a unique person.* He was realizing that more and more as time went along.

"I'm going to make a sandwich. Would you like one, too?"

she asked.

"Yeah, I guess," he said. The burger hadn't filled him up, and he was still hungry. He stood and walked toward the kitchen but tripped over another upended end table and crashed with it to the floor.

"Are you alright?" she asked, running back toward him.

"Yeah. We'll have to fix this place up tomorrow," he said, shrugging off his irritation. It wasn't his night tonight. If she wasn't so cute, he'd be more upset.

"Well, if you're sure," she said, helping him stand and set the end table back up.

Her gentle touch sparked a fire in him. "Thanks," he said, gazing into her eyes as he stood.

She gazed back for a moment. "Do you like peanut butter and banana sandwiches?" she asked.

"What?" he asked, coming back to earth.

"Peanut butter and banana sandwiches. That's what I was going to make," she said, patting his arm as she pulled away.

"I don't know. I've never had one, are you sure they go together?" he asked.

"Trust me," she said, turning and heading into the kitchen. "They're my favorite."

"Hmm. If you say so," he said.

She pulled a half loaf of wheat bread off the counter and peanut butter out of the cupboard before grabbing a banana and slicing it. She finished making the sandwich and brought it over to him, setting the plate on the coffee table with a glass of milk.

He picked up the sandwich and tried it. "Not bad," he said, after taking a bite and washing it down with the milk. "This might be my new favorite snack."

She retrieved her sandwich from the kitchen and sat down next to him. "You have good taste," she said, before taking a bite.

There was a knock on the door.

"Who could that be? It's after midnight," she mumbled, shielding her mouth with her hand. "It must be Mrs. Griffith."

It was hard to understand her with her mouth full, but he got the gist of it. "I'll get it," he said, standing. He thought about getting his gun, but the landlady would have locked the outside door, so he didn't. He strode to the door and hooked up the bolt chain before opening it a few inches. "Mrs. Griffith, how nice to see you."

She stood in the hallway with her gray hair rolled up in brightly colored curlers, peering at him over the top of her glasses.

"What can we do for you?"

"I thought I heard something up here a while ago. Same thing I heard earlier in the evening when I came in from gardening in the backyard, like something hitting the floor. Is everything okay?"

"Sure," he said, standing in front of the crack in the door. He didn't want her to see the state of the apartment and ask questions. It was best to keep things undercover for now to keep Tarryn's name out of the paper. That could happen since she'd just published her article, and it was of public interest.

"It was probably noises in the pipes or something. This warm weather can do that to them." He didn't know if that was true or not, but it sounded plausible to him. He hoped she'd buy it. She gave him a strange look. "By the way, did you notice anyone unusual in the building today or maybe a little while ago?" he asked quickly to get her mind on something else.

"Unusual? No. Why?" She looked over his shoulder. "Tarryn?" she called.

"I'm right here. Don't worry, everything's fine," Tarryn called back.

"Well, okay," Mrs. Griffith said. She looked back at him, and her peer turned into a glare. "Keep it down up here," she said.

"Sure thing," Brock said, closing the door after her. He walked back to the sofa and sat down.

"You didn't want her to see what happened, did you?" Tarryn asked. "That's why you didn't open the door. You want to keep it a secret. We're different from each other in that way, aren't we? You want to cover everything up, and I want to make everything public. We're an odd pair."

"I didn't think of it that way," he said. "I suppose you're right. I'm just trying to protect your privacy. So, you think we're a pair?" he asked, grinning.

"I didn't mean it that way," she said, smiling, before standing and taking her plate into the kitchen. She glanced back over her shoulder. "Maybe we're just odd."

"Maybe," he said, laughing. He finished his sandwich and helped clean up the dishes before heading back to the sofa.

"Can you sleep now?" he asked.

"Yes, I guess. If I don't think about Todd. Can you?" she asked.

"I think so," he said. "See you in the morning."

"Goodnight," she said, grabbing her teddy bear off the sofa and going into the bedroom.

She shut the door, and he stretched out on the sofa. He reached over and turned off the lamp. The light shining under the bedroom door flicked off, and he laid there in the dark, thinking about the way Tarryn's cheeks flushed pink when he looked at her and hoping she'd get a good night's sleep.

CHAPTER 5

Tarryn opened her eyes the next morning, and for a moment, she forgot where she was. Then she remembered the events of the night before and suddenly realized that Brock was sleeping in the other room, or at least she thought he was. She hopped up and peeked in the living room. Yep. He was there. A welcome sense of relief rushed over her. His presence made her feel safe.

She walked over and grabbed her phone off the floor, where it rested in a pile of clean but wrinkled underwear that had obviously been tossed out of the dresser. It was set on silent, and she hadn't checked it since she got back from dinner last night. She bit her lip nervously as she typed in the passcode, hoping she hadn't inadvertently missed an important deadline or meeting. She planned to stay away from the White House, even if it was scheduled, until she was sure it was safe to go back there after the warning she'd received from the man by the river. His hostile threats still scared her. She checked her email first. There was a long list of things to open, but the first thing she tapped on was an email from her editor. It said she had a meeting later that morning at the paper. She walked past the bedroom door on her way to the bathroom.

"Brock, it's morning," she said, satisfied to see him stir and reach for his phone on the coffee table.

"Thanks," he said, rolling onto his back with the phone in hand. He looked at it and sat up. "Six o'clock? I've gotta get going."

"Right now?" she asked.

"Yeah. I'll be back to help you clean up later. I have to get to the White House," he said.

"Okay, sure," she said, waiting while he stood and slipped on his shoes. She wished he wouldn't leave in such a rush. Her break-up with Todd had left her feeling abandoned and Brock's leaving accentuated that fear.

"See ya," he said, grabbing his gun and holster off the coffee table.

He dashed out. The door slammed shut and then opened again.

"Lock the door after me," he called out before the door slammed shut again.

"Okay," she said softly to herself in the sudden quiet of the room. She suddenly felt empty and lost. A pang hit her in the pit of her stomach as she realized she was genuinely alone. Even Todd had abandoned her. How could it be over with him? It couldn't be. Maybe she'd stop by his place and see if she could talk some sense into him. If she told him, it was all a misunderstanding and that she'd spend more time with him and not write so much, maybe everything would be okay. Yes. That's what she would do, maybe this afternoon. She padded solemnly through the living room to the door and locked it before heading back to the bathroom to get ready. It was probably best to do as Brock said.

After showering and dressing, she cleaned the apartment. Nothing appeared permanently damaged, but it was definitely a mess. Her chess set was upside down in the corner, and pieces were strewn across the floor near the baseboard. She returned the chessboard to the end table and restored the pieces to their squares, all the while wondering who would do this.

She continued tidying up. It didn't take her long to make

it presentable again. She turned a small, swivel rocker next to the end table over and set it up straight, but just as she did, she saw a tiny, round tin on the carpet that looked like miniature shoe polish. She picked it up and turned the tin over. It emitted a strong scent of peppermint. What kind of shoe polish smelled like that? "Tobacco?" she said aloud, reading the tin. "Chewing tobacco." Whoever had ransacked her apartment must have dropped it. She shivered and walked over to put it in the sink. Holding something the intruder had held and thinking of him being in her apartment scared her. And suddenly she was reminded of the man in the park. He had smelled the same way. *Maybe it wasn't chewing gum she'd smelled. Maybe it was chewing tobacco. He could be the same man that did this. She'd have to show this to Brock and see if it could be dusted for fingerprints if she hadn't messed them all up.* She grabbed a Ziploc bag and put the tin in there instead.

She was going to eat something, but her stomach hurt, either from angst or the peanut butter and banana sandwich she'd eaten in the middle of the night. She wasn't sure which. It didn't matter. She had to get going, anyway. Her laptop was at the newspaper, and she had to get some research done before the meeting. She wasn't sure if she was ready to publish another article after being threatened in the park, but she needed to write it anyway.

It seemed important to pull information together and try to find out what was going on. If she could interview an economic advisor or investment fund manager, maybe she could come up with a fresh angle for a story on the financial markets. Then, she could run it by her editor and see what he thought about a follow-up article. And if she were honest, she needed to be around people. She didn't feel that safe in the apartment with Brock gone. His strong, calming manner soothed her.

The morning was brisk and clear as she walked down the street to the bus stop. She inhaled the fresh air. It revived her a bit and made her stomach feel better. But before she'd gone too far, she decided to make a detour to the university. She didn't want to wait until this afternoon to see Todd. If she just said the right thing, maybe she still had a chance with him.

She picked up her pace, feeling her mood lighten further as she neared the campus. The trees lining the sidewalks were a vibrant green, and the Georgetown neighborhood had an air of vitality as if nothing could be more satisfying or important than whatever intellectual pursuits they were engaged in. As she neared Todd's building on the outskirts of campus, she was surprised to catch sight of his navy jacket. She'd assumed he'd be inside studying. But then she realized he was walking his dog. Just as she was about to cross the street, a girl walked up to him. They talked for a while, and when she moved in closer, Tarryn stepped behind a tree to keep from being seen. Just as she did, Todd pulled the girl to him and kissed her solidly on the mouth.

Tarryn's heart hit her hard against her ribs. It wasn't possible. They were going to be married. He'd bought her a ring. How could there be another woman? Her breath came in short gasps, and she wondered if she was hyperventilating. Her stomach clenched, and nausea hit her again. What if the breakup speech was all a lie and another woman was the real reason he broke up with her. Had she been too busy and too trusting to recognize the signs he was cheating? She doubled over and held her stomach while still keeping an eye on them.

The two of them went inside together, and she crouched for a moment, pressing her hand to her forehead to brush away a film of sweat and trying not to throw up. It seemed like the whole world was spinning out of control, and she was a top whirling along with it. She didn't know what to do.

And then, suddenly, everything stopped, and she knew exactly what to do. She didn't give herself a chance to overthink it — she'd done far too much of that lately. She took a deep breath, crossed the street, and headed for the door to confront him. But as she neared the steps, she saw something that gave her another idea. "The jerk should really clean up after his dog," she said and figured out there was a way to get him back instead, and it wouldn't take her long to do it. Fishing a tissue out of her pocket, she went to work.

She rang the bell after she finished and ran back across the street. When he came out moments later and hopped around yelling at her, she yelled back and suppressed a smile before continuing on her way. It wasn't like her to do what she did, but then again, maybe it was. She'd just never been pushed to her limit before. She felt better anyway and no longer nauseous, although she still felt horribly betrayed. Maybe she'd tell Brock about it later. But then again, maybe not. She'd have to wait and see. She picked up her pace to keep from being late for the newspaper. She didn't want to head back to the bus stop and wait for the bus, so she walked toward Foggy Bottom. Georgetown was busy this morning with the few students who stayed for the summer bustling about, probably trying to make it on time for their summer classes. She dodged people here and there as she hurried through and on to Foggy Bottom. As she neared the Metro, she passed the research lab where Professor Hall was walking down the steps.

"Tarryn," he said. "Are you going in, or can I talk to you for a minute?"

"I'm on my way to work, but I can spare a minute if you'd like," she said, relieved to have someone to chat with. Talking to Professor Hall would get her mind off of Todd, and she really wanted to do that. "Actually, if you'd like to walk with me, we can chat on the way."

He swung a book bag over his shoulder and fell into step with her.

"I've been thinking about your story, but what I want to

talk to you about is something specific to one of your conclusions. Where did you find the data on the hedge funds you mentioned in your article? I'm specifically referring to the Harrington Hedge Fund. Was it in a prospectus from the Harrington fund, or did you find it on the internet or in the library, or did you ask someone?"

Tarryn wasn't that surprised by the question, given the seriousness of her conclusions.

"I did talk to a few people about it if that's what you want to know," she said, dodging the question. She wouldn't reveal her sources if that's what he was after. "But I also used research from others, especially at the lab, along with interviews with investors, and I wrote the article accordingly. Why?"

He paused for a moment before continuing. "Was the article based on the same data and sources you footnoted in the thesis you wrote for your international finance course? The thesis was distributed by the internal university press and available to scholars online, and I read it."

"Well, yes," she said, amazed that he had taken the time to find and read her thesis. "Is there something I missed?"

Professor Hall slowed to a stop at a crosswalk and turned to her. "You could say that," he said, looking directly into her eyes. "But you're not the only one that missed it. There are a lot of smart, very powerful people who missed it, too, and they're going to be really mad when they find out the truth. It's a truth that needs to be told, but only by someone who's strong enough and savvy enough to do it. You know who's going to be even madder?"

Tarryn slowly shook her head.

"The people who already know the truth and don't want it to come out." He paused before continuing. "I think I may have talked to some of them — one of them anyway. That's why I'm telling you. You've uncovered the tip of the iceberg. It's up to you if you want to uncover any more. But if you do, you need to be careful," he said, gravely.

"What do you mean?" Tarryn asked, suddenly frightened by the look in his eyes.

The blinking sign at the crosswalk turned green, but she didn't move, and he didn't either. People behind them jostled by, and someone yelled an obscenity at her. But she still didn't move.

"What do you mean, Professor Hall?" she asked again.

"This is bigger than you know," he said. "Study your article. Reread it and retrace your steps. You were smart enough to write the article, so you're smart enough to figure out what it says."

He abruptly walked forward to cross the street and left her staring after him with her mouth open. Why was he talking in riddles? A car with tinted windows made a right from the side street, and she waited for it to pass. She had a funny feeling there were eyes on her, and she wished Brock was with her.

"Professor Hall," she called out. He was on the other side of the street by then. "Wait. Tell me what you mean."

He glanced back over his shoulder. "Figure out what it says," he called out as the crosswalk light blinked red in front of her, and he disappeared into the far crowd.

She waited for the light to change again and shook her head to clear it. What could he have been talking about? She would have to read through her article again when she got The U. S. News Chronicle's office. There must be something in it she hadn't seen, but she couldn't imagine what it was.

She made it the rest of the way to the office without incident and rode the elevator to the third floor. She stepped off the elevator to the smell of coffee and freshly ground pencils. The newsroom was hopping like usual. Reporters talked on phones and typed on laptops while a TV mounted high on the wall blared the 24-hour news in the background. Her editor, Andy, was right in the middle of it all, calling out orders to everyone.

"Hey Stanford, hightail it to the Hill," Andy shouted to a man with thinning hair standing by the wall. "They're taking a roll call vote."

"Sure thing," Stanford replied as he turned and headed for the elevator.

He grinned and waved to her as he passed by. His name wasn't Stanford. It was Justin. But Andy sometimes called people by the name of the school they went to.

"Tarryn. You finally made it," he said when he saw her. "Thought you decided to take the day off."

He stuck a pencil behind his ear and rolled up the sleeves of his poorly pressed shirt. One of the buttons stuck out a little bit over the slight paunch in his belly. She hoped it wouldn't pop off and show her more of him than she wanted to see.

"No. I just had a late start. I'll get right to work," she said, pretending to look for something in her purse to ward off further questions. He was a great editor but kind of annoying and nosy, too. She stifled a sigh when he walked toward her.

"Your story made a splash, I'll say," he said. "Calls came in all day yesterday and the day before. Good work. Write another one, 750 words. Have it on my desk by the end of the week."

"Same subject?" Tarryn asked, thinking about her tentative plans to write a follow-up, maybe without her name attached.

"White House response to today's dip in the stock market and forecasts on future fluctuations," he answered, walking away. "Come up with something."

"Okay, sure," she said.

She walked to her desk and sat down, relieved to see her laptop where she'd left it. She opened it and pulled up her original article. Professor Hall's words still resonated with her, and she wanted to read it and see what she could find. About halfway through, she noticed that she hadn't mentioned the Reardin fund, a feeder fund to the Harrington hedge fund, which was something she remembered footnoting in her thesis. Maybe that had something to do with what Professor Hall was referring to. She made a note to talk to him about it tomorrow. Maybe he could shed more light on what he was talking about. Her watch showed she had about a half an hour before the meeting, so she settled in and began researching her next article. She was plagued with moments of yearning while she searched the internet and also thought of Todd jumping up and down on his steps and yelling. She really got him back. But then she remembered a funny joke he told and started to feel sad about their break-up again. She had to get her mind on something else. She spent the next half hour doing research before heading to the meeting.

Surprisingly, the meeting centered around other stories around Washington and didn't concentrate on hers or the economic news. She supposed it was because the hype about the economy was out already, and *The U. S. News Chronicle* editors wanted to keep the DC coverage well-rounded by publishing reports on other things. She wouldn't let herself think it was because they'd been threatened and muzzled into silence by someone who didn't like her article as she felt she had been. Political silencing of media outlets was known to happen in the district, but she didn't think her newspaper allowed that — but then again, maybe. She looked at Andy, calling out story ideas and pointing at reporters, but he didn't catch her eye. *Would he allow the newspaper to be silenced?* She didn't think so. And he had asked her to write a short follow-up article. But it could depend on who they were dealing with or what the consequences of continuing to publish controversial economic news would be.

The meeting went well, and they brought in lunch, but she was relieved when it was over so she could spend the rest of the day writing. She looked up later when someone bumped her desk. It was Clark from the mailroom.

"Oops. Sorry. Guess I should look where I'm going,"

he said, steadying a mug of pencils and handing her several envelopes. By the way, great story, Tarryn. I hope I can write like that someday."

"Thanks. You'll get published soon enough. I read your latest obituary. It was great. You really emphasized the important points."

"Do you think so?" he asked. "I was trying to keep it real but soft, you know what I mean?"

"I think I do," Tarryn said, not sure if she did or not. She'd written obituaries on her first summer job as an undergrad and knew how hard it was. "It was really good."

"Thanks. Oh, by the way," he said again, "Someone stopped by the mailroom earlier in the afternoon and said to give you this." He handed her a small, blue envelope the size of a thank-you card. "He was pretty adamant that I give it to you in person."

"Oh, thanks," Tarryn said, taking it and scrunching her eyebrows together. Who would come by the office and not just have reception call up to her? "What did he look like?"

"The guy? Tall, dark hair, very polished. It was kind of strange to see him in the mailroom. The suits usually keep their distance. And he acted strange, too. He shielded his eyes with his hand like he was looking for something. I couldn't really see his face. But he was wearing a thick, silver ring with some sort of insignia on it. Anyway, I've gotta go pick up a courier package for the printer," he said and walked away.

"Bye," Tarryn said as she picked up a pair of scissors and sliced open the envelope. A shakily written note on blue stationery inside read — *"Be careful what you write. Be careful who you talk to. Ask the professor what this means."*

Tarryn sucked in a breath. The professor? Was the note referring to Professor Hall? A man who brazenly left a note like that at an office must think he was above the law. She glanced around before stuffing it in her purse and shoving her wheeled chair back from the desk. It was time to head home. She needed to show this to Brock. And she needed to show it to him now.

CHAPTER 6

Brock dashed up the stairs to the second floor of the Dirksen Senate Office Building on Capitol Hill, hoping he wasn't late for the private, off-the-record meeting with the White House press secretary and prominent area journalists. Jodi Conlon, the press secretary, had texted him that the meeting had been rescheduled for a new time and location, probably for security reasons. And this was it. He found the room and knocked on the polished wood door before entering what turned out to be a medium-sized conference room painted a dark, somber green. Mini-slatted Venetian blinds let in a little light through a window that looked out over Constitution Avenue from which he'd just come. Several men and women in suits were already sitting around a table talking, and they looked up when he walked in.

"Good morning," he said. "Hope I'm not late."

"Not at all," Jodi said, standing and walking over to him.

A man in a dark suit who had been standing behind her chair followed her.

"Everyone, I'd like you to meet Special Agent Brock Spencer. He's monitoring the meeting at the direction of the FBI. He has my full cooperation and I hope yours, too," Jodi said.

The others nodded, although Brock noted a few sideways glances and averted eyes. But that wasn't unusual when people found out he worked for the FBI, so it didn't bother him. The man in the suit strode past him. Brock recognized him as Secret

Service. He could be temporarily protecting the press secretary.

"I'll be right outside the door," the man said to Jodi. Call me if you need me. He pulled open the door and left.

Brock was surprised he didn't acknowledge him, but sometimes that's the way it was when he showed up. He looked around. Riley Keagan sat across from Jodi at the table, and he nodded when Brock looked at him. Brock was surprised to see him there as he assumed Riley would confine himself to meetings at the White House. But maybe as a presidential economic advisor, he considered it his duty to be part of a conversation about a controversial article on the economy. Jodi had told Brock the article was what the meeting was about. A woman sitting next to Riley smiled and ran her fingers through her long, blonde hair. He recognized her as a finance expert from a news show she'd been a guest on. He nodded, and she smiled again.

"Well, I guess it's time to start the meeting," Jodi said after checking her watch. She turned and walked to the table, and sat down.

Brock remained by the door in a stalwart stance with his hands behind his back. It was a good place to listen and find out more about what was going on with the fallout from the article. Maybe someone even knew who Tarryn's sources were and would mention that. She might have discussed them with a fellow journalist. As he scoped out the room and noticed the famous faces, it struck him as odd that a meeting like this was set up in the first place. He wondered who had set it up and why.

Jodi cleared her throat. "I'm sure you all know about the recent article on hedge funds that was in the U. S. New Chronicle. Maybe you've even read it," she said.

A few people chuckled.

"Okay, you've probably all read it," she continued. "Laura is passing out copies of it for us to refer to." She gestured toward the blonde who had stood and was walking around the table.

Jodi continued. "The White House is well aware that there is a possibility of an economic downturn and possible recession due to the anomalies in the stock market and unusual hedge fund activity reported in the article. I've convened this off-the-record, emergency meeting to convey information the White House has obtained that directly contradicts the story's claims and to determine how best to move forward with news coverage during this situation."

"Contradicts the story?" a white-haired man with a very deep tan at the end of the table said. "What do you mean? And why all the hush-hush? What's this all about?"

Brock suddenly recognized him as the national news anchor of a Sunday morning political show. Another recognizable reporter jumped in.

"I second Kent on that," she said, looking at the man who had just spoken. "Why isn't this information imparted in a press conference instead of a backroom meeting?"

"Normally, it would be," Jodi said, seeming flustered. "But because of the possibility that further news leaks could lead to more economic upheaval, a more private setting was decided upon."

"News leaks? That wasn't a news leak. That was a bonafide story," the reporter said.

"Not according to the information we've just handed out," Jodi said. "As you can see, if you turn to page 6, many of the details in the article were greatly exaggerated and erroneously reported. A more accurate portrayal of the state of the economy is included in the memo for use in future reports. I hope you'll take advantage of this information to better inform the public and, hopefully, calm the fears the previous article engendered."

"Even if that were true, which I doubt that it is, that doesn't make it a news leak," Kent said. "There's no reason to assume that this article was based on anything other than legal sources."

Pages rustled as those around the table flipped through the memo. A few people commented and asked questions before the meeting became more heated.

"What is this? A propaganda campaign?" Kent said loudly, flipping a page and tossing the memo on the table. "We're not a bunch of idiots here. The White House can't just put out its own version of the news."

"Well, I wouldn't say that's what it is," Jodi said. "It's just a correction and a more accurate account of the current situation."

"Yeah, right," Kent said, standing. "I've heard enough."

"Me, too," another reporter said.

People around the table stood as Kent headed for the door. They milled around and followed him out as Jodi loudly stacked and shuffled papers at the table. Riley Keagan remained seated, talking on his cell phone. Brock stepped aside to let the others pass. Just as he did, Laura sidled up to him and handed him a folded piece of paper. He was going to hand it back but noticed it had his name on it. He folded it again and stuck it in a pocket inside his vest without looking at her. The last time someone had passed a note to him, he'd been the object of a crush in second grade. He was slightly amused. She was attractive but not really his type, and he was more interested in the "out to save the world" doe-eyed girl he'd met.

"Later, maybe?" she asked. Her eyes glinted playfully. "I like men with guns."

"Yeah, no," Brock answered, angling away from her. That seemed like a strange thing to say.

"Another time?" she asked, barring his way. "I'll make it worth your while."

She was aggressive, too. "I'm sure you would," he said. "But I have other plans. See ya." He opened the door and walked past the Secret Service agent, who he assumed would handle whatever was bothering Jodi, and headed for the stairs.

"See ya," she called after him.

He took the stairs down to the street. Constitution Avenue was busier than it had been earlier in the day, probably because of the lunch hour. He walked to the FBI office on 4th Street to see what was happening. Before he headed inside, he remembered Laura's note and stopped under a tree on the red brick walk in front of the building to read it. He was surprised to find it wasn't the come-on note he had expected.

"The Big Guy says to stay out of this one," it said. "Leave the girl alone."

He shook his head impatiently as he refolded the note and stuffed it back in his vest pocket. "The Big Guy?" Who was "the Big Guy?" Maybe it was whoever had instigated the meeting. "The girl" could be a disparaging reference to Tarryn, but that would mean someone knew they had been together. And that would mean he was being watched. He was torn between confirming his original assessment of Laura as strange and entertaining the possibility that she could be an undercover agent or, perhaps, a corporate lackey relaying a message. He wasn't sure which. Either way, she was on his radar now. He made a note to find out more about her and her cryptic note. He continued on his way to the office. The field office was jumping when he got there. A call had just come in, and the evidence response team was scrambling to address it.

"Hey, Brock. Good to see you, buddy," his friend Gabe called out to him on his way out the door. "Come by Saturday for dinner. I'm having a barbecue. Bring a date if you want."

"Sure," Brock called back. "What time?" But Gabe was already gone, leaving him to wing it as far as time was concerned. He wondered briefly if Tarryn might like to go with him. He'd ask her later.

He spent the rest of the afternoon at his desk, making calls and checking into Leo Harrington's background information since the Harrington Hedge Fund was prominently mentioned in Tarryn's article. It turned out that not only was he an investment genius, he was quite an art aficionado, as well, with vast collections of priceless paintings in houses around the world. Brock couldn't help but wonder where all of his money originated. He was obviously extremely wealthy. He planned to check into it further.

While he was at it, he decided to find out more about Tarryn. She wasn't in the FBI database, but he hadn't thought she would be. She wasn't the criminal type. He Googled her instead. Her story was prominent, of course, but there wasn't much about her other than the fact that she worked for the U. S. Chronicle and was a recent graduate of Georgetown. He did find some background on her family, though, if the inferences he made from the search results on her last name and Washington, DC, were correct. Her father had been a diplomat to a small country in Europe, and her mother was the granddaughter of a late senator. They definitely had ties to Washington. He wondered if her article had caused any problems for them. He made a note to find out more before logging off and leaving the office.

It had been a long day, and he was ready to go home. He wanted to shower and change, but the thought of going back to his apartment by himself grated on him. Besides, Tarryn needed help putting her apartment back together, and he'd said he'd help. He crossed the street and texted her a quick message, then smiled and boarded the bus. He stopped for Chinese take-out after he got off and headed down the street to her place, clutching a white paper bag and savoring mouthwatering whiffs of Kung Pao chicken. She was waiting for him on the stoop when he got there.

"I'm so glad you're here," she said, motioning him inside.

Her face was drawn and taut, and he wondered if something more had happened regarding her story.

"What is it? What's wrong?" he asked, glancing toward

Mrs. Griffith's door and thankfully not seeing anyone before following Tarryn up the stairs.

She led him into the apartment before answering and grabbed something off the kitchen counter before going to sit on the sofa. He set the bag on the counter and looked around. He was surprised to see it looked pretty good. She must have been busy. He walked over to join her. When he neared her, she held something out to him.

"Here," she said. "I want you to see this."

"What is it?"

"A note warning me or threatening me. I'm not sure which," she said.

He snatched it from her and read it quickly.

"What do you think it means?" she asked.

"More of the same," he said, shaking his head. He couldn't believe this was happening to her. "More threats, more harassment. I can only guess what it means. It would probably be a good idea to show this to the professor it mentions. Do you know who it's referring to?"

"Yes. I'm pretty sure it's referring to Professor Hall. I'll see him soon, and I'll tell him," she said.

"Good," Brock said, handing the note back. He stood for a second, rubbing the back of his neck before sitting next to her on the sofa and meeting her eyes with his.

"Have you thought of writing under a pen name?" he asked. "For your own protection?"

She shook her head. "If I do that, people won't know where the information is coming from. It's like I'd be hiding and tossing spitballs or something. There's no room for public discourse if no one knows who to talk to about the information or where it's coming from. That doesn't seem right," she said.

"It's not right for your life to be in danger either," Brock said.

"I suppose. But I still want to inform the public. Is that so wrong?"

"No. I see your point. There has to be some sort of way for you to do that and stay safe at the same time. We'll have to keep brainstorming solutions. Now that I think about it, my grandmother's in the stock market. My grandfather had a lot of investments, and when he passed, they went to her. I think she actually might be in a hedge fund, too. I'll have to check."

"Might be a good idea," Tarryn said. "Oh, there is one other thing. I found a tin of chewing tobacco at the apartment when I was cleaning up."

"Chewing tobacco?"

"Yes. I don't know where it came from. I put it in a Ziploc bag in case you need it for evidence."

"We'll see. What we really want to do is keep an eye out for anyone with a tobacco habit. It could be the guy that broke in."

"Okay," she said.

"Hey, let's quit talking about work and have some dinner. I brought Chinese," Brock said, hoping to change the mood.

"Is that that wonderful smell?" Tarryn asked. "I haven't had take-out in a long time. Let me get some wine."

"Perfect," he said.

He followed her into the kitchen. She had a casual sway to her walk that captured his attention. And the fact that she didn't seem to realize how sensual it was intrigued him. She pulled a bottle of Pinot Grigio out of the refrigerator and set it and wine glasses on the counter. "Will this do?" she asked.

"Sure," Brock replied, taking the bottle and pouring them each a glass. He handed her one and lifted his. "To you," he said, gazing at her and losing himself in her wide, earnest eyes.

"What for?" she asked.

He snapped back to reality. "For following your dreams,"

he said, "and taking on the world. I'm in if you'll let me be. You're onto something here, and I want to follow along and help find out what it is."

She blushed. "Really? Thank you. With your background, you could be a big help. We could accomplish a lot together," she said, raising her glass to his.

"To us, then," Brock said, clinking her glass. "I mean to us finding things out together," he added.

She nodded. "To us," she said.

She lowered her eyes and her glass and sipped her wine before hesitating and setting her glass on the counter. Her lips glistened, red from the wine, and he leaned toward her, mesmerized. She abruptly picked up the bag and moved it to the table.

"You okay?" he asked, wondering if he'd unintentionally offended her.

"Yeah, sure. It's just that I saw Todd this morning, and I can't stop thinking about it."

"You saw Todd again? I thought it was over between you two," Brock said, surprised. She was so devastated yesterday.

"It is," Tarryn said. "Now."

"What do you mean?" he asked, a little more loudly than he'd intended. He was suspicious of Todd's involvement in the break-in, and Tarryn could provide potential information about it. Beyond that, he reminded himself, her love life was of no concern to him.

"He got upset with me again," she said. She set stoneware plates on the table and motioned Brock to sit down.

"Why? What happened?" He pulled out a chair and sat down, cringing at the sharpness in her voice. Cool it a little. One of his academy instructors in interrogation techniques had told him more than a few times. You don't want to scare them off. You want them to trust you. This wasn't an interrogation, but the principle still seemed to apply.

She scooped some chicken and rice onto his plate and hers and sat down across from him.

"Why should I tell you?" she asked. "It doesn't have anything to do with you."

"True," he said, softening his voice. "But it might have something to do with all the craziness that's going on around you, and I could help with that." If it did, he'd love to go over there and give that jerk a piece of his mind unless he was involved in the more sinister aspects of the situation. In that case, he'd lay low and keep an eye on him.

She seemed to ponder his words before continuing. "Maybe. Let's eat a little first. I'm not sure you're going to want to hear this over dinner."

"Okay," he said.

They ate for a while in silence. He was starving, and the food was good. He didn't want to pressure her, but he wanted to know what she was going to tell him. Finally, he couldn't stand it anymore.

"Okay, so what happened?" he asked, setting his fork down and wiping his mouth with a napkin.

She set her fork down, too, and took a sip of wine before answering.

"Well," she said, eventually, "Todd was walking his dog when I got to his apartment, so I stood across the street and watched him while I tried to get up the nerve to go talk to him." She paused for a moment as though trying to decide whether to continue.

"Makes sense," Brock said, prompting her.

She nodded. "Anyway, this girl came by who obviously knew him, and he kissed her right outside on the sidewalk." Her voice cracked. "The whole story he told me was obviously a lie to cover up being with another girl," she said, shrilly.

"Oh, no," Brock said. "That's rough. What's the matter with this guy?" He'd known something was wrong. It hadn't occurred to him that it was another woman. He'd thought Todd's actions were related to the break-in at Tarryn's apartment and to the fallout from her story. But maybe, from Tarryn's point of view, this was just as bad or worse. He moved to comfort her, but she held up her hand and continued talking.

"That's not the end of the story," she said.

"I'm sorry. Go on," he said.

"So anyway, he was so caught up with this girl, who really wasn't that pretty anyway..." Her voice quivered.

"It's okay," Brock said. "Take your time."

"... that he didn't clean up after his dog," she continued. "So, I went over there after they went inside and picked up the "you know what" with a tissue and put it on the doorstep. Then I rang the bell and went back to the sidewalk."

"You what?" he asked, a little more loudly than he'd intended.

"You don't have to yell. I was doing him a favor. It's the law to clean up after your dog," she replied, raising her voice in response.

"If you say so," he said, chuckling. "What happened then?"

"I don't know if I should tell you."

"Well, you told me this much. You might as well finish the story," he said.

"Hmm. Okay," she said after contemplating for a moment. "But you have to promise not to arrest me."

He almost laughed, but she seemed earnest. "I promise," he said, crossing his heart.

She went on. "Todd opened the door and saw me. He stepped out of the house right into the dog...into it. He started yelling and screaming. He told me he was going to sue me."

"Sue you? You're kidding. What'd you do then?" Brock asked.

"I told him he wasn't a real lawyer yet and to get lost. And then I left," she said.

Brock sat for a moment, taking in what she said. "You're right. That's pretty bad. Remind me never to get on your bad side," he said eventually. "Now I know what you're capable of." He patted his mouth with a napkin to hide a grin.

"Well, nobody's perfect," Tarryn said, sharply.

"No, no," he said, holding up his hands. "I didn't mean anything by it. It's not as bad as when my girlfriend in college broke up with me and dumped ice cream in my lap."

"Oh, no," she said.

"Yeah. A hot fudge sundae with maraschino cherries and the works. It didn't come out in the wash either," he said, shaking his head.

"Oh, okay," she said, more quietly. "That's pretty bad, too. Well, I didn't know I was capable of that, either. But now I do, and I'm ready to move on."

"Are you?" he asked, daring to hope she was.

"Yes, I really think I am," she said, nodding.

She nodded so forcefully that he wondered if she was kidding herself.

"Something tells me you're not being completely honest with me," he said, hoping to draw her out more.

"Well, maybe," she said slowly. "I'm ready to move on now in my head, anyway, if not in my heart. I just need some time to recover."

"I understand," he said. "Breaking up is never easy."

"Thanks for listening," she said. "I feel better now that I told you what happened."

"Sure thing," he said.

"Would you like dessert? I have apple pie," she said,

standing.

"Sounds good," he answered, leaning back in his chair and watching her move.

"So am I in the clear, or what?" she asked, giving him a sideways glance and maybe the hint of a smile.

"In the clear? Oh, yeah. Don't worry. You don't get handcuffs for breaking up with your boyfriend. In fact, just the opposite. This lawman's on your side," he said, grinning.

"Good. Thanks," she said. She placed a plate with a slice of apple pie topped with whipped cream in front of him. "By the way, I asked Mrs. Griffith about putting another lock on the door. She said she would, but it will take a day or two for the locksmith to get here. I'm still feeling scared," she said. She had that frightened little girl look on her face again.

"Do you have a friend you can stay with?" Brock asked. "You really shouldn't be alone."

"No. I'll be fine," she said, sitting down across from him with her slice of apple pie.

She didn't look fine. Maybe he should stay with her.

"You know," Brock said, "when I was a kid, I had a math teacher who gave me demerits for not doing my homework. One time, when he said he was going to call my parents because I didn't do it, I told him the smell of paper made me throw up. He still gave me an F, but it's true that I don't like homework or paperwork. If anything happens to you, I'm going to be filling out paperwork until I'm old and gray like he was. So why don't you let me stay here tonight and make sure whoever broke in doesn't come back?"

She paused before answering. "All right. It makes me feel better to have you here anyway with everything that's going on. You can take a shower here if you want." She smiled. "I'd hate to have you turn old and gray because of me."

He smiled back. "Good. It's settled then," he said, taking

a bite of apple pie.

He looked forward to spending another night with her regardless of how uncomfortable it was sleeping on the sofa. She was something, all right, and she sounded better than she had in a few days. Maybe she really could move on now. He hoped so. He hoped she'd move on in his direction.

CHAPTER 7

Tarryn jumped back the next morning when hot grease splattered her from bacon strips frying in the pan. She'd gotten up early to make breakfast for Brock before he headed back to his apartment, which he'd said last night he was going to do first thing in the morning. She forked the bacon onto a paper towel and slid the pan off the burner before folding scrambled eggs together and sliding that pan off the burner, too. She popped wheat bread into the toaster and called Brock to the table.

"Smells good," he said, standing from his seat on the sofa and ambling into the kitchen.

"Hope it is," she replied, blotting spots of grease on the fluffy, pink bathrobe she was wearing.

His sandy blond hair was endearingly tousled, and his chin sported a scruffy shadow, which added ruggedness to his usual, cleaned-up look. She liked it. She wished she'd had time to run a comb through her hair before he saw her, as it was probably even more tousled than his was. But judging from the way he moved closer to her, he didn't seem to mind.

"I hope you like a big breakfast," she said, pausing to look up at him as goosebumps tickled her arms. His nearness was enticing. Having him around to talk to mitigated the pain of losing Todd, and that made her feel close to him.

"It's great," he said, smiling. He leaned forward, and she suddenly wondered if he was going to kiss her. But he only took the napkin from her and patted her robe.

"You missed a spot," he said, grinning before handing it back to her.

"Thanks," she said, shivering as she watched him stroll over and take a seat at the table. She bit her lip and busied herself, filling plates with food.

The savory, comforting smells of her childhood filled the kitchen, and she was reminded of weekends at home when they had gathered as a family on Saturday mornings. The kids would set the table while her dad made hot, buttered toast, and her mother fussed over the stove. There was always a lot of laughter amid the chores. One time, their dad had dropped a piece of toast on the floor, and their dog, Chester, had grabbed it in his mouth. He'd dodged everyone chasing him around the kitchen before running into the other room and stuffing it under the sofa. They laughed so hard. She missed that. She missed them. Maybe someday she could have her own family and make memories like that.

"Hey, do you want to go to a barbecue with me this evening? One of my friends invited me, and I'd love to take you with me if you'd like," Brock said, as she walked over and set a steaming plate down in front of him. "That is if you can tear yourself away from writing for a while. You mentioned you had another deadline," he said.

"What? Oh, yeah. That won't take me that long. I guess I could go," she said, feeling her heart flutter at the hopeful way he looked at her.

He did have beautiful blue eyes, and she hadn't been out for a fun evening in a long time. Besides, she wasn't sure she wanted to write more stories until she figured out what Professor Hall was talking about. She wanted to know what he saw in her article that she didn't see. Maybe she'd go to the research lab this afternoon and talk to him if he was there. She might be able to fit in a quick game of chess, too, if someone was available. She sat down across from him.

"By the way, do you play chess?" she asked while she was thinking about it.

"Chess? Maybe a little. I know enough to know I have to keep the king safe. Why?" he asked, stuffing a forkful of scrambled eggs in his mouth.

"No reason. I thought we could play sometime if you want, that's all," she answered.

"Sure," he mumbled through a mouthful of eggs. "Anytime. If I'm around."

They chatted as they ate, and Tarryn was interested to find out that Brock had family in Detroit, since she was from Michigan, too. He mentioned a younger brother he was close to, and it reminded her of her younger brothers, who she seldom saw now but still loved and missed. The more she talked to him, the more it seemed they had in common, and she liked that. It sounded like he had a nice family, although his father had passed away when he was young, and he missed him sometimes.

"What happened to your father, if you don't mind my asking," Tarryn said, relating to his feelings of loss when thinking about her fractured family. "Was he sick?"

Brock hesitated before answering. "No, he wasn't sick. He was caught up in a bad situation, and, well, I don't really want to talk about it," he said, looking down.

"Sure. I understand," she said, wondering what made this gruff, seemingly solitary man look so lost. "You don't have to if you don't want to. I just thought it must have been hard growing up without a father," she said, softly.

He looked up and gazed at her for a moment until it seemed he decided to say something. "Actually, it was hard, really hard. I don't know if I should tell you this because I don't usually talk about it, especially with people I don't know well. But for some reason, I think you'd understand."

"Understand what?" she asked, gazing back. In his eyes, she saw deep sadness and a desolate vulnerability. Now, she really wanted to know what it was.

He was silent.

"I'm listening if you want to talk about it," she said, softly.

He looked away. "My father was murdered in front of me when I was a little boy," he said.

"What?" Tarryn couldn't believe what he'd told her. It seemed like such an incongruous background for someone with his casual yet impenetrable way. "What do you mean?"

"Well," he said, pausing before looking back at her and continuing. "Let me tell you what happened. My father gambled a lot and bet at the racetrack. One night, some men came to the house to collect. He didn't have the money, so they beat him. They beat him to death. I still remember his cries for help and my mom screaming for them to stop from the kitchen where they held her. Thankfully, my brother was at a friend's house and didn't see it. There was nothing I could do. I tried. I ran down the stairs from my bedroom and started punching them. But this big guy, the guy in charge, slammed me with an uppercut. It laid me out flat on the floor. I still have this scar on my chin that was cut by the ring he wore." Brock pointed at it.

Tarryn stared at him, unable to trust her voice after the shock of hearing what he had said. "I s-see," she said after a moment, hearing herself stutter slightly. "I wondered how you got that. That must have been a terrible experience."

"Yeah. It was. I'm pretty sure the reason I'm an FBI agent is because I want to keep people like the ones who murdered my father away from society. I want to find them and take them out via prison or otherwise. It helps me feel better. It gives me a sense of justice."

"I understand," Tarryn said, taking note of the fire that had replaced the hurt in his eyes. "I do. I'm sorry you went through that." She saw him in a different light now. He wasn't just a guy off the street who wanted to protect her. He was a deeply hurt human being struggling to overcome a traumatic past. She respected him for that, and it made her want to know even more about him. But before she could say anything more, he pushed his chair back from the table.

"I better go home," he said abruptly, standing.

"Sure," she said, as he walked by her. He picked his holster up from the coffee table and put it on.

"Sorry I have to leave so soon," he said. "But I haven't been home in a few days, and there are some things I have to do, like bring in the mail and paper and change my clothes. And thanks for the offer of a shower, but I want to wait until I get home for that, too. It's a little personal to use yours."

"Is it? Okay. I'm sure you'd like to do that," she said, grinning. "It's okay if you leave. You have to go back there sometime anyway," she said.

"Yeah," he said. "It's not a great place, but it's where I live. Here, I'll write down the address. You can come over when you're done at the lab, and we'll go to the barbecue together, okay?" He jotted his address on a notepad on the counter and handed it to her.

"Thanks," she said. "I'm not sure how long I'll be at the lab, but I want to talk to Professor Hall about my article if I can. I'll come over after."

"Great. And call me if you need me. You have my cell number, right?"

"Yep, in my contact list," she said.

"Good. See you later," he said, walking to the door. "And lock this behind me."

"I know," she said. "I'm on it," she added, surprised at herself for saying the phrase she'd heard him say often enough.

She followed him to the door. "Oh, and Brock," she said. "Yeah?" He turned.

"I'm glad you told me about your father."

He pulled open the door and hesitated before responding. "I'm glad I did, too," he said, as he stepped into the hallway. "Thanks for listening."

She waved as he walked down the stairs, then closed and locked the door. She turned and leaned against it, letting out a deep breath as she looked around the apartment. The silence without him bothered her. There was something about him that drew her in. Maybe it was the way he scrunched his face up when he talked about the seriousness of her situation or the way he leaned toward her when emphasizing a point. Or it could be the way he trusted her with the trauma in his past. She didn't know what it was. It surprised her to think that she missed him when she'd only known him for a few days. But she did. What he'd told her made her feel closer to him. And he made her feel safe when he was around which was something she didn't feel right now without him. She cleaned up the dishes before showering and changing, and heading out the door.

Mrs. Griffith shook her head as Tarryn passed her, carrying groceries and coming in the door. "Doesn't your lawyer boyfriend ever change his clothes?" she asked, frowning. "I saw him when he left earlier."

Tarryn laughed. "He does, but not always. It's hard to explain," she said.

"I would imagine it is," Mrs. Griffith said as she sidled past her. "Spare me the details," she continued, raising her eyebrows before disappearing inside.

Tarryn grinned and walked down the stairs. It was a beautiful, sunny day, although somewhat humid, and she took her time walking to the lab. She didn't need to meet Brock until later in the afternoon. When she got to the research lab, she hurried up the outside stairs. She opened the door and stopped cold. She perceived the same eerie silence she'd noticed the last time she'd been there. It seemed odd. But, then again, everyone was probably upstairs. It had become the new place to be.

She headed toward the kitchen, but no one was there. Coffee wasn't made either. An announcement on the corkboard near the refrigerator said students had the day off for professional development day. That could explain it. It was disconcerting to be so on edge all the time, and all because of her story. She walked back toward the stairwell, glancing into the empty living room, then jogged up the stairs. Hopefully, at least Professor Hall had made an appearance, and she could show him the frightening note she'd received and also ask him if his concerns about her article involved the Reardin feeder fund she'd footnoted in her international finance thesis.

She stopped on the top step and glanced around the open room. The desks were empty as were the sofas and chairs and the chess table near the window. The aisles between the bookshelves in the back were empty, too. It was almost too quiet, even for the library atmosphere of the lab. A sudden chill ran down her back. Something was wrong. She felt it.

An almost imperceptible noise caused her to hesitate before stepping past the railing onto the second floor to investigate. Was it water? She inched across the floor toward the back of the room. As she neared the bookshelves, she realized the sound was a low, intermittent drip, and she wondered if the roof was leaking. But that didn't make sense. It wasn't raining.

"Is someone there?" she called out.

No answer.

"Hello?"

Silence. A ray of sunshine glinted through the window, and something on the chess table caught her eye. She moved toward it. What was it that bothered her? Then she saw it. The white king was tipped over on its side on the chessboard, the universal sign for resigning the game to an imminent checkmate by an opponent. Professor Hall had taught them the sign. But who would do that on an unplayed chessboard? All the other pieces were in perfect order as though ready to start a game.

"Professor Hall?" she called out, tentatively.

And then she smelled it, the pungent smell of something raw and fresh. The hairs on the back of her neck stood up. She backed away from the table slowly, glancing sideways at the bookshelves before turning to leave. But the dripping continued, and she had to know what it was. She turned back around and headed toward the shelves. It seemed to come from the back corner where the copy machine was.

She crept down a dim aisle between dusty stacks of old books. She stopped and peered around the edge of the bookshelf. She screamed when she saw him.

"Professor Hall!"

She rushed toward him but jolted to a halt at his blank, unseeing stare. He sat upright on a straight-back chair in the corner with his back against the wall and his head tilted sideways. His legs splayed horribly in front of him, and a rash of dark-red-streaked papers lay scattered next to him on the floor, along with the mangled, black frames and smeared lenses of his smashed glasses. She gasped when she realized the streaks were from the blood that had dripped from a gaping wound on the side of his head and pooled onto the floor next to him.

"Professor Hall!" she screamed again.

Then she put her hand to her mouth in horror. Should she go to him? She jerked back suddenly as she realized that his wound was fresh. Whoever did this could still be in the lab. And now the murderer knew she'd seen the body.

She covered her face with her hands to block out the horrible scene and ran for the bookshelves, where she cowered on her knees in an aisle. But she couldn't help peering through her fingers to see if anyone had followed her. It didn't seem so. She was alone and entombed in the lab with Professor Hall. Her body shook with terror. She had to get away. She crawled desperately down the aisle. When she reached the end, she glanced both ways before jerking upright and bolting for the stairwell.

She was almost there when she heard a sudden noise. It sounded like the click of a gun. She ducked and screamed when wood splintered on the railing in front of her. Someone had shot at her. She dodged right and swung around the railing to race down the stairs as footsteps pounded across the floor above her. When she reached the bottom of the stairs, she yanked the door open and ran outside.

She didn't stop running until she turned the corner and jumped on a bus that was just about to pull away from the curb. She boarded and dropped into a seat, breathing heavily as she stared out the back window and watched the sidewalk fade from view behind her.

CHAPTER 8

Brock pitched his cell phone on the sofa and stalked around his apartment after trying to reach Tarryn for the third time with no answer. He hadn't gone to the barbecue. He was too worried. She'd never shown up, and she hadn't called either. He was torn between wondering if he'd said something wrong and offended her and thinking that something had happened to her. He shouldn't have left her alone. Whoever trashed her apartment could still be hanging around. The latter idea gained the upper hand in his mind, especially as dinner time came and went. He'd made do with a grilled cheese sandwich and had made an extra one for her in case she showed up. It didn't make sense that she would stay at the research lab this long. He was concerned. There was no getting around it.

He grabbed his phone and headed out. It was warm on the street in the thick, steamy way that DC often was in the summer, and by the time he reached the Metro, his shirt was stuck to his back. He tugged at it, breathing a sigh of relief as he took a seat in the relative coolness of the train. But he was still on edge. When he reached the station in Foggy Bottom, he sprinted up the escalator to the street and headed for the lab. His worst fears were realized as he approached it. Yellow caution tape surrounded the building, and police swarmed the area. Something was terribly wrong. It was obvious. A sharp pain stabbed him in the chest as he realized that whatever it was might involve Tarryn.

"Stand back," an officer shouted. "This is a crime scene."

"FBI," Brock called out, flashing his badge.

The officer walked over and inspected it.

"Yeah, okay," he said. "What are you here for?"

"I know someone who does research here. I was just walking by. What happened?" Brock asked, trying to keep his voice flat and unemotional even though he didn't feel that way.

"Looks like a professor got shot this afternoon. Professional hit, maybe. That's what they're saying. Doesn't look like it to me. But that's the word."

"Professor Hall?" Brock asked, shocked in spite of his effort to remain aloof but relieved that it wasn't Tarryn.

"Could be," the officer said. "I didn't get the name."

"Why doesn't it look professional to you?" Brock asked.

"Too sloppy. Whoever did this was probably someone who knew him, not a hitman," the officer said.

"Hmm," Brock murmured, considering the information. "Yeah, and why would a professor be the target of a professional hit?"

"Exactly," the officer said. "Doesn't make sense. But that's what they're saying. He was evidently a real smart guy involved in some pretty high-up stuff, and the detective thinks he could have ruffled some feathers."

"I see," Brock said, nodding and silently agreeing with the initial assessment. It could have been a professional hit. It could have been someone working for Harrington and looking for Tarryn or targeting Professor Hall. They could have traced the background sources for Tarryn's article and found out about the research lab.

"Was anyone else shot or hurt?" Brock asked."Maybe a woman?"

"No, but a woman found the body. Why do you ask?"

"Just covering the bases," Brock replied.

The officer tilted his head. "You say you knew someone here?" he asked, whipping out a notebook.

Brock backtracked. He didn't want to implicate Tarryn by giving out her name. "Just in passing — only enough to want to know if they're okay."

"What's their name?" he asked, clicking his pen.

"It's not important now that I know what happened," Brock said, casually waving his hand. "Mind if I go in?" He forced himself to stay calm.

The officer looked up and stared at him for a moment as though gauging his authority.

"Help yourself," he said, flipping the notebook shut and walking toward a patrol car.

Brock ducked under the tape and hurried up the steps to the lab. If Tarryn had been at the lab that afternoon as she had planned but hadn't seen Professor Hall, maybe someone at least knew where she was. If she didn't know about his death, he wanted to be the one to tell her so he could break it to her gently when he saw her again. The door was open, and what looked to be plainclothes detectives and more officers were milling about inside. He slipped in slowly and tried to be inconspicuous. It didn't work.

"Who are you?" a man dressed in khakis and a navy polo shirt asked, beelining his way over to him.

"Brock." He flashed his badge again.

This time, the response was more open.

"Detective Marley. Come with me. I want to show you something," he said, gesturing to Brock to follow him as he headed up the stairs.

Brock cast glances around the townhouse as they went. It was comfortably decorated in a shabby chic kind of way but noticeably absent of students or laymen until he reached the top of the stairs. A young woman in a gauzy skirt was sobbing and blowing her nose while talking to an officer.

"Carla here found the deceased earlier this evening. She came to do research and found her professor shot instead. It was quite a shock for her to find him dead behind the bookshelves," Marley said.

"I can imagine," Brock said, following him past her and through the room to the bookshelves. It was quite a studious looking place with its overstuffed armchairs, rows of bookshelves, and computer desks. He could imagine Tarryn here writing or reading a book. At least now he knew she hadn't found the body. He didn't think so anyway.

"His name's Professor Hall. He was an international finance professor and researcher. No one's moving the body until the coroner gets here. Let me warn you. It's pretty bad."

Brock followed him down an aisle between the bookshelves and gasped when he reached the other side. Marley was right. It was bad. He hadn't seen a mess like this in a long time. It looked like the professor had been shot point-blank in the temple. Brock swallowed hard to quell his rising nausea. He never got used to the things people did to each other. It reminded him of what had happened to his father, who had also died in a violent act, an incident that had propelled him into his life of seeking justice for terrible wrongs. He hoped Tarryn hadn't seen this. It was too bad Carla had. He was suddenly terrified that Tarryn had met or could meet a similar fate if he didn't get to her soon.

"You're right. It's not good," Brock choked out, taking in the gruesome scene. "Any idea what the papers are he's holding?"

"Some sort of financial thesis according to what we could make out written below the title on the front. We're not disturbing anything right now, even if the rest of the pages are legible with all the blood on them, which they probably aren't. Everything stays put."

"Financial thesis," Brock said, rubbing his chin and thinking of Tarryn. "Any thoughts on who wrote it?"

"The name was smudged."

"What about the title?" Brock asked.

"Looked like it said, "The Blue Analysis," whatever that means.

"The Blue Analysis?" Brock asked sharply, shocked at hearing Tarryn's last name but hoping he didn't sound that way.

"Yeah. But like I said, we're not looking into this any further right now," Marley said, looking at him quizzically.

"Right," Brock said. *Could Tarryn have written the financial thesis Professor Hall was holding when he died?* He didn't want to mention the possibility and risk putting her in a difficult situation with the police.

Marley gave him the once over, seeming to contemplate whether to confide in him further before continuing. "You know, we could use the assistance of the FBI in this thing. The off-campus police aren't much help. This is more than they usually handle. The way this was set up to happen with no one else around makes it seem professional, but I'm not ruling out the possibility that the professor could have known his assailant. I won't block any assistance you might offer."

"Good to know," Brock replied, handing him his card. "Call me if you find out anything?"

"Sure thing," Detective Marley said.

Brock pivoted and hurried for the stairs. He was about to rush down them but stopped abruptly when he noticed a notch in the stairwell banister. A chunk of wood was missing from the railing near the top of the stairs.

"Detective Marley," he called, turning and raising his arm.

Marley came over.

"Looks like something shaved off the wood here," Brock

said. "Could have been a bullet. What do you think?"

Marley bent and looked at it. "You're right. I'll have my guys check it out." He waved some officers over.

Brock waved and continued past the crying woman, who was still talking to the police officer, and past the officers at the bottom of the stairs. He wanted to get to Tarryn's apartment as soon as possible. He hoped he'd find her safe there with some plausible excuse as to why she hadn't come to his place. Maybe she wasn't really over Todd yet and had decided it was too soon to see someone else. That could be it, although it would have been nice to show up at the barbecue with her on his arm. He was sure his friends would like her. But he'd rather have the reason she bailed be due to it being too soon after her break-up to date rather than due to her having witnessed Professor Hall's death. He picked up his pace as he reached the sidewalk and headed toward her place.

The front door of the apartment building was unlocked. He stepped in and took the stairs up to her apartment two at a time. He knocked furiously on the door. No answer. He knocked again.

"She isn't there," he heard from below. It was Mrs. Griffith's thin voice. "Stop all that knocking."

He walked back down the stairs. "How do you know?" he asked when he was partway down.

"I saw her leave this afternoon, and I haven't heard her return," she called up.

He hastened down the rest of the way down until he reached her. She looked at him strangely.

"Looks like you finally changed your clothes," she said, dryly. "But you look all sweaty. What do you want?"

He dispensed quickly with the small talk. He didn't have time for it. "Tarryn was supposed to meet me this afternoon," he said, "and she never did. I'm afraid something's happened to her."

Mrs. Griffith's eyebrows shot up. "Why would you say that?" she asked.

"Because something happened to make think she's in danger. If she comes back here, tell her to call me." He pulled his card out of his shirt pocket and handed it to her.

"FBI? Brock Spencer? I thought your name was Todd," she said, tilting her head and looking at him suspiciously.

"Yeah, well, it's not. You can call me, too, if you need to," he said.

"Why would I need to?" she asked. "What's going on?"

"I can't tell you right now. I have to find Tarryn," Brock said. "But if anyone comes around looking for her, don't let them in, and keep the front door locked."

He yanked the door open and left her standing there with her mouth open. Back on the street, the evening had descended into a dusky, purple twilight. Headlights blinked on here and there, highlighting the darkening shadows as he shuffled down the sidewalk. *Where could Tarryn possibly be, and why hadn't she called him?* He'd thought they were closer than that. It would be dark soon, and the thought of her alone and desperate on the street scared him. He couldn't think of any other reason for her disappearance than that she knew about Professor Hall, which would mean she'd seen the gruesome scene he saw. *That would make anyone run.* He wouldn't allow himself to think that whoever killed Professor Hall had taken her or perhaps even killed her, and that's why she didn't call him, but it was in the back of his mind.

He shoved his hands in his pockets and walked back to the Metro in Foggy Bottom. *Where would Tarryn go if she thought her life was in danger?* It probably was, and she probably knew that by now. She could be hiding somewhere with her phone turned off and the tracking disabled. *But where?* And then it struck him. She was probably at the newspaper office. If she was there, he'd have to wait until morning to find out since he had no way of getting in while the building was closed. He thought for a moment. Maybe he could talk to a security guard. They might have one there.

He took the Metro back into town, where he walked to The U.S. News Chronicle offices. A few lights were on on the higher floors, but the glass front doors required a passkey to enter. He didn't see a security guard. He stood staring up at the lighted windows and desperately wondering if Tarryn was up there hiding. At least she'd be safe if she was. After a while, he shook his head, feeling defeated at his inability to locate her. He walked back to the sidewalk and headed down the street. He needed to talk to Mickey at the bar. When he walked in, Mickey greeted him in his usual way and set a double scotch down in front of him. He squinted at him slightly.

"Did something happen? You don't look so good," he said.

"You could say that," Brock responded, taking a long swig of the smoky scotch to relax himself, enjoying the coolness of the bar. "Someone I know got hurt pretty bad, and I just came from there."

"Oh, sorry to hear that," Mickey said. "You want to talk about it?"

"Not right now," Brock said. "But there is something I do want to talk about."

"Sure, just a second," Mickey said, waving another bartender over to a customer and leaning in to listen. The bar was hopping on a Saturday night, and the music and talk were loud.

Brock took another sip of scotch and leaned forward. He hoped Mickey might give him a lead on possible suspects in Professor Hall's death. "I need to know if you've heard any more reactions to the Tarryn Blue story, especially in relation to the Harrington Hedge Fund. Anyone been talking about that? Economic advisors or anything?" he added, thinking of Riley

Keagan. He'd sure like to know what Riley was up to after seeing him in the meeting at the Senate building — not that he expected him to be capable of murder. He was pretty sure he knew him better than that.

Mickey rubbed his chin and appeared to ponder the questions. "Not really. No more than usual, I mean, in relation to a major news story. Oh, but there was one thing, now that you mention it. Leo Harrington bought a big place in Georgetown recently. He's running for office next term, and it looks like he thinks he's going to win."

"He's moving here?" Brock asked.

"Yeah. He probably already has, although he owns other houses, so he's probably not there all the time."

"You're probably right," Brock said. "Thanks for telling me. That's good to know."

"No problem. I'll be right back," Mickey said, heading over to talk to some customers.

Brock gulped the rest of his scotch, enjoying the warm buzz it gave him, and scanned the room. A few senators were sitting at a table in the corner, laughing and sucking down beers. Grady, the reporter Tarryn had ditched in the Rose Garden, was sitting near them, and Brock turned around quickly to avoid being recognized. But a few moments later, Grady sat down next to him.

"Hey Todd, where's your supposed girlfriend? I looked for her in the press room, but she hasn't shown up since the reception. What's the deal?" he asked.

"No deal," Brock said. "We're spending a lot of time together, and she can't be everywhere at the same time."

"Yeah, right. Even at work? She's hot on a major story."

"Yeah, well, she's hot on me, too. I gotta go." Brock stood and turned to leave.

"I'm not buying it," Grady said. "You're not her boyfriend."

You don't know anything about her."

"Whatever you say," Brock said. "Hey, Mickey, put it on my tab. See ya."

Mickey looked up and waved, and he waved back as he headed for the exit. He had to get back to his apartment.

"I'll be watching you," Grady called after him.

"You do that," Brock said, scoffing as he walked out the door.

But once he was out on the dark street, concern for Tarryn overwhelmed him again. He didn't want to wait until morning to find her. He changed direction and headed to the FBI field office. Maybe he could find out more about the hit on Professor Hall, and maybe he could enlist some help to determine Tarryn's current location. Not everyone would have gone to Gabe and Macie's barbecue tonight, and maybe someone was working late over the weekend. As he neared the multi-storied building and its bricked walkway, bushes rustled under a nearby tree. He heard her before he realized who she was.

"Brock, it's Tarryn," she whispered loudly. "Please help me. Professor Hall is dead. I'm so scared."

He jolted upright. "Stay low. Keep out of sight," he whispered back, keeping his normal pace. "Were you at the research lab?"

"Yes," she replied quickly.

"Someone could be watching you. Stay on the grass and head through the parking area to the back of the building. I'll go in the front and come back to let you in. I'll wave to you from the middle back door when it's safe."

"Okay," she whispered.

"Don't let anyone see you," he added, heading for the front door.

His heart was racing. He didn't know if it was from relief at knowing she had come to him for help or fear that someone had followed her. It was probably both. She knew Professor Hall was dead. She had to have been at the research lab, and there could be people after her. He had to keep her undercover so that anyone looking to harm her wouldn't know where she was or that she was with him. He hoped no one had seen her talking to him. She'd be okay if she did as he said and stayed out of sight, but what if she didn't? There weren't that many trees and bushes to hide behind. He unlocked the front door, trying to appear calm, and stepped inside the building. He swung the door shut behind him and raced to the back of the building to bring Tarryn in.

CHAPTER 9

Tarryn headed through the parking area for the back of the building as Brock had directed. She kept her head down and shadowed the few trees and bushes on the side, staying away from the streetlights. She'd never been so scared in her life. After riding the buses for a while after her escape from the lab, she'd gotten off near the FBI building after dark. She'd come here instead of going to Brock's apartment because she already knew where it was. Trying to find his apartment in her shocked state was more than she could handle. Plus, she didn't want to leave the relative safety of the government sector for a less populous residential area in case someone was following her. She'd hoped someone would let her in and contact Brock if she showed them his business card, but the office was closed. They were probably all still at the barbecue, or maybe it was too late on a Saturday. She'd been hiding in the bushes with her phone on silent for at least an hour when he showed up. She couldn't believe her luck that he had. But now she had to make it inside the building. When she reached the back, she stayed in the shadows and watched for Brock to signal to her. A man sporting a scraggly beard and dressed in jeans and a black t-shirt walked down the sidewalk by her hiding place and laughed.

"Hey, baby. How ya doing? Looking for a place to sleep tonight?" he asked.

She gasped when she realized he'd seen her. She should

have been more discreet.

"I'm waiting for a friend," she said in what she hoped was a casual manner. If he didn't realize how afraid she was, he might go away.

"I could be a friend," he said, grinning and moving closer. He stared at her, and the grin left his face. She didn't know if it was because of the way she looked or because he had an ulterior motive. "Man. You look like you need one."

"Thanks, but no. I really need to wait for my friend," she said, casting a desperate glance at the doors. Maybe she could make a run for it.

She stepped out of the shadows. Just as she did, Brock bolted out of the middle back door and dashed toward her spot in the bushes.

"Here he is now," she said, stunned as she watched him run toward her. He had the physique of a football player.

The man turned and looked toward Brock, whose face was contorted in a fearsome expression.

"Shit," the man said under his breath.

He took off running and disappeared into the night around a far corner. Brock reached her and grabbed her arm.

"You're coming in right now," he said, gruffly, pulling her with him. "Did you know that man?"

"No. Of course not. Should I?" she asked, trying to catch her breath and calm her racing heart.

"No. But you can't be too careful. He could have been following you," Brock said, keeping her close to him.

"Maybe, but I rode the bus for a long time before coming here, and I made a few transfers," she said.

"Good," he said. "That could have helped lose someone. You didn't go back to your apartment first, did you?"

"No. I'm not that dumb," she said, shortly, surprised at her sudden irritability and annoyed that he sounded condescending again. She could take care of herself, at least in usual circumstances. It was hard to hand that responsibility over to someone else, especially someone who kept showing up and telling her what to do. But she had no other choice now.

He didn't seem to notice. Or maybe he did. He gave her a sideways grimace. They reached the door. Brock yanked it open and guided her inside with his hand on the small of her back. It felt proprietary but nice. He made her feel safe. When the door closed behind them, she breathed a sigh of relief in the welcome silence of the building. He led her to an elevator. She tripped as she stepped inside, and he grabbed her arm, steadying her.

"I was afraid something had happened to you," he said, holding her gaze.

She shivered at the obvious concern in his voice.

"You did the right thing coming here," he said, searching her eyes. "You were there, weren't you? You saw Professor Hall dead."

Tarryn looked down. Hearing him say Professor Hall's name brought back the horrible scene at the lab, and she couldn't form words to express her feelings. If she acknowledged what had happened to someone else that would make it real, and she didn't want it to be real. She wanted to keep it to herself and think it hadn't happened.

"Are you okay?" he asked, brushing a tendril of hair off her face.

"Y-Yes," she answered, kicking herself for stuttering. She should have known that would happen after what she'd seen. "I c-can't."

He pulled her to him. She stopped talking and buried her face in his chest.

"I understand," he said. "Take your time. No one should have seen what you saw. You weren't there when it happened, were you? You didn't see it happen, did you?"

The desperation in his voice touched her deeply, especially in the state she was in. Her stuttering, of which she was so ashamed, didn't appear to faze him at all. He seemed to only fear that she'd been even more traumatized than he thought. She shook her head without lifting it from his chest.

"Good. At least, that's something. And the perpetrator may not have seen you if he'd already left," he said. The elevator doors opened. "We'll talk more about this later."

She let out a breath, relieved he didn't press her for more details. Her arms and legs were trembling, and she didn't want to fall apart in front of him while reliving the scene. Luckily, he assumed the perpetrator had left before she got there. He gently released her, and she followed him off the elevator and through a glass door into an office area filled with desks surrounded by windows. The lights were low but still on.

"There must be someone here," Tarryn said, glad that her stutter seemed to have faded. "The lights are on."

"Could be the cleaning people," Brock said. "They're probably in the break room. Come over here to my desk." He led her to a spot in a far corner near a window. It didn't seem as though anyone would be able to see them from outside because of how far up they were. "Have a seat," he said, pulling a wheeled chair over from another desk.

She sat down with a sigh and waited while he glanced around the room. When he seemed satisfied they were alone, he sat down next to her in his desk chair and grabbed two bottled waters out of a file drawer. He handed her one, along with a crumpled bag of peanut chocolate candies.

"Here, drink this, and try to eat something. It's on me," he said, giving her a charming half-grin.

"Thanks," she said, eyeing the ancient-looking candy suspiciously. She needed to protect her churning stomach.

"Don't worry. They're fine. I'll rustle up something more

later. Now, can you tell me more about what happened?" he asked, leaning forward.

Tarryn wiped a damp palm on her shirt before wrestling her favorite blue-coated candy out of the bag and popping it in her mouth.

"Well," she said, after crunching on it for a minute and swallowing it with a swig of water, "you're right. I was there. I saw Professor Hall." She paused when the scene flashed before her eyes. "B-but." *Damn. The stutter was back.*

"It's okay. Take your time," Brock said.

The chocolate tasted stale and bitter. Tarryn took another swig of water. "There was someone else there. He sh-shot at me."

"He shot at you?" Brock asked loudly, sitting up straight.

"Y-Yes," Tarryn replied. "I didn't see him. I ran down the stairs and outside before he shot again. And then I came here."

Brock nodded. "You did the right thing," he said again. He sat up, turned to the desk, and jotted a few notes on a pad.

"Are you sure no one can hear us?" Tarryn asked, looking around. Something struck her as strange. *Did she hear footsteps?*

Just as she said that a man stuck his head around the corner of a partition next to the desk. Tarryn jolted back.

"Brock, I thought I heard you," he said.

"Gabe?" Brock said. "I didn't see you. What are you doing here?"

"I was by the window in the back. I saw you looking around. I came to the office to make a few notes on a case. The barbecue ended earlier than I thought. Where were you anyway? Oh, sorry," he said, looking at Tarryn. "I didn't mean to interrupt."

Tarryn took a breath and tried to relax. She hoped he hadn't overheard their conversation. Everything bothered her now after the trauma of seeing Professor Hall dead. Still, it seemed odd that Gabe hadn't told them he was there. He could have been eavesdropping. Before she could say anything, he continued.

"You're Tarryn Blue, aren't you? I recognize you from the coverage your article received on social media. There was an image of you."

She nodded.

"I met her at a Rose Garden reception at the White House a few days ago, and she came to me for help," Brock said.

"What's going on?" Gabe asked.

"Are you the only one here?" Brock asked Gabe.

"Yes."

Brock glanced at Tarryn. "Okay if I tell him?" he asked.

She nodded again, surprised that he consulted her but glad that he did. It made her feel protected to think he put her feelings above the curiosity of his colleague.

"There was a shooting in Foggy Bottom this afternoon. A professor was killed. Tarryn was in the building soon after it happened, and someone shot at her. She's in danger."

"I'll say," Gabe said, directing his gaze toward her. "You came to the right place and the right person." He looked at Brock before continuing. "This is the first I've heard of it. Is it being covered up or something?"

"Probably," Brock said. "The local guys, MPD, think it's a professional hit, and they'll want to keep it quiet until they can find out who put the word out for the hit. They want FBI help, too."

"That's kind of unusual. It must have been bad," Gabe said.

"It was," Brock said. He glanced at her, and she looked away.

"Oh, sorry," Gabe said. "Are you okay?"

She nodded, unable to trust her voice.

"Why is someone after her?" Gabe continued.

She heard the words, but they sounded far away. Her head spun with a vision of Professor Hall's contorted, blood-streaked face. She leaned over and put her head between her knees.

"She's not okay," Brock said, ignoring Gabe's question and placing a hand on her arm. "I'm bringing her back to my place. If I don't, she could end up in protective custody, and I don't want that to happen to her."

"I'll drive you. Let me lock my desk," Gabe said, walking away. "I'll pull up in the back, and you can get in with Tarryn," he said, over his shoulder. "Grab the lights on your way out."

"Okay," Brock said. He rubbed her arm. "Take a deep breath."

The nausea that had hit her receded slowly as her thoughts returned to the present. "I'm sorry. I don't know what happened," she said. "Everything got blurry."

"Yeah. We'll get you back to my place, and you can sleep it off. You're probably still in shock," he said.

He helped her to her feet after putting the desk in order and guided her toward the door, where he turned off the lights on their way out. She blinked to clear the haze from her eyes as she leaned against him. She was starting to understand what shock was after experiencing it over the last few days, and she didn't like it. It was nice to know Brock understood what she was experiencing. They made it down the elevator and to the back door, where a black car was waiting at the curb.

"Okay. That's Gabe. Keep your head down and walk slowly next to me. We're just a couple of late-nighters leaving work together with a friend. Nothing to rouse suspicion," Brock said.

She stepped forward, placing one foot deliberately in front of the other and trying to stay upright. She felt like she was floating. It must be the shock that made her lightheaded. Brock held her arm, and they walked together to the car, where she slid into the back seat and felt him slide in beside her. The door thunked shut, and the car pulled away from the curb.

The ride to Brock's place was quiet and tense. Maybe it was her tension, or maybe it was the overall intrusion into the world of Professor Hall's murder. Tarryn didn't know. She gazed out the window at the passing lights of the district as they traveled through the lettered and numbered streets and state-named avenues near the Capitol. The Capitol itself was a shining dome of light rising into the dark night sky. She sucked in a deep breath as she contemplated her place in this glowing seat of democracy and her obligation to keep the people informed with her writing. It was almost too much to think about now after Professor Hall's death. Washington wasn't just the idyllic, powerful place holding the key to her hopes and dreams anymore. It held a dark underside as well, and she didn't know if she could overcome it, emotionally or through her writing. She trembled, feeling stifled and uncomfortable with the silence. Brock stared out the window, and Gabe remained quiet in the front seat.

They stopped at a stoplight. She suddenly felt completely alone. It was a new world to her now after the murder, and she wondered if she could navigate through it. *Who could she trust?* She looked at Brock again to scan his expression, but his face was turned from her. She looked back out the window at strangers passing by. They seemed so calm and normal, not like she felt at all. The light turned green, and the car continued on. She bit her lip, cringing when she tasted a salty drop of blood. It reminded her of the dripping blood at the lab. And that reminded her of the smeared papers Professor Hall was holding. She couldn't recall much because of the trauma of seeing him dead, but very faint images of words on the front page entered her consciousness. It suddenly struck her. "The Blue Analysis" — her financial thesis. That's what the professor had been reading when he died. She moaned and sucked in a breath, scrunching her eyes shut to block out the memory.

"What's wrong?" Brock asked.

"Nothing, just tired, that's all," she said, quietly. She didn't want to tell him what she remembered — not yet anyway — and risk having him think her writing was responsible for Professor Hall's death. If it was, the killer could have known something about her thesis that she didn't know in the same way that Professor Hall had. She had to find out what Professor Hall wanted her to figure out about her thesis before she told Brock about it.

Gabe turned left on a dark street. *Where were they going?* Her heart beat faster. She didn't even know where Brock's apartment building was. She glanced around nervously. *No sign of it. Did she really know these men she was riding with and what they were like? What if she didn't?* She put her hand to her chest, which ached from the incessant pounding of her heart. *How did she know she could trust them?*

"Are you okay?" Brock asked quietly.

She turned to him and breathed a spasmodic sigh of relief at the kindness in his concerned expression.

"Yes, I guess so. I'm just on edge, that's all," she said.

"Understandable," he said. "We're almost there. Hang in there."

"Thanks," she said. "I'll try."

She leaned back, feeling better and remembering how safe she'd felt with Brock at her apartment. She could trust him. He was trying to help her. She just couldn't get the bloody picture of Professor Hall out of her mind, and it was making her wary of everything and everybody.

"Here we are," Gabe said after a moment. "No one followed us. You're good to go."

"Thanks, man. I owe you one," Brock said, opening the car door.

"No problem," Gabe answered. "I'll wait until you get inside."

"Yes. Thank you," Tarryn added, sliding across the leather seat to follow Brock out the door. *It was quite a nice car. Gabe must have an extra source of income unless they paid FBI agents more than she imagined.*

They headed across the parking lot, and Brock slid a card into the door lock. The door clicked, and he pulled it open. He guided Tarryn into the building and turned to wave at Gabe as he pulled away. Then he led her up the stairs to his apartment and inside.

"Whew, we're here," Brock said, when the door closed behind them. "Let's get you a shower and a place to sleep. You look like you need it. I'll show you where they are."

"Thanks," Tarryn said, reveling in the cool air-conditioning and glancing around at the gray-walled, contemporary decor. It seemed a bit stark but livable. "I didn't know I looked that bad."

"No offense," Brock said quickly. "You just need some TLC. Do you want something to eat or maybe a stiff drink?"

"No." She sighed. She had no energy left to do anything else. "I just want to go to bed."

"Sure. This way. You can have my bed. I'll sleep in the living room."

The bedroom was painted gray, too, but the bed looked inviting with its plump, white comforter and silver throw pillows. She kicked off her shoes and dropped into the softness, not bothering to pull back the covers. Brock covered her with a light blanket that had been folded near the bottom of the bed.

"You're safe now," he said, tucking it in around her. "Try to rest. I'll see you in the morning."

A warm feeling of contentment settled over her. It's what her mother used to say to her when she was a child. "Okay. Goodnight," Tarryn mumbled as she closed her eyes and drifted off toward sleep.

She awakened later in the cool dark of the bedroom to the

hum of the air conditioner kicking on. Where was she? Oh yeah, Brock's place. And Professor Hall was dead. The realization hit her, and she jolted up and slid out of bed, shaking. Her friend and mentor was gone, never to be seen again except perhaps for his bloody face in her tortured dreams. She turned on the lamp and found her way to the bathroom. She used it before sucking down Dixie cupfuls of cold water and splashing her face. In the dim light of the bathroom mirror, a ghost stared back at her, hollow-eyed and unrecognizable. *Was that her?* She stared back. *It was. It was the ghost of her former self.* She would never be the same after this, and neither would her friends at the lab, she was sure. Her whole world had changed. The life she'd worked so hard to build was different.

A surge of heat coursed through her body. She clenched her fists and stared at the lost specter staring back. Whoever killed him had to pay. She'd find out who it was somehow and use the power of the pen to bring him to justice. Her investigative skills would come in handy, and so would Brock and the FBI. She stood, collected herself, and then headed into the other room. Brock slept on the sofa, curled up under a throw. His presence made her feel safer. He'd help her. She was sure of it. She went back to the bedroom and climbed into bed, noticing a framed print of a Seurat pointillism painting of a Sunday afternoon outing she loved hanging above the backboard. It made her feel better. *Brock certainly had an eye for art, something she hadn't expected to find in a rugged lawman. It could be another glimmer of a sensitive side to him she wouldn't mind exploring further. But that was for another day.* She turned off the lamp and closed her eyes before drifting off to one last thought. *Professor Hall's death would not be in vain.*

CHAPTER 10

Brock twitched awake the next morning and blinked his eyes shut again when a ray of sunlight stabbed them through the vertical blinds shielding the balcony. He pressed his palms to his scratchy eyelids and rubbed them. For a moment, he didn't know where he was. He wasn't used to waking up on the sofa. He sat up groggily and swung his legs to the floor. And then it hit him. Tarryn was there. He jumped up to check on her. She was still sleeping under the blanket on his bed, her light breaths wisping a silky lock of hair over her flushed cheek. He caught his breath, stunned. *She was so beautiful*, so *vulnerable, so unfairly marred by tragedy*. He gazed at her, wondering what she dreamed of and if she'd respond to his touch. He reached out gingerly to smooth her hair back but hesitated when he neared the warmth of her. He had no reason to wake her.

He left her side and made a quick stop in the hall bathroom before ambling into the other room to check his phone, scrolling through a long list of emails on his way to the kitchen. There was one from Gabe asking how things were going and mentioning that he'd alerted Kip Castleman, the Assistant Director in Charge at the FBI field office, to the situation. Brock cringed. He didn't know how Kip would react to Tarryn being at his apartment if Gabe had told him she was there. He probably had. But Brock couldn't help feeling this was the best way to handle things. Given that Professor Hall had been reading a financial paper at the time of his death, which could have been Tarryn's thesis, Brock didn't want her to turn herself in and risk being considered a suspect in the professor's murder, especially in her current emotional state. She was better off with him.

Brock replied that they were still sleeping and wondered if he'd hear from the field office soon or if they'd investigate further first and contact the Metropolitan Police Department. He hoped they'd do that. He preferred to forgo outside communication and concentrate instead on Tarryn. Despite her bravado and quick thinking in the face of danger, she'd obviously been pretty shaken up last night. He understood, given what she'd seen. It wasn't a sight for a layperson. Overall, she'd handled it pretty well. The crime scene had shaken him, too, and he'd been doing this for a while. There were a few other messages he planned to reply to later. Unsurprisingly, the local news app showed no hint of a story about the professor's murder. This was clearly one that was going to remain under the radar. He pocketed his phone and went into the kitchen where he started the coffee and grabbed two mugs out of the cupboard. He turned when he heard a footstep.

"Thanks for letting me sleep in," Tarryn said, padding over and leaning on the kitchen counter. "Coffee smells good." She yawned. "You look great, probably a lot better than I do. How'd you do that?" she asked.

"I got up and got ready before you did, that's all," he said, glad she thought he looked good but wondering how to read her. Was she just making small talk? He was still getting used to having a woman around and dealing with the feelings she invoked in him.

She didn't look too bad either, even though her shirt was rumpled and her hair was tousled. She was barefoot with her faded jeans unbuttoned. Except for the dark circles under her eyes, she looked better than she had last night. Sleep must have helped. There was more color to her face. In fact, she was strikingly lovely. It was her high cheekbones or maybe her creamy complexion. He couldn't pinpoint the reason.

"Hey, it's the weekend," he replied, smiling and pretending along with her that nothing was out of the ordinary. *They were just a regular couple spending time together.*

"Mind if I take a shower?" she asked.

"Sure. Go ahead. I'll have coffee and breakfast ready when you get out. Toaster waffles, okay?"

"Yes. Great," she said. Her face suddenly crinkled into a frown. "Oh, my friend, Carla, called after I took my phone off silent this morning. She's pretty broken up over Professor Hall." Her eyes welled up with tears before she continued. "She found him later after I had left, and she called the police. She said everyone who works at the lab is horrified, and the police blocked the entrance to the lab indefinitely. I guess she talked to everyone or texted them. She was advised by an attorney she knows not to say much about it, but she wanted to tell me and some other friends. I didn't tell her I was there and had found him, too, because I didn't feel up to talking about it. Is that okay? It was awful hearing about it again." She brushed tears off her cheeks.

"Yes. Of course. I can see how hard this is for you. Keep it to yourself for now. It isn't public yet, if it ever will be. The news of his death may have to stay word-of-mouth between those in the research lab and kept out of the public eye." He felt bad for her and understood her obvious grief and empathy for her friends, but he wanted her to be aware of the stark reality of the situation she was in after the murder.

She looked at him. "Why? He was a friend of mine. People should know he passed so they can pay their respects."

"Things don't always work out the way you want them to," he responded tersely, slightly perturbed at her continual insistence on making things public. "Some things are better kept quiet." He didn't add that it was possible it was a professional hit. He didn't want to alarm her, and he didn't want it to possibly end up in the newspaper if she wrote about it.

"But it's not right. He was a wonderful person. This should never have happened, and now no one can even know he's gone? That goes against all my principles that the public has the right to know and make their own decisions about things." Her gaze was direct and earnest.

"Yeah, I know," Brock continued, trying not to sound exasperated. "But not if it puts other people's lives in danger or hinders an investigation, which it might do depending on what the motive was for his murder. It might have to do with what was revealed in the article."

"My article?" Tarryn asked, looking stricken.

He lowered his voice. "I didn't mean it to sound that way. It may have to do with what's going on and the information revealed, that's all. It's not your fault."

She still looked stricken. "I don't know what to think anymore," she said, pulling away from the counter.

"You didn't tell Carla you were here, did you?"

"No. She probably thought I was at my apartment. I know enough to keep my location secret. I'm not dense, remember? She wouldn't have told anyone anyway if I asked her not to. I just didn't want to get into it."

"I didn't mean…"

Before he could finish, she turned and headed toward the hallway. "I'm going to take a shower," she called over her shoulder.

He kicked himself as she walked away. He'd been working on softening his tone of voice around her, but he obviously hadn't perfected it yet. He'd noticed that she shied away from him occasionally and took offense at things he said. He hadn't wanted to upset her, especially now when he knew she was hurting. He turned and grabbed breakfast sausage out of the freezer just before his phone rang. He slammed the door shut and answered it after dropping the box on the counter.

"Gram?" he asked, surprised to see his grandmother's name on the phone.

"Brock, I'm so glad you answered," she said.

Her voice sounded thin and strained.

"What's up?" he asked. "Something wrong?"

"I don't know what to do. I had to call you. Riley called and told me to check on my investments. Something to do with a downturn in the markets. So, I…"

"Riley Keagan?" Brock asked.

"Yes. He calls once in a while. So, I called my financial advisor, and he told me some of my investments are gone. I had no idea things were so bad, or I would have paid the fees to take it out and put it elsewhere. But there are always restrictions on withdrawals, too. Anyway, now I'm stuck. Your grandfather would have been so upset. He wanted me to be set for life when he passed, and now look at what happened." Her voice shook.

"Wait, slow down," Brock said. "Who told you you'd lost investments?" It surprised him that Riley had called his grandmother. He was friends with him, but he didn't know Abby was. If Riley had called her, things must really be heating up in the markets. As a presidential economic advisor, he was privy to information other people didn't know. He hoped his grandmother wasn't caught up in the looming economic downturn in the financial markets mentioned in Tarryn's article.

"My financial advisor," she replied. "I just hung up from being on the phone with him. There must be some mistake."

He heard the panic in her voice, and it resonated in his heart. His grandmother needed him, and he loved her dearly.

Okay, try to relax. I'll come over later and talk with you," he said. "Do you have any investments left?"

"Yes, I have some, but many of them are lost," she said, her voice cracking again. "And have you seen the news? I turned on the 24-hour news channel this morning after Riley called. It sounds like things will get worse. I don't know what to do. What if I lose everything?"

"Hang tight. We'll figure out what's going on," Brock said. "Try not to panic."

"I'll try, but I'm very worried. I need the income for the stables and the horses," she said. "And we're hoping "Truly Yours Only" could win in the spring races."

"I know," he said. "We can talk when I get there. And I may be bringing someone with me."

"Someone with you?" His grandmother's tone changed to the bright tone he was used to. "A girl, you mean? Are you seeing someone?" She was curious, as always, about a possible girlfriend for him, and his statement seemed to put her troubles behind her.

"Well, I wouldn't say that, but she is a girl," he replied. "And she knows about investments."

"Really? Well, all right. If you come in time for dinner, I'll have Chef whip up something special. I'll let him know you might be here," she said. "And allow a little more time than usual. There are construction slowdowns once you get to Virginia."

"Okay. Thanks, Gram. Try not to worry. We'll find out what this is all about," he said.

"Thanks, honey. You're a good grandson," she said. He exchanged goodbyes with her and hung up.

He dumped the sausages into a frypan and covered them before turning the burner on low. How could his grandmother's investments be gone? This financial crisis was hitting a little too close to home. The coffee machine beeped, and he poured a steaming cup, breathing in the pungent aroma and taking a tentative sip. The rich, savory blend warmed him, and he relaxed.

But not for long. Tarryn walked back into the room.

"Wow," he said, tensing as he looked up. "I mean, do you need something?" She looked amazing, wrapped up in one of his plush spa towels. Her shoulder-length hair dripped water on the carpet, but he didn't care.

"Yes. The shower went cold on me. I don't know what to do."

"Sorry. That happens sometimes. I don't know why. Give it a few minutes, and it will warm up again."

"Thanks, but I'll just get dressed," she said, starting to turn.

His brain felt muddled. He tried not to stare at her, but he couldn't stop himself. "Wait. You don't have to go," he said.

"What?"

"Well, of course, you do have to go. You have to put clothes on. I mean. I just thought if you want breakfast, it's almost ready."

Her eyebrows inched up. "I think I'll finish getting ready first if that's okay. I'm dripping wet."

"Sure, sure, whatever you want," he said, backtracking to cover up his awkward words. "Go ahead and do whatever you need to do. Towel off or, um, dry off or whatever."

"Yeah. Thanks, I will," she said, heading back the way she came.

He sighed and plopped into a kitchen chair just as his phone rang. "Yeah, hi, Kip," he said, bracing himself for whatever the Assistant Director had to say.

"Do you have the girl?" were the first words out of his mouth.

"Yes. She's in the other room," Brock replied.

"Don't let her out of your sight and find out what she knows about the hit. We'll cover it from this end but keep her secure while we find out who's behind this," Kip said.

"I'm on it," Brock said.

"Don't enter the District tomorrow or the next day. Her either."

"Got it," Brock said.

"And keep me posted on any new developments," Kip said.

"Same," Brock replied.

"And one other thing," Kip said.

"Yeah?"

"Keep your distance from her. Got it?"

"Yeah," Brock said.

Kip hung up, and Brock hung up right after he did, feeling chagrined. He'd keep his distance. What made Kip think he wouldn't? Did he think he didn't have any self-control or something? Ridiculous. He had more self-control than most people. He prided himself on it. And Tarryn was just a somewhat annoying, gung-ho journalist who had gotten herself into a convoluted mess. At least Kip hadn't fired him over the situation. His strong words resonated with him. Tarryn was definitely in danger, and it sounded like he was, too. They must have determined that it was a professional job. It was all the more reason for him to get out of town with Tarryn and go to his grandmother's place in Virginia for a few days.

She came back with her shirt smoothed out, and her jeans buttoned up, obviously leaving her hair to dry naturally. She smelled faintly of soap and mint and must have found the new toothbrush and sample tube of toothpaste he'd left out for her.

"Have a seat," he said, pulling out a chair for her.

She did, and he set a plate of waffles in front of her as he sat down across from her with his own food.

"How do you feel about heading to Virginia for a few days?" he asked. "You could use the vacation after what you've been through, and it would get you out of town and safe, too. My grandmother invited us to her horse farm."

"Your grandmother?" Tarryn asked, taking a sip of the orange juice he'd poured earlier.

"Yes. She lives on a big estate near Middleburg with horses and everything. She breeds them. She comes to DC sometimes for fundraising galas and political parties. Mostly, though, she stays on the farm."

"That sounds amazing. I love horses," Tarryn said. "I already called in sick to the Chronicle this morning, so they won't be expecting me in the office tomorrow. As far as I know, no one there knows I worked at the research lab, so they probably don't know about Professor Hall being killed and won't tie my absence to him." She looked down at the table.

"Are you okay?" he asked.

"Yes. Sure. I was just thinking about him," she said.

"That's understandable. It may take a while for you to recover. Say. What do you say we finish up here and get going?" he asked, hoping to help her feel better by changing the subject.

"Okay. By the way, I checked the news app on my phone. There's nothing about Professor Hall. But news about the economic instability is all over social media and the internet. We'll have to see what happens tomorrow when the stock market opens."

"I agree. My grandmother told me she's lost some investments," Brock said.

"Oh no," Tarryn said. "That's awful."

"Yeah. Maybe you might have some insight into what's going on with her accounts?"

"I don't know. Maybe. I'd have to see what she's got."

"I'll talk to her and show her the article. When she finds out you're the Tarryn Blue that wrote it, I'm sure she'll let you look at them. She's scared she's going to lose everything. That scares me, too."

"Most people feel that way, I think," Tarryn replied. "No one wants to lose money."

"Yeah. Let's clean up here and get going. I'd feel better having you out of town even though I'm pretty sure we're safe here for now. No one followed us home last night. But you never know. If someone knows you're with me, they could find out where I live. And with all the talk that goes on around DC, it wouldn't take long for my location to get around."

"Even when you're in the FBI?" Tarryn asked.

"I don't know," Brock said. "I don't know how big this thing is."

"But only Gabe knows I'm with you," Tarryn said.

"And possibly your landlady. She could probably deduce that you're with me since I gave her my card. And you said she was a gossip."

"You gave Mrs. Griffith your card?" Tarryn asked. Her eyes widened. "When?"

"I went to your apartment looking for you after the murder, and I ran into her," Brock replied, wishing he'd kept that to himself when he saw her face.

"After the murder? You were at the research lab, too?" Tarryn asked, surprising him by throwing her arms up in seeming dismay. She was more upset than he'd thought she'd be.

"Wait. Hold on," he said, raising his hands, palms out. "When you didn't show up to go to the barbecue, I got worried about you, and I headed to the research lab in case you were still there. It was cordoned off as a crime scene. I checked it out and went to your apartment to look for you, but you weren't there either. That's when I gave her my card. I told her to call me if she saw you."

Tarryn shook her head. "I don't like this. Professor Hall gets murdered, and now you're following me around, all because of my story? And now Mrs. Griffith knows you're from the FBI, too? This is awful. You're right. Probably everyone will know now. She's such a gossip. How could you do that?" she asked, loudly.

"I said hold on," Brock said, keeping his hands up. He hoped to calm her down by showing he wasn't a threat. "You don't have to worry. It could give you protection from nosy people who know the FBI is involved and stay away from you because of it. However," he said, pausing to think and then looking straight at her, "if the person who shot at you finds out I was looking for you, he could come after me looking for you."

"What? This is just terrible," Tarryn said, frowning. A crease formed between her eyebrows.

"Well, at least he won't be coming after you while you're all by yourself," he said. "That would be worse."

Her frown receded as she nodded slowly. "I see your point. I couldn't keep running and riding buses forever to stay away from a killer."

"Exactly," Brock said. "You had to get help sometime. And I'm glad you came to me. Together, we can fight this off and keep you safe. Are we okay now, or are you still upset with me for following up on you?"

She glanced up. "I guess we're okay," she said, more calmly. "But don't do things behind my back anymore. You don't have the authority to do that, at least not in my book. No one asked me about any of this. Tell me first."

"Got it," Brock said, lowering his hands and starting to clear the table. He understood her need for privacy, but he was determined to keep her safe. And now that the FBI was investigating a murder at the lab where she had been a researcher, he did have a reason to find out more about her. But he didn't want to upset her by telling her that. He took the plates to the kitchen, and Tarryn helped him load the dishwasher.

"Let's get going," he said, when they were through,

heading for the door.

"I'm right behind you," Tarryn said. "*I'm* following *you* this time."

"Right," Brock said as they headed out the door.

CHAPTER 11

When Brock drove through the open, wrought iron gate onto the long, paved driveway leading up to his grandmother's house, Tarryn couldn't help feeling impressed. It was a stately address with stretches of lush, green grass lined with wood and split-rail fencing. Horses grazed here and there, occasionally shaking their manes as their dark, shiny coats glistened in the sun. It was a beautiful scene and more than worth the nearly hour-long drive. They hadn't talked much on the way, although Brock had mentioned that no one was following them. She hadn't wanted to speak of the murder. It was too painful and too fresh in her mind, even though she'd felt a lot safer after they crossed the Potomac and left the now nerve-wracking atmosphere of DC behind. She wanted to keep it to herself until she could process what had happened. Then maybe she would talk to her friends about it. Brock had appeared caught up in his own thoughts, as well, as they drove through the peaceful Virginia countryside. But he spoke as they neared the gracious, stone-front mansion.

"Have you been to Virginia before?" Brock asked, glancing over at her.

"I think I visited around here when I was a child, but I don't remember much about it other than that my mother took my sister and me horseback riding a few times," she said. "It was before my brothers were born. It's lovely."

"Yes. It's my favorite place to be," he said. "And my

grandmother is my favorite person."

"Really?" Tarryn said. "I can't wait to meet her."

Brock pulled up and parked out front, and Tarryn walked with him up a few steps to the door. She breathed deeply of the crisp, clean air perfumed with the scent of lavender and freshly cut grass. It soothed her nerves and refreshed her at least enough to make herself presentable, she hoped. Brock rang the bell. After a short pause, a delicately featured, petite woman with coiffed, white hair opened the door and smiled at them.

"You made it," she said with a hint of a Southern accent.

"We did, with no problems. Gram, I'd like you to meet Tarryn," he said, gesturing toward her.

"Lovely to meet you, dear. Please come in, both of you," she said, stepping aside. "We can have refreshments in the living room. Chef made sweet tea and lemon cake."

"Sounds great," Brock said, following Tarryn into the house with his hand on the small of her back.

The light pressure of his hand gave her chills, and she almost swooned as he guided her forward. He was so sure of himself in every way, including how he touched her.

"Gram loves her sweet tea," he said.

"That's true," his grandmother said, laughing. "It comes from growing up a little further south. But we have unsweetened tea, too, and lemonade if you prefer. And you may call me Abby if you'd like."

She led them into a beautifully furnished living area with pale-taupe sofas and antique wood tables grouped around an elegant, white marble fireplace. A gold-framed portrait of a woman in riding clothes standing by a horse hung on the white wall over the mantle. Tarryn walked over to it.

"This is lovely, and the pale blue hue of the sky in the background is exquisite," she said.

"Do you like it? I picked it up at one of the shops in town

several years ago," Abby said. "It's by a local painter."

"Very nice. It's very pleasant and evokes a feeling of calmness," Tarryn said, trying to control the quiver in her voice. The shock of the day before was still very much with her, even in the calmness of her current surroundings.

Abby nodded. She had a bemused expression, and Tarryn wondered if she'd inadvertently said something wrong. Abby walked to the coffee table and poured a glass of tea from what looked like a Waterford Crystal pitcher.

"You're right," Brock said, joining Tarryn and perusing the painting. "Are you okay?" he whispered after a moment, giving her a concerned look.

She nodded, grateful that he was kind enough to ask.

He looked back at the painting. "It's nice that it's seen with a new pair of eyes. I've seen it so often that it's become commonplace, but now that I look at it again, it's quite striking. It reminds me of a Degas painting with the way the meadow is depicted in the background. The woman next to the horse actually reminds me of Gram. It captures the tone of what it's like living around here, too. Everyone has horses. They're a part of everyday life."

"That's true," Abby said. "I didn't know you thought the woman looked like me. She does a little, I guess." She tilted her head, contemplating the painting before addressing Tarryn. "Have we met before? You look familiar."

"I don't think so," Tarryn replied, wondering if she had met her when she was a child riding horses with her mother and didn't know it.

"Maybe not then," she said, smiling. She looked at Brock. "And please forgive me if I seem forward, but has something happened to bring you here? It's not just my investments, is it? I get the feeling something more is wrong. You both look a little stressed."

Brock glanced at Tarryn and then looked back at his grandmother before answering. "You're onto me, Gram, in your usual perceptive fashion," he said. "Something did happen, and it involves Tarryn. I may have led you to believe she was my date for the afternoon, but she's not. She wrote a controversial article about the economy that's been all over the Internet. That could be why she looks familiar. I only met her a few days ago. She's in danger, Gram, and she came to me. I brought her here to get her out of DC."

"My goodness," Abby said, putting her hand to her heart. "How awful. But why is she in danger? What happened?"

"I can't tell you right now," Brock said. "But I hope it's okay that we hide out here for a while — at least until we figure out a way to deal with the problem."

"Of course it is," Abby said. "I may look timid, but I can be pretty formidable if someone messes with my grandson." She turned to Tarryn. "Or someone he's helping. Come over here, dear. Take a seat on the sofa and have some tea. It will refresh you and make you feel better." She held out a clear glass filled with ice and tea and topped with a lemon slice.

Tarryn took it from her gratefully. "Thank you," she said. "I can really use this." The glass was cold, and the tea was fresh and fragrant as she took a sip. She sat on the sofa to rest. Abby poured more tea for Brock and herself and sat next to Tarryn.

"So, are you from around here? How did you two meet?" Abby asked her.

"It's not quite like that, Gram," Brock said quickly, clearing his throat and sitting across from them on another sofa. "You don't have to ask her personal questions. She's not my date. She's on the run. I'm just here to give her support."

"Oh, yes, of course," Abby said. "I didn't think that at all. But you must have met somehow. I was just interested."

Tarryn felt like it was her turn to come up with an answer.

"We met in the Rose Garden at the White House," she said. "I was covering a press conference, and your grandson helped me out of a difficult situation with another reporter."

"Did he? How wonderful. And you're a reporter covering the White House? What an interesting job. Is your family from Washington?"

"Not anymore. They live in Michigan, but my father was Ambassador Blue. Perhaps you know him."

"Really? Now that you mention it, I have heard the name, perhaps in passing, at a party. Well, this is just wonderful. I can't imagine any trouble you're in being too difficult to solve with your connections and my grandson's help. Things will turn around before you know it." She sipped her tea, then smiled at Tarryn. "You know, Brock can be very useful at times, as I'm sure you noticed in the Rose Garden. He's a good man for a pretty girl to have around, don't you think?"

Tarryn glanced at Brock who seemed to have become enthralled again with the painting and wasn't looking at her. "Yes. Yes, I do," Tarryn said.

"I think he and the FBI are a good fit, too, don't you? They pay him a steady salary," Abby added.

Tarryn nodded and took another sip of tea to avoid talking and tried not to look amused. She hadn't been expecting Brock's grandmother to try and set them up, but it seemed like that's what she was doing. She sat in silence for a moment, wondering what Abby would ask her next. But Brock jumped in first.

"How about some lemon cake, Gram? It sure looks good. Is that powdered sugar dusted on top?"

"Yes. Let me give you a slice," she said, reaching for a china plate.

Brock glanced at Tarryn and winked. She smiled back. He obviously thought Abby was trying to set them up, too, and was leading his grandmother in a different direction.

"Would you like a piece, Tarryn?" she asked.

"No. Thank you. The tea's enough for me," she answered.

"Lemon cake was always your dad's favorite. Did you know that?" Abby asked Brock.

"Yeah. I remember," he said, taking the plate. "For his birthdays, he asked for lemon cake while the rest of us asked for chocolate. It was standard for him." He took a big bite of cake.

"Yes. I miss him. When his horse won in the spring races, that's what we celebrated with," she said, with a faraway look in her eyes. She paused for a moment before adding. "But that was a long time ago before he started betting on the horses and gambling and playing the stock market — before he lost his life. She stopped abruptly, seeming flustered, and glanced at Tarryn. "I'm so sorry. Enough about that. We have other things to talk about."

"No, that's okay," Tarryn said. "I don't mind talking about Brock's father."

"Well, I do," Brock said, stabbing another bite of cake with his fork. "Let's move on to something else, shall we?"

"Of course, dear," Abby said. "Forgive me if I reminisce. If you're planning to stay a few days, I'll have Melinda make up the guest rooms. It will be so nice to have visitors for a while." She tapped her finger on her lips. "And I'll speak to Chef about the menu. Is there anything you prefer to have or not have?" she asked Tarryn.

"No. Anything would be fine," she answered. Abby was the most gracious hostess. She made her feel welcome and special, something she hadn't felt for quite a long time, especially since her parents' divorce. That had left her feeling lost and unloved in the same way Todd had made her feel with their break-up. It was nice to be treated with genuine care and sophistication again.

"Good. I think we'll have Rock Cornish game hens and wild rice then. This will be fun," Abby said. "And you can ride tomorrow, too, if you'd like. Do you ride?"

"Oh, not really, but I love horses. I had a few lessons as a child," Tarryn said.

"Did you? Wonderful. Brock, you'll have to take her out to the creek in the far pasture and show her the waterfall." She tapped Tarryn on the knee and leaned toward her. "It's more of a rocky rapids than a waterfall, but it's lovely." She turned to Brock. "You can ride Sunrise, and Tarryn can ride Rosalind. And Chef can prepare a picnic," she said, lightly clapping her hands.

Brock set his plate on the table. "Hold on, Gram. I'm not sure Tarryn is ready for that," he said, glancing at Tarryn. "She's had a rough few days."

"Oh, no. It sounds wonderful," Tarryn interjected, sitting up straight. "I could use the recreation. I've been cooped up and working for so long."

"Well, if you're sure," he said, sounding hesitant.

"It's settled, then," Abby said. "If you'd like to meet the horses, go ahead. I'll talk to Chef about dinner and to Melinda about the guest rooms. You two go on and head out to the stables."

Abby followed them to the door. It seemed that what his grandmother said was usually adhered to. "Thanks for the tea," Tarryn said, smiling as Abby assured her she was welcome and waved them on their way.

When the door shut, Tarryn turned to Brock and grinned. "I can see why she's your favorite person," she said. "She's very cordial."

"That comes from all the social gatherings she attends and the parties she gives. She can talk politics with the best of them. She's not as well-versed in finance as you are, though. I'm still hoping you can give her some insight into her financial situation later," he said.

"I'll try."

She walked with him through a gate and down a dirt path,

enjoying the coolness of the countryside. It was so much nicer than DC with its thick, sweltering air. She wondered if Carla was okay, given the desperate way she'd sounded this morning. Maybe she'd call her later and Jamie and Paul, too, to see how they were doing. Losing Professor Hall, especially in such a violent way, was certain to have been a shock to all of them as it had been to her. Panic suddenly struck her, and she turned to Brock.

"Do you think my friends are safe? Should I call them and warn them that someone could be after me and maybe people Professor Hall knew?"

"No. The FBI is on it. I'm sure they're keeping anyone perceived to be in danger under surveillance. And we'll hang out here until I get the all clear about you."

Tarryn nodded. She supposed it was okay that he was taking charge again, although it bothered her that he was so direct about it. She needed someone to take care of her for a while, but it was hard to hand over her independence to someone else all of a sudden, especially someone who seemed to take it and run with it. "Okay," she said. "I'll probably call them tonight or tomorrow to see how they're doing."

"If you're up to it," Brock said.

"Yes," Tarryn replied, tersely. "If I'm up to it. I'm starting to feel better."

"Good," he said.

They reached the stables, and she followed Brock into the dim interior. It smelled like hay and warm leather mixed with earthy smells of dirt and dusty wood. It was pleasant in a way, perhaps because it reminded her of horseback riding with her mother long ago. Brock walked over to a horse who had hung its head over the door of the stall.

"This is Rosalind," he said, "the horse Gram thought you might like to ride."

Tarryn petted Rosalind's nose. It felt like crushed velvet. "She's beautiful," she said.

"Yes. And over here is Sunrise," he said, stepping over to the next stall. "I usually ride him when I visit."

Tarryn stayed put, rubbing Rosalind's nose. After a moment, Sunrise's head appeared over the door of the next stall, and Brock petted him.

"I don't know where Jackson is. He's the stable hand. I'll introduce you tomorrow when we go for a ride," he said.

Tarryn leaned toward Rosalind. "You're a pretty girl, aren't you? You're a pretty girl," she said. Rosalind shook her mane. "I think she likes me. I hope so."

"Of course, she does. She knows a good person when she meets them," he said. "Just like I do." He glanced over at her.

She smiled at him. He was much nicer when he wasn't acting like a gruff lawman and much less annoying to be around. They petted the horses for a while, and Rosalind nuzzled her as she turned to leave. She rubbed the horse's nose again, glad that it seemed they'd made friends with each other and looking forward to riding the next day. They left the stables, and Brock showed her more of the grounds. They couldn't go everywhere because the estate was so large, but he gave her an overview of the area before they headed back to the house. Tarryn thought it was one of the more opulent and beautiful farms she had ever seen, and Brock seemed to be in his element. She pictured him riding a horse, wild and carefree, with his sandy blond hair blowing in the wind, so different from the strait-laced special agent he presented himself to be. She shivered pleasantly and followed him inside. Abby was waiting for them in the living room when they returned, and she showed them upstairs.

"You can sleep here," she said, leading Tarryn into a spacious, white bedroom with flowered curtains and windows overlooking a back garden. "It used to be Brock's aunt's room.

And Brock can sleep in his dad's old room like he usually does," Abby added.

"Sure thing," Brock said.

"Now, let's go to dinner, shall we?" Abby asked.

Before they'd even reached the bottom of the stairs, Tarryn's mouth started watering. Dinner smelled wonderful. By the time they entered the sumptuous dining room with its carved crown molding on the ceiling and its elegant, floral wallpaper, she was more than ready to eat. And the menu didn't disappoint. The game hens were perfectly done, and the side dishes were delectable, all prepared by the traditionally trained chef who turned out to be an amiable middle-aged man with a penchant for pleasing their palates. They thanked him profusely before he retired for the evening and left them with their coffee and tiramisu.

"What a wonderful meal," Tarryn said again, after he left the room. "And the tiramisu is the perfect ending."

"I'm so glad you're enjoying it," Abby said.

"By the way, is that a marble chess set on the side table?" Tarryn asked.

"Yes, do you play?" Abby asked.

"A little."

"We could play after dinner if you'd like," Brock said. "I remember you asked me once if I played."

"Yes. Do," Abby said. "It hardly ever gets used."

"Okay," Tarryn said. "If I can keep my eyes open. Everything's been so wonderful, and I'm so much more relaxed than I was."

"Good. That's what you need, dear. You can forget about your troubles while you're here. Of course, you're more than welcome to head up to bed anytime."

"Thank you. But I might play a little chess first. I'm always up for a game."

"Whatever you'd like," Abby said, pushing back her chair and standing. "If you don't mind, I think I'll take my coffee and sit by the pool for a bit. It's lovely this time of night. That way, you two can get to know each other better."

"You can stay, Gram," Brock said.

"Please, stay," Tarryn said, turning toward her. "We're having such a nice conversation."

"Thank you. I'm sure you two have things to discuss, and I want to make a few notes for Chef about the menu for tomorrow. Perhaps we'll talk more some other time." She smiled impishly and headed into the other room.

Brock was shaking his head in seeming defeat when Tarryn turned back to him.

"I'm sorry. I don't know why she's acting this way," he said.

"I'm flattered that she seems to like me enough to want us to get together," she said.

"It is pretty obvious, isn't it?"

Tarryn grinned. "Sort of."

"Tell you what," he said, standing. "Why don't we have that chess game now?" He went to the side table and returned, balancing the chessboard and pieces before setting them on the dining table. He sat down and pushed the sculpted black and white pieces around until they were perfectly aligned. "So, are you pretty good?"

"I can hold my own," Tarryn said, moving her plate over to one side. "Actually, I was in a chess club over the last few years at the research lab, and I picked up a few things. Professor Hall was our mentor." Her voice cracked. "I'm sorry."

"It's okay," Brock said. "I'm sure he was very good."

"He was. He really was, and everyone liked him. I can't believe he's gone." She squeezed her eyes shut to hold in the tears, but it didn't work.

"Here," Brock said, handing her a napkin. "This will help. How about I play the white pieces and go first?"

She nodded and blew her nose, grateful that he was getting her mind on the game. He moved the king's pawn forward two spaces.

"Classic move," she said, moving the same piece in black up to meet it.

"That one, too," he said.

"Oh, so you do play," she said, raising an eyebrow.

"Only once in a while," he said, scanning the board. "The last time I played was with Riley, an old friend from college. He comes out here with me occasionally when he can get away from the White House. He's a pretty good player — in fact, he always wins."

Tarryn looked up quickly. "Not Riley Keagan," she said.

"Yes. Do you know him?"

"Sure. I mean, he's an economic advisor to the President. Of course, I've heard of him," she said, feeling her mouth drop open. "He's your friend?"

"Yeah. Don't be so surprised. He's just a regular guy," Brock said, moving his knight forward.

"If you say so." She stared at him, wondering what else she didn't know about this self-contained special agent. "So, you lead with your horses, huh?"

"Yep. In life and in chess," Brock said, chuckling. "Just like my dad, although he wasn't very good at chess."

"This ought to be an interesting game," she said, matching his move. "I do, too."

"I don't think that's a good move for you," he said.

"What?" she asked, looking up.

"That move. You're leaving yourself open for "check" in a few moves."

"No, I'm not. I know what I'm doing. I've been playing

this game forever."

"Maybe so, but that doesn't mean you couldn't use a few pointers," he said.

"Pointers?" she asked, exasperated. "I don't need pointers."

"Whatever you say," he said, moving another pawn.

She brushed off her annoyance and continued. They played for several minutes before she got him into checkmate.

"There," she said. "How about that pointer?"

"Ha ha," he said, sarcastically. He grinned. "Any other pointers you want to give me?"

Her cheeks warmed from the way he looked at her. "Not at the moment," she said.

"Oh well. I'm tired anyway," Brock said, shrugging. "What do you say we get a good night's sleep so we can be fresh for the picnic tomorrow?"

"I'm game," she said.

"Shake on it?" he asked, holding out his hand.

"Okay, sure." She clasped his hand lightly, and he gripped hers in return. She shivered at the contact.

He smiled and released her hand before standing and putting the board and pieces back on the sideboard.

"At least you didn't tip my king over before you checkmated me," he said, over his shoulder. "That's what Riley always does. I guess he thinks it's amusing to let me know he's beat me. I don't think it's that funny."

Tarryn froze, reminded of the king tipped over on the chess set at the research lab when she found Professor Hall dead. She'd thought the man who had shot at her in the lab was probably the same man who had threatened her in the park. But now she remembered that she hadn't smelled peppermint at the research lab like she had at the other places like her apartment where she assumed he'd been. Maybe the shooter was someone else. "Riley did what?" she stammered.

"Never mind. It's not important," he said.

He walked over and pulled her chair out for her. She hesitated, processing what he'd said. Tipping the king over wasn't such an unusual thing to do, was it? Perhaps not. A lot of people probably did that, although the imminent loser usually tipped over his own king in deference to the opponent. The opponent wasn't supposed to tip over the imminent loser's king. But did it really matter? And did it point to someone as a killer? Probably not. She was just on edge lately. She wanted to say "goodnight" to Abby, but she wasn't around. When they got to the guest room, Brock stood outside the door with her for a moment.

"I'm really glad you came out here," he said. "You're safe here, and I hope you can sleep well." He paused and ran his fingers through his thick, sandy hair. "And it's been nice spending time with you."

She tried to smile, feeling an attraction to him but suddenly wondering if she really was safe with him. But, of course, she must be. He worked for the FBI, and his friend, Riley, worked at the White House. The background checks for both positions were probably exhausting. "Thanks. It's been nice spending time with you, too," she said, smiling more easily now. She turned the doorknob and pressed against the door, but it didn't move.

"Oh, here, let me help you. You have to turn the doorknob hard, or it sticks," he said, reaching for it.

"Don't be silly. I can open a door," she said, annoyed that he was taking charge again. She wasn't a child.

He touched her hand before she moved it, and a pleasant tingle raced up her arm. She pulled away.

"Oh, sorry," he said, as he continued to lean in next to her.

She felt the warmth of him. "No, that's okay, that's fine." She folded her hands, then released them.

He turned the knob and pushed the door open, brushing

lightly against her arm as he did so.

"Oh, well, it looks like it worked," she said, feeling the tingle again. "Thanks."

"Yeah, well, no problem," he said.

She stood with him, feeling awkward, until he slowly moved away.

"Okay then, try to rest, and I'll see you in the morning," he said, briskly, turning and walking down the hall toward his room.

"Goodnight," she said, looking after him before heading into her room and closing the door.

She laid down on the bed and put her hands behind her head, staring up at the ceiling and trying to sort through the emotions that coursed through her mind. She didn't know what all her feelings were or if they were personal or professional, but she could identify one thing. She wanted to spend more time with the intriguing, enigmatic, and impossibly condescending Brock Spencer.

CHAPTER 12

"Now, as long as we're up here, why don't we take a look at some of your investment statements," Brock said to Abby late the next morning. "I'm assuming they're in the converted bedroom office. Tarryn is a finance whiz, and it might help to see what investments, such as yours, have been affected and make sure nothing out of the ordinary is going on.

"Are you sure you don't mind, Tarryn?" Abby asked.

"Not at all. It would be my pleasure," she replied. "I'm hopeful we can find something."

They followed Abby to a door at the end of the hall. It was a beautiful morning, and the sunshine boded well for their picnic this afternoon. He'd thought about Tarryn last night. Something about her made him want to be around her. Maybe it was the way her lips curved into a half smile when she contemplated something he said or the way she never let him get away with anything condescending, no matter how unintentional it might be. She stood her ground. That's for sure. And he liked that.

"Here we are," his grandmother said, opening the door.

It was a smaller room than many of the others, though still generously sized, with built-in shelving and a large wooden desk. It smelled faintly of orange wood polish. A few overstuffed armchairs and a brown leather sofa resting on a Persian rug filled the remaining space. Along with various books, classics, and others, the shelves held framed photos, including one of him as a child, and several sculptures of horses in various sizes, some of them bronze. Abby walked over to the desk and pulled envelopes out of a drawer, and set them on the desktop.

"These are statements from the last quarter for the investment funds that my financial advisor told me are currently dipping."

"Sounds like more than a dip from what you told me," Brock said, dropping into a nearby chair.

Abby flinched.

"I'm sorry," he said, "but I think it's important to look at this economic downturn with our eyes open, and that includes your investments."

His grandmother nodded.

Tarryn stepped behind the desk and placed her hand on Abby's arm. "Why don't I take a look and see what I can find," she said, softly. She picked up an envelope, removed some papers, and spread them out on the desk.

"Hmm. The Reardin Fund. That's a coincidence," She sat in the leather rolling chair behind the desk and lifted the papers, looking at them more closely.

"A coincidence? What do you mean?" Abby asked, sounding out of breath.

"Oh, nothing. Please don't worry, at least not yet. I'm just looking at the statement to see what I can find."

"Why don't you have a seat over here, Gram?" Brock said, gesturing to an armchair next to him. "We'll relax while Tarryn has a look at things."

"Alright, dear."

"Is the 10% rate that's listed one of the usual rates of return on this fund?" Tarryn asked after a while.

"Yes, every year," Abby replied.

"Every year?" Tarryn asked.

"I think so," Abby said. "It's the publicized rate. Many

of my friends are in the fund as well. That's how my husband initially found out about it. It's been a very safe and steady investment."

"Hmm." Tarryn paused. "Well, that is a nice rate, especially if it's continuous. But isn't this a feeder fund to the Harrington Hedge Fund?" She shuffled through the pages. She paused and read a few paragraphs. "Looks like it is."

"I guess so," Abby said. "Why?"

"No reason. I just didn't expect the guaranteed rate of return to be listed at the beginning of the year in the prospectus. It's odd, isn't it, that it's a guaranteed rate instead of a projected rate when it's listed before the year even started?"

"I don't know," Abby said. "No one's ever brought that up before."

Tarryn's eyebrows furrowed in their same familiar crease, and Brock wondered what it was that could be so concerning to her. She set the papers on the desktop. "I'll tell you what. Why don't Brock and I look through the statements tomorrow, and I can make some notes then. This could take longer than I had anticipated."

"Are you sure? If there's something wrong, we don't mind waiting while you look into it. Right Gram?" Brock said.

"Yes, of course," she said.

"Thank you, but I'd like to think about it for a while and come back to it later. That's how I figure out what's bothering me about things," Tarryn said.

"Well, at least you got a start on things," Brock said, standing. Something was clearly bothering her, but he didn't want to pursue it while Abby was so obviously concerned and upset her more.

"Yes. That's a good idea," Abby said, standing. "I've had quite enough of this financial situation myself. We can all use a break. Now, why don't you two head out. I don't want you to be stuck in here any longer and end up being late for your picnic."

Tarryn turned to Brock. "I'll meet you at the stables in a half an hour. I want to make some calls."

"Sure," he said, following her and Abby out of the room.

Later on, he stood by the fence outside the stables and adjusted the saddle on Sunrise before turning to check the saddle on Rosalind. Tarryn was meeting him soon to ride out to the creek with the picnic lunch Abby's chef had packed for them, and he wanted the horses to be ready. He was looking forward to relaxing and getting his mind off of his grandmother's investments. He couldn't help wondering how precarious Abby's financial situation really was. The horse farm held a lot of memories for him from his visits as a child after his father died and even now from his visits as an adult. He couldn't fathom its loss if the money supporting it disappeared. Sunrise stamped his foot, and Brock jumped back just as Tarryn appeared at his side.

"Sorry. Didn't mean to startle you," she said when he sidestepped to avoid bumping into her. "Or your horse," she added.

"No. That's okay. I'm glad you're here," he said. "The horses are ready to go." He gave her a once over, nodding in approval. She wore her faded jeans and had changed into one of his white t-shirts, and she looked cute and surprisingly chic. "Are those the boots I bought?"

"Yes," she replied. "They fit with a little room to spare. I feel like a real horsewoman in them."

"Well, you'll need them for the heels in order to keep your feet in the stirrups. I'm glad they fit."

"I'm glad you were thoughtful enough to buy them for me. When you said you were going into the town nearby after breakfast, I didn't know you were going shopping for me," Tarryn said, smiling. "What a nice gift."

"Glad you like them. That's why I asked you what shoe

size you wore," he said.

"I wondered about that," she said, laughing. "I just thought you thought I had big feet."

Brock grinned at her self-deprecating sense of humor. It was endearing to see this casual side of her as she relaxed in the country, away from the hustle of DC. He wiped perspiration from his damp brow with his sleeve. It was shaping up to be a warm day. "Did you have a chance to call your friends?" he asked.

Her smile turned to a frown, and he mentally kicked himself. He wanted to keep the atmosphere light and fun for their afternoon out.

"Yes, I did. Carla's still in quite a bad way, and Jamie and Paul are both devastated. Paul did say that there will be a funeral for Professor Hall this week — I guess just family and a few friends. I want to go to it," she said.

"I'm sure you do, but we'll see," Brock said. He looked away. It was hard to watch her beautiful face contort into grief. "Let's see what happens this week." He hoped she'd listen to him and take his advice, although she was under no obligation to do so. But he did have her best interests at heart, and he wanted to keep her safe.

"Okay," Tarryn said, seeming to acquiesce. But the furrow between her eyebrows deepened as she tapped her lips. She seemed to gather her thoughts for a moment before she spoke. "The stock market opened at about the same as it was on Friday, but that could change by the end of the day."

"All the more reason to keep an eye on it," Brock said, and he suddenly wanted nothing more than to touch her and to smooth away those worry lines.

"Okay, but I'm still planning to take another look at Abby's investment statements," she said. "I talked to Carla and Jamie about my concerns about the consistent annual rate of return, and they think I'm on the right track in looking into it. It just doesn't make sense that the rate of return was guaranteed rather than projected at the beginning of the year in the prospectus. I don't know why that doesn't bother anyone."

"Well, it bothers me," Brock said. "My father was in an investment fund, and the money he lost when it failed set him on a trail to destitution and despair. It was so long ago that I don't know the particulars or what the name of the fund was, but I don't want what happened to him to happen to other people or to my grandmother. It could have been affiliated with the Harrington Hedge Fund in some way. If something's wrong, I want to know what it is so I can help make it right. That's why I became an FBI agent."

Tarryn looked at him. "I respect that. That's very honorable of you," she said.

"It's the way I feel," he said.

She nodded. "Anyway, my friends both said they'd help in any way they can in determining the underlying cause of the economic downturn, which could be related to unusual hedge fund activity. They're especially interested in finding out if what I wrote in my article had something to do with Professor Hall's death, which I told them was possible."

"Good. They could be a big help," he said. "They have a personal stake in this, too. When you figure out what's bothering you, and if it comes to something, I'll tell my boss and alert the authorities. Maybe you can even write another story if you take my advice and write under a pen name. But later. For now, let's go for that ride, shall we, and quit talking about this? We both need some distractions to help us relax."

"Sounds good," Tarryn said, her tone brightening. She turned to the horse she was going to ride. "Hi, Rosie," she said. "Are you ready for a picnic? Can I call her Rosie?"

"Sure. Jackson calls her that," Brock said. "He left to mend a fence after saddling the horses. I'll help you up if you want." He walked over to her and put his left hand on the rounded saddle horn, lightly touching her arm with his right hand. "Put your left foot in the stirrup."

"I remember how to do this," she said, tersely, raising a booted foot and slipping it into the stirrup before grabbing the horn and allowing Brock to help her up.

She was light and very easy to lift. As he touched the soft curves of her waist above her hips, he was surprised at the mesmerizing effect such a simple action had on him, and he scrunched his eyes shut to clear the haze that overtook him before opening them again.

She swung her other leg over the saddle and into the right stirrup. "I did it," she said, taking the reins in her left hand and sitting up straight. "Ready to ride."

He smiled at her. "You're a natural," he said, walking over to his horse and mounting. "Let's go."

Brock led her toward the gate just as Jackson showed up, pocketing his phone in his canvas work pants and opening it for them. He was a small, hardworking man known around town for jockeying horses that won races, and he did a good job of taking care of the horses at the farm. Brock hoped nothing would happen financially with the farm that would keep him from continuing to do that.

"Thanks, Jackson," he said, riding through. "This is Tarryn, the woman I told you about."

Tarryn nodded.

He gave her a long look with the dark eyes that some women called sultry and nodded back. "Hi. Hope you have a good ride," he said, shutting the gate after them. "I'll put the horses up for you when you get back."

"Sure thing," Brock replied, wondering if Jackson knew her or maybe had seen a picture of her. Or maybe he just thought she was as attractive as he did. He might have to get used to other men looking at her if he was going to be around her. But now that he thought about it, that might be hard to do. He relaxed his jaw when he realized he was gritting his teeth.

He headed toward the creek. It was a beautiful, warm afternoon, and the air pulsated with the undulating hum of early cicadas as they rode down a dirt path that cut through the grassy fields to the far side of the farm. It never ceased to amaze him, this vast expanse of earth and sky that was his heritage but could truly belong to no one. *It was the world's. It was everyone's and no one's.* But his grandmother had told him it would be bequeathed to him and his brother when she passed. If that happened, he would do whatever he could to be worthy of caring for it. *It was his destiny, even more so than his calling to be a seeker of justice.* As they neared the creek, he glanced back. Tarryn rode a few steps behind him, slightly swaying to the muted clop of Rosalind's hooves.

"We leave the path here," he called back, gently tugging on the reins and steering Sunrise off the dirt road. "We'll head through the low grass to the banks of the creek. See that willow tree up ahead?"

"Yes," she called out.

"We can spread the blanket underneath and have the picnic there," he said.

A clean, fresh scent reminiscent of a new rain mingled with the soothing gurgle of burbling water to signal the presence of a hidden waterfall. Brock breathed deeply and sighed. He loved it here, and he hoped Tarryn would, too.

He glanced back when Rosalind snorted. The horse shook her head. "She knows we're near the water," he said. "She likes the creek, and she's probably thirsty."

"We're almost there, girl," Tarryn said, patting the horse's neck.

Suddenly, Rosalind reared back and squealed. A

copperhead snake slithered through the grass. Before Brock could react, Rosalind took off running. He caught a glimpse of Tarryn as she sailed past him, gripping the reins.

"Help," Tarryn called out as she sailed past him, gripping the reins.

She hunched forward in an awkward twist and appeared to be slipping sideways. Fearing she'd fall off and hit her head, or be trampled, or worse, he jolted upwards in his saddle and pushed Sunrise into a gallop. Tarryn wasn't that far ahead, but Rosalind's frantic pace made it difficult to catch the runaway horse. When he finally neared Tarryn's side, he shoved her back up in the saddle and grabbed the saddle horn.

"Whoa. Pull up on the reins," he shouted, trying to retain his own balance on Sunrise. "Now."

Tarryn seemed dazed but did as he asked. Rosalind began to slow.

"Whoa," Brock said again, more quietly, as the horse came to a restless stop next to him. "Keep a tight hold on the reins." He dismounted and walked around to help Tarryn do the same. He took the reins from her and talked soothingly to Rosalind until she eventually stopped her agitated, stationary trot. Then he wound the reins around the saddle horn and held a hand out to Tarryn.

"I'm sorry," she said, leaning into him as he helped her down. "I didn't know what to do. She wouldn't stop."

"You're fine," he said. "You did great for someone who hasn't ridden since they were a kid. At least you didn't fall off."

She turned in his arms and looked up at him. "Thanks to you," she said, her voice sounding shaky. "Looks like you rescued me again."

He grinned. "That's what I do. Remember?" he asked.

She nodded, but the expression on her face was still serious. "How could I forget? You do it so well."

He gazed at her for a moment, his body tensing at the closeness of hers. *She was so delicate and so vulnerable. But she wasn't his in any personal way, and she was off-limits as far as his boss, Kip, was concerned.* He released her slowly, keeping his eyes on hers, then wrenched his gaze away and glanced around. "Well, at least we're close to the willow tree. Why don't we walk the rest of the way and lead the horses on foot?" he asked brusquely to mask his feelings. He pivoted and walked over to Sunrise.

"Good idea," she answered, sounding relieved or maybe a little puzzled.

He hoped she was relieved. The whole purpose of going on the picnic was to relax, not get more tense. He grabbed Sunrise's reins and led him forward next to Rosalind.

"Is everything okay?" Tarryn asked when he was next to her.

"Sure. Yeah. Why?" he asked, hoping his face didn't show the frustration he felt. How did he end up in this impossible situation with a beautiful woman he couldn't have anything to do with? He'd better watch himself, or Kip would be on his case. On the other hand, who was Kip to tell him how to deal with a woman?

"No reason," she said. "It's just that you seem a little angry."

"No, not at all. Unwind the reins from the saddle horn, and let's get going."

"Okay, sure," Tarryn said. "Whatever you say."

He ambled ahead, leading Sunrise toward the creek. Tarryn's soft murmurings to Rosalind let him know she was close behind. When he reached the water, he let Sunrise drink and moved sideways to allow Tarryn to do the same with Rosalind. He pulled a soft, cooler bag holding the picnic lunch, a small thermos, and a red, gingham tablecloth out of a saddlebag.

"That's the waterfall over there," he said, tilting his head in its direction. "We can set things up over here to stay out of the sun. There's a nice, shady spot under this branch up here."

Tarryn paused for a moment and peered downstream. "It's very nice, just like Abby said. But it does look more like water falling over rocks than an actual waterfall. It sounds musical," she said.

"It is kind of," he said.

She followed him to the tree and helped him spread everything out on the grass underneath it before plopping down next to the tablecloth. Brock followed suit. They sat together, taking in the scene as the horses stopped drinking and stood quietly together under another tree near the water.

"Cold chicken is the best picnic lunch there is," Tarryn said, picking up a drumstick. "Abby's chef is the best." She took a bite of the chicken and gave him a thumbs up.

"He really is," Brock said, grabbing a drumstick himself. "He's new. Her other chef was good, but he retired. He used to pack picnic lunches for my brother and me when we visited when we were kids after my dad died. It was fun."

"I'll bet it was. Would you like some iced tea?"

"Sure," he said.

She poured him a plastic cupful from the thermos and handed it to him before pouring herself a cup as well.

"I like kids," she said and took a sip of tea.

"I do, too. I want to have a few someday," he said. Surprised when she didn't respond, he filled the silence. "What about you?"

"I don't know," she said, looking down. "I like them. I really do, but I don't know if I want a family of my own or not. I know what it's like to lose one. I came from such a wonderful, happy family growing up. We all loved each other and supported each other, but when my parents divorced, everyone separated into their own little shells. There was so much animosity it became unbearable. No one talks to each other anymore. I seldom hear from anyone. It's the worst feeling in the world to lose something that was so important to you and so much a part of your soul. I couldn't risk losing that again."

"I'm sorry that happened to you," Brock said. "That must be very painful."

"It is," she said. "I feel lost without them every day. And sometimes, when I wake up in the morning, it's all I can do to get up and go to work. But I have to write. It helps soften the pain. I lose myself in my stories and my writing, and I don't think of the bad things then." She pulled a handful of grapes off a cluster and gave him some before popping a few in her mouth.

"He ate the grapes, contemplating her words before saying, "But just because that happened to your parents and your family doesn't mean it would happen to you and whoever you married. Don't give up on marriage because of something that happened in your past that you had no control over. You have a lot to give, Tarryn, and someone would be very lucky to have you."

She glanced at him and then looked away. "Todd didn't think so," she said, quietly.

"Todd blew it. He's in the past, too," Brock said, trying not to raise his voice when he thought about that two-timer. She needed tenderness, not his usual bravado, which she tended to shy away from. "He didn't know a good thing when he saw it, and he missed his chance." He scooched closer to her on the cool grass and touched her arm. "The right person for you won't do that. He won't give up on you. And you won't give up on him. He'll come along someday. I know he will. Don't give up on love, Tarryn. It's out there. It's waiting for you. You just have to find it — or let it find you."

There was a short silence during which she leaned closer to him, returning his gaze as she put her hand over his hand on her arm. "What a lovely thing to say," she said eventually.

Her touch was smooth and gentle.

"And if it does," he said, gazing deeply into her glistening, brown eyes, "If love finds you, let it in. Okay? Let the love in."

She gave him an almost imperceptible nod, and he leaned slowly toward her, unable to control his yearning for her. She closed her eyes as he pressed his lips to hers. They were warm and soft. He pulled her to him and kissed her more deeply, losing himself in the pleasure of the kiss. She put her arms around his neck, returning his embrace. Her response surged through his senses, relieving the tension that had been building between them. This was right. He felt it. And no one other than Tarryn was ever going to tell him otherwise.

CHAPTER 13

"Okay, here's the deal," Tarryn said the next day, smoothing last year's year-end statement out in front of Brock on the desk and handing him the investment fund prospectus.

Brock had followed her to the office after lunch after Abby told her she had laid out the prospectus and statements for the Reardin feeder fund on the desk for them. Tarryn had just finished reviewing them again. As he leaned in next to her, his arm brushed hers, and despite the tingling it caused in her body, she tried not to think about his kissing her at the picnic. She didn't have the time or emotional energy to dwell on romance when there was a looming economic crisis to deal with and a funeral to go to in the future. Plus, Andy, her editor, had called and wanted another story about the economy as soon as she could pull it together. She hoped to get back to the office soon and write it. She'd already made a lot of notes. She steeled her emotions and looked up at Brock.

"If you take out all the financial jargon and cut through the legalese in the prospectus, this is what it basically says. On January 1st, the rate of return to investors for the year from the Reardin Fund was guaranteed to be 10%. Investors in the Reardin Fund have the same rate of return as the Harrington Hedge Fund because it's a feeder fund to the Harrington fund and parallels the earnings," she said.

"Okay," Brock said, flipping quickly through the

prospectus and looking at the statement. "I'll give you that. Then, at the end of the year, on December 31st, the rate of return on the fund was 10%. It says that right here." He pointed to the bottom line. "That's perfect, right? What's the problem?" He squinted and rubbed his chin.

"The problem is that the Harrington Hedge Fund should have emulated the returns of the market given its investments and the split/strike conversion strategy it used," she said.

"What's that?"

"It's a way of buying and selling stock options to minimize risk on an underlying asset such as an index fund which contains many different stocks."

"Okay. So?" he asked.

"So, the rate of return for the stock market last year was significantly more than that, closer to 15%. I know that from my reading and keeping up on the financial markets."

"What does that mean?"

"That means that the fund wasn't correlated to the rate of return on the market. The safe, conservative rate of return of 10% that was advertised and drew investors to the fund was determined by something else. And, on top of that, it was guaranteed before the year even started. There's no way anyone could have predicted what the market was going to do. It could have gone down."

"I don't understand. What are you saying?" he asked.

"That the fund's return isn't based on the market, even though by its nature, as stated in the prospectus, it's supposed to be. The stated gains must be based on something else. And the fact that it's the same every year is impossible. The only possible answer is that it's not a bonafide hedge fund. It's a fraud."

"A fraud? A big fund like Harrington Hedge Fund? How would he get away with it for this long?"

"Well, think of how people relate to him, especially his

investors and those in the financial world. They think he knows everything, and he did run a stock exchange for a while. They trust him. That goes a long way in investing."

"I suppose you're right," Brock said, nodding.

"Plus, he's paying his investors good, steady money on the returns," she added. "It's hard for people to turn that down, even if they have qualms about its origin. He makes a lot of his own money on commissions just for running the fund and that could easily run into the millions of dollars for himself."

"I see," Brock said.

"As I see it," Tarryn said, "the real problem isn't that Harrington is so smart that people don't understand what he's doing. The problem is that most people do understand what he's doing, but they believe him when he tells them that they don't. This doubly confuses people who really don't know what he's doing. That leads everyone to believe that he's smarter than they are. That's how he gets people to invest in something that doesn't make any sense without any repercussions."

"Got it. So, you're sure it's a fraud?"

"Yes. It's a fraud," Tarryn repeated, looking at the numbers again. "The posted consistent annual rate of return probably brings in new investors who put up new money to keep the fund going. And that money could just be going into a bank account or even pocketed. It's probably a Ponzi scheme."

"What's that?" he asked.

"That's when money put in by new investors is used to pay investors who are already in. It only works until it doesn't, like when there aren't enough new investors. I don't know how this could have gone undetected, but it looks like that's what it is."

"Wow," Brock said. "If that's true, and there aren't enough new investors, it sounds like the scheme could go south real fast, especially with the economy slowing down. And in a hedge fund the size of Harrington's, it could very easily take other financial institutions down with it. That's probably what caused the fears of the economic downturn your article suggested. Savvy financial people reading the research in your article deduced the risk, but they didn't know why or that it was due to an underlying fraud. Now we know why."

Tarryn nodded. "You're right. You picked up on this financial information very quickly. Professor Hall must have known this was all a fraud, too, after reading my thesis for the international finance class and picking up on the too good to be true, consistent annual rate of return on the Reardin fund, which he would have known was a feeder fund to the Harrington fund. I didn't mention that fund or its rate of return in the newspaper article, so the general public wouldn't have seen that information. That's what he was trying to tell me to figure out. And Harrington and his cronies must have somehow found out that the professor knew about the Ponzi scheme. Professor Hall or someone he trusted must have told them what he knew and probably that he read my international finance thesis. That's why they k-killed him." She pressed her lips together, upset that her stutter had returned.

"Hold on a minute," Brock said, holding up his hands, palms out. We don't know who killed Professor Hall. It could have been Harrington, but let's not jump to conclusions until we find out what the police and the FBI uncover."

"Okay, but the professor did tell me that he mentioned his findings to someone, and he seemed concerned about the fact that he'd told them. He could have shown them my thesis, too," Tarryn said.

"Hmm. I wonder who that was," Brock said, rubbing his chin. "That could very well have gotten him killed."

Tarryn flinched.

"I'm sorry," Brock said. "I didn't mean to be so blunt.

Regardless, this puts us in more danger now if someone involved finds out we know it's a fraud. They won't want it to be exposed. You'll have to keep this to yourself."

"What?" Tarryn shook her head. "I should have known you'd say something like that."

"Something like what?" he asked.

"You know, keep everything private, don't tell anyone, even though my first instinct is to tell everyone I know," she said.

"Yeah, I know," Brock said. "Let's not argue about that right now and go with my instincts on this one. I want to keep you safe."

"Okay," she said. "I'll keep it to myself for now."

"Good." He paused and walked over to the window.

Tarryn wondered what he was thinking as he stared out at the rainy day. It could mirror her own thoughts about what would happen to them and everyone else if the economy went south. Would she lose her job? Would she still have a place to live? And what about all the people who lived paycheck to paycheck? Could they survive an economic downturn? She strung words together in her head, thinking of possible angles for her next economic story. It was important to keep the public informed, as much as she could, anyway, without endangering herself or outing an FBI investigation of Professor Hall's murder. His death struck her consciousness again, and she dropped her head into her hands. How could he be gone? He had been so kind and generous in sharing his expertise. She needed him to help her with what she was discovering. But maybe he'd given her enough of a hint before he died. It seemed so. He'd said he told someone else what he found out and regretted it. Maybe he'd known what might happen to him and had told her what he did in order to save her life. She couldn't let his death be in vain.

"Oh, man," Brock said.

She looked up as he turned from the window and pressed

his hand to his forehead. He ran his fingers through his tousled, sandy hair, and she couldn't help but melt when he looked at her with sad, puppy dog eyes.

"What about my grandma? If you're right about the fund, her investments are in real danger."

"Yes," Tarryn said, standing and walking over to him. She touched his arm. "Hers, and everyone else's in the feeder funds or in the Harrington fund itself. It's a huge financial operation."

"Okay, let me think," he said, rubbing his temples.

"Let me help you," she said, pressing her hands together and touching her forefingers to her lips. She closed her eyes, then lowered her hands after a moment and continued. "We have to report this to the Securities and Exchange Commission as soon as possible. If we keep this a secret from the public, as you suggest, the authorities can look into Harrington's finances before he finds out we've figured this out. That might be a good thing. The SEC may be able to mitigate any losses and shore up the fund. That could keep a lot of people from losing a lot more money."

"Well, that's good to hear," Brock said.

"Although probably not all of it," she said, a crease forming between her eyebrows. "I'm going to make some more notes for my next article." She went back to the desk, picked up a pen, and scribbled a few things on her nearby notepad. "You know, once this becomes public, which it eventually will, we'll have a whole new set of problems."

"What do you mean?" Brock asked.

"I'm not sure yet. I'm still working it out," she said, jotting down a few more things.

"Okay. Well, this is good as far as it goes," Brock said. "But one thing really bothers me. Why didn't the SEC know all this already?"

Tarryn looked up. "I'm not sure. Maybe the prospectus wasn't filed properly with them, or the yearly update wasn't made. Somebody dropped the ball."

"Or maybe somebody at the SEC is involved," Brock said.

"It could be," Tarryn said, "although the writing in the prospectus is pretty obscure. Maybe the people at Harrington were able to talk their way out of it if someone was suspicious and keep the SEC convinced things were on the up and up."

"Could be," Brock said, "but it's hard to understand why someone didn't call him on this."

"Or maybe someone high up in the government is involved, and they vetoed an SEC investigation," Tarryn said.

"I'm on it," Brock said, yanking his phone out of his pocket. "I'm reporting this information to my boss." He turned and walked into the other room.

Tarryn used the opportunity to write more notes. Things were going well with Brock today. He'd seemed irritable and frustrated yesterday afternoon but since they kissed at the picnic, he'd been more attentive and calmer. She hoped that would continue because she liked being around him when he was more relaxed. She stopped when she heard footsteps.

"I talked to Kip, my boss. He's going to put somebody on it and get back to me," Brock said.

"Good," Tarryn said, leaning back in the office chair and tossing the pen on the table. *All this number crunching was making her tired.* She glanced over at him, thinking she'd make a quip about how often he talked to his boss, and gasped. His face was ashen, and he was gripping his phone.

"What is it? What's wrong?" she asked.

"The stock market is plummeting. Kip told me while I was on the phone with him, and I looked it up. Look." He showed her his phone screen. "The story's exploding on the Internet."

Tarryn bolted straight up in the chair. "I have to call my editor," she said, grabbing her phone out of her pocket. "I shouldn't have put this on silent while I was looking into these numbers, but I wanted to concentrate. He's probably trying to call me." She tapped the buttons on the phone quickly. "Hi Andy, it's me. Yeah. I'll be in tomorrow." She paused. "Sure. I'll write another story on the economy right away. Got it. Bye." She hung up and clicked onto the Internet, where she perused the information streaming in. "Looks like there's panic selling of stocks going on," she said. "That's why the market is falling so fast."

"Oh no. That can't be good," Brock said.

"It's not," Tarryn said. "Can we head back to the District?"

"Kip said we could head back tonight," he said.

"Can we go now?"

"We'd better stick with Kip's advice. Your laptop's at your work, anyway, isn't it?"

She nodded, and he continued.

"So, you won't be writing until you get there anyway. You can stay at my place and go to the newspaper tomorrow."

"Okay. I guess that would work," she said.

"Just stay away from the research lab. It's cordoned off as a crime scene," he said.

"Yeah, I know. Carla told me, and you told me before. What am I going to do for clothes, though, if I don't go back to my apartment?"

He rubbed his hand over his face and took a deep breath, seeming to recover from the news about the stock market. "Funny you should mention that," he said. "Follow me."

"What? What do you mean?" She stood and followed him down the hall to his room.

He walked to the closet. "When I bought the boots yesterday, I picked up a skirt and blouse for you, too. Hope they work." He pulled a white gauze skirt and a taupe blouse out of the closet and handed them to her.

She gasped. "They're perfect," she said. "How'd you

know what I'd like?"

"I've been around you long enough to get an idea of your style," he said. "It looked like you."

"Thanks," she said, taking them from him.

"Oh, and the sales lady added these when I told her your situation," he said, looking away and slipping her a package of underthings. "I guess you're all set now."

"I think so," Tarryn said, amused at his obvious discomfort when he handed her the package. "Don't worry. I'm glad you thought things through."

"Okay, well, good," he said, glancing up at her with a sheepish expression.

She peered around the bedroom. It was spacious like all the rooms but decorated in a more masculine way with dark wood furniture and Wedgewood blue curtains. "Is this really where your dad slept when he was a child?" she asked.

"Well, I think he was in high school when they moved here," Brock said. "But yes, this is his room. It used to have his horse racing trophies displayed, but they're all in the closet now. And over here on the dresser is a picture of him at college graduation with Gram and my grandfather. Oh, and that's my aunt standing on the other side of them." He picked it up and looked at it before showing it to her. "I think Gram set the picture out after my grandfather passed on. He had everything related to my dad cleared away after they fought about his gambling." He set the picture back on the dresser. "Why do you ask?"

"No reason. I just wondered. It must be nostalgic sleeping in here."

"It is a little," Brock said.

Abby walked in looking sophisticated and lovely in a silver blouse and white linen pants. Tarryn caught a whiff of Chanel perfume.

"There you are," Abby said. "I didn't see you in the office, so I came looking for you. What's this?" She pointed at the skirt and blouse Brock had given Tarryn.

"Oh, just something Brock picked out for me," Tarryn said. "I thought I'd wear it to dinner."

"How nice. You've always had good taste," Abby said to Brock.

"Thanks. I don't want to alarm you, Gram, but the stock market is falling. We need to head back tonight," Brock said.

"What? Falling? What do you mean? How much?" she asked.

"I'm not sure exactly or what it means for you yet," he said. "But it's not good news. I just thought you should know."

"Oh, dear," she said, putting her hand on her heart.

"Try not to worry," Tarryn said, patting Abby's arm. "We'll do everything we can to find out what's going on."

"I'm sure you will," Abby said, patting her hand.

Tarryn thought of that conversation when she headed down the bannistered staircase to dinner that evening wearing her new outfit and the taupe, suede ankle boots Brock had bought her. She hoped she hadn't been too hasty in reassuring Abby about her investments. It seemed possible that she could lose everything, but she hadn't wanted to mention that and risk upsetting her. What a terrible situation.

The dinner that evening was as elegantly served as the ones before, and Tarryn enjoyed the cured country ham, roasted carrots, and chess pie the chef had whipped up. She felt pretty in her new outfit, and her cheeks warmed when Brock glanced at her more than a few times and smiled. By the time dessert was served, she was pleasantly relaxed and basking in his continued attention. She'd had such a nice time on the farm, and she didn't want to leave. But knowing Brock would still be with her made her feel better.

"Before you go," Abby said, turning to Brock. "I thought

I'd tell you that my friend, Millie, called to see how we were doing because I'd told her you were coming with your friend. She said Leo Harrington is having a big fundraising party at his new estate in Georgetown, and I'm going to be invited. He's the famous art connoisseur planning to run for office, you know, and he just moved to Georgetown a short while ago. I don't think he needs the money, but he probably wants the political connections. Anyway, I think I'll go. It's so nice to have another art lover in the social circuit."

Tarryn nearly choked, and she covered her mouth with a cloth napkin to keep from spitting out her pie. She hadn't mentioned the Harrington fund and its connection to the Reardin fund to Abby, and she was surprised that his name came up. She looked at Brock, who returned her gaze before looking at Abby.

"Leo Harrington?" he asked, seeming surprised. "Are you sure he's the one planning to run for office and not a relative and that it's his mansion?"

"That's what Millie said. Isn't that something? I think he lives in New York, but he has a place around here now, too," she said. "I guess he's been to Virginia in the past a few times betting on the horses, but I didn't know that."

"Well, that is something," Brock said. "If you find out more about it, I wouldn't mind coming with you. His art collection is renowned worldwide, and I'd love to meet him."

"Yes, of course," Abby said, smiling widely. "I'd love to have my grandson come with me. Your art history major would stand in good stead with Mr. Harrington, I'm sure. I'll let you know."

"Thanks, Gram. Now, if you don't mind, I think we should be going," he said, pushing his chair back. "I'd like to get home before it gets too dark."

"Well, if you must. It's been lovely having you here," she said. "And you, too, Tarryn. It's been so nice spending time with you."

"Thank you," Tarryn said, trying not to look flustered at the coincidental turn of events. It seemed odd that Abby would be apprised of an invitation to Harrington's home on the same day they were visiting her. But there was probably nothing to it. Brock had said she was active in the Washington social scene, and people could be calling her all the time. On the other hand, someone at the farm could have alerted Harrington or someone he knew that she was there — Jackson, maybe? She'd caught him looking at her strangely a few times, and he'd been noticeably absent the two times she'd visited the stables. But maybe that was stretching things a bit. She had to take into account how hyper-alert she'd been since the murder when she made assumptions. "Likewise, I'm sure," she added, hoping she sounded nonchalant.

She followed Brock up the stairs to gather her things before heading back down with him and saying "Goodbye" to Abby. They stepped out into the cool air, fresh from the earlier rain, and made their way across the driveway to the car. The evening had faded to a dusky twilight, and fireflies blinked here and there as they loaded their meager things into the trunk. When they finally waved to Abby and pulled away from the estate, it was nearly dark, and Brock flicked the headlights on as they started down the drive to the main road.

"I'll miss it here," Tarryn said. "It's so beautiful."

"We'll come again," he said.

Tarryn nodded, thrilled at the prospect of returning with him someday. He'd said it so casually. It was as though they were obviously a couple. Were they? She didn't think she'd mind if they were. But she'd have to wait and see. He was still gruff and rough around the edges at times, and she wasn't sure what his actual intentions were toward her. He hadn't tried to kiss her again. Did he like her, or was she just someone he picked up during a crisis in her life and had a passing fancy with? That was possible. After what she'd been through with Todd, it seemed anything was possible, even with a man she trusted. And she hardly knew Brock, after all, even if he had kissed her — and even if she'd liked it.

CHAPTER 14

Brock switched on the radio and tuned into a contemporary music station as he drove through the gate and left the farm to turn onto the main road. He was glad to be heading back to DC, even though the short respite had been refreshing. Kissing Tarryn at the picnic had given him a warm glow that he wanted to continue, but she'd seemed more interested in Abby's investments than she had in romance. He'd wanted to kiss her again, but he never got the opportunity. It seemed as though she was pulling away for some reason. Maybe she didn't feel the same passionate feelings for him that he felt for her. He could have misread her, although he hadn't thought so at the time. He shook his head and turned his thoughts to something else.

Finding out more about the economic crisis and keeping on top of developments was uppermost in his mind, too. Now that Tarryn had deduced that the Harrington fund was a Ponzi scheme, he wanted to follow up on that, as well. It was interesting to find out from Abby that Leo Harrington had bought the mansion in Georgetown for himself and not a relative, which is what Mickey had told him was the rumor at the bar. And he wanted to find out who had killed Professor Hall unless that had already been accomplished. He hoped it had been since Kip had given him the go-ahead to return to Washington with Tarryn as long as he went straight back to his apartment tonight. Kip's okay made Brock more optimistic about her safety going forward, something he'd been extremely concerned about since the professor's murder. He drove for a while, relaxing as he listened to the soft love songs emanating from the speakers.

"Abby seemed quite taken with you," he said, after a bit, hoping to draw her out. Traffic was sparse, and the road was dark except for a few headlights here and there in the distance.

"Do you think so? I hope so. She's very nice, and I like her, too," Tarryn replied.

"Yeah, I do. She actually told me that when you left the room one time. Sorry, she came on so strong. Gram's been hoping to see me hitched for a long time," he said.

"Hitched?" Tarryn repeated.

"Sorry. That's a vernacular. Married, I mean," he said.

"Yes. I know what it means. I'm not dense, remember? I was just surprised to hear you say it," she said. "She does seem to want that."

There was an awkward pause during which Brock struggled to think of something more to say to diffuse the tension. He hadn't meant to offend her. Anything to do with marriage was probably a touchy subject with her after her recent break up with Todd. "I know you're not dense," he said. "I was just trying to be clear."

"Oh, I see," she said.

It didn't sound like she did see from her tone of voice. "It's what she wants, not me," he said, quickly. "For me to get married, I mean."

"Um hmm," she said.

"I mean, it's not that I don't want to get married or that I wouldn't want to get married to you. I mean, anyone would," he added, thinking of Todd and hoping to soften his words. "It's just that that's not what I was thinking."

"Of course not," she said.

He sighed. "Maybe we should talk about something else,"

he said, feeling like he was rambling on. He hoped he hadn't hurt her feelings. She was so sensitive about things, and he was still trying to figure out how to deal with her. She'd been through a lot lately. "Anything bothering you?"

She was quiet for a moment before answering. "Not really, except that I'm a little concerned that Abby brought up Leo Harrington's name at dinner. It gave me the shivers for some reason. I felt like he knew where I was. Did he?"

"Well, no. I mean, how would he?" Brock asked, surprised at the question but not that surprised that she had qualms about Harrington. He, too, had been blindsided by Abby's revelation that Harrington had bought the estate and was planning to run for Congress. Mickey had told him at the bar that the rumor was that Harrington bought the estate for a relative running for Congress. And now it looked like it was for Harrington himself.

"That's what I'm wondering. Did anyone know we would be there?" she asked.

He thought for a moment. "It sounds like Abby told Millie I was coming and bringing a friend. But that's all. Although now that you mention it, I did tell Riley I was heading out for a few days with someone, but I didn't tell him your name. Why?" Where was she going with this?

"Riley Keagan?"

"Yes," he replied.

"Hmm. His name has been coming up a lot lately," she said.

"Riley? Riley's cool. He's a good guy. Don't worry about it. Abby knows a lot of people. It was inevitable that she'd meet Harrington sometime now that he's part of the Washington social scene. It's just going to be sooner rather than later. That's all. It's a coincidence," he said. She really was on edge if she suspected Riley of keeping tabs on her and informing Harrington or someone who knew him. Riley was about as well vetted as anyone could be given his position as an economic advisor. He wouldn't be chasing around after a reporter even if she was drop-dead gorgeous — and annoyingly proud. Where did she get off treating him like an unsophisticated rube anyway?

"Maybe," she said.

He shrugged off his irritation and continued driving and listening to music, feeling alone with his thoughts. After a while, fat drops of rain pelted the windshield, and he turned on the wipers. Traffic picked up as they neared Washington, and he sped up to lose a tailgater who was somewhat obscured by the rain. After they'd crossed the Potomac River and continued on, the news broke into the music stream, and Brock turned the radio up. Three large banks had closed their doors that afternoon and refused to allow withdrawals by panicked customers. It seemed the downturn was worsening, possibly heading toward recession.

"I'm going to interview the bank presidents and CEOs," Tarryn said, almost to herself in her quiet way, seeming to snap back to the reality of their situation. "I'll make calls tomorrow." She paused. "I hope they'll talk to me."

"Don't worry. Anyone with an ambassador and a senator in their family tree has a lot of pull in this town," Brock said.

Tarryn gasped. "How did you know that?" she asked.

"What?" he asked, glancing over at her. Oh no. Did he say the wrong thing again?

"How did you know my grandfather was a senator?"

"I didn't. Well, I mean, it's common knowledge, isn't it?" he asked, kicking himself for mentioning it.

"No. It isn't common knowledge. I've never told anyone. And my family lives in Michigan so they've certainly never told you. How did you know that?"

He didn't answer. He didn't know what to say.

"Have you been looking into my background?" she asked,

raising her voice.

"Wait. Hold on a minute," he said.

"No, I'm not going to hold on," she said. "You always say that. You have, haven't you? Wait. Is that what this is all about? The FBI and everything? I'm such a pushover. That's what this is, isn't it? You don't care about me. You're investigating me for the FBI, aren't you? This is all a ruse to find out more about me. Just because you're good-looking and charming, you think you can get away with anything. I should have known. You looked sleazy when I met you."

"Sleazy? Now, hold on a minute," Brock said again, trying to mitigate his temper and gain the upper hand in the situation, which seemed to be spinning out of control. "I'm not sleazy. I'll admit that I did an Internet search on you and found out about your grandfather. I mean, it's history. He was a senator. I didn't mean any harm. That type of information is public knowledge if it's on the web. Besides, I thought you were the one who thought everything should be made public." The rain stopped, and he turned off the wipers.

"That's not the point. The point is you went behind my back to find out things about me instead of asking me," she said. "That's creepy."

"It's not creepy," he said. "It's what I do for a living. Anyway, that was before I got to know you. I didn't know anything would happen between us. It just did. And I'm happy it did," he said, before she could jump in with a reply. "But I didn't plan any of this. It just happened."

"Really," Tarryn said, scoffing. "I find that very hard to believe. You're not seeing a girl that goes to Georgetown either, are you? Like you told me in the park that first night, you supposedly coincidentally ran into me. You're stalking me."

"No. Hold on," he said again. "I wouldn't call it that. You always think you're right, and you're not. It's a good thing I was there to run off that guy that threatened you."

"I'm not holding on," she said, raising her voice. "And I don't think I'm always right even if I am."

"See," he said.

"No, I don't see," she said. "I am right. Things were just a little too convenient for you, weren't they? That first night when I met you, schmoozing your way into my apartment so you could stay overnight, then getting me overnight in your apartment a few days ago, and then yesterday, kissing me?" She spat out the last two words.

"Now, wait a minute," Brock said. "My kissing you had nothing to do with investigating you. I'm not investigating you." He tried to keep his eyes on the road and talk to her at the same time. He wished he could just look at her and concentrate on what she was saying so he could come up with better answers.

"Really?" she asked. "I think you are, and I think it did. You found out everything you needed to know and more."

"Okay, that's enough," he said, exasperated. She was impossible to argue with. "I told you, I didn't plan this. It just happened. I should have told you earlier that I was investigating the article and its sources. I'm not assigned to investigate you, specifically, but the fact that you wrote it makes you integral to the investigation. And you should have been told."

He slowed down and glanced at her again as he turned a corner. The streetlights cast an eerie glow on her face, illuminating her tense expression.

"Yes. I should have been," she said. "You should have told me a long time ago. And long before you kissed me." She grabbed her purse off the car floor. "I have to go. Drop me off here. I'm calling a ride."

"I can't drop you off here. It's in the middle of the District. It's dark, and it could rain again," he said.

"I said drop me off. Stop the car. Now," she said, throwing

her arms up in the air.

"What? No. Well, okay. Okay. Don't get so upset," he said when she stamped her foot on the mat. "Geez."

He stopped at the next light. He didn't know what else to do. He couldn't keep her against her will even if he had been advised to take her straight back to his place. Tarryn swung the door open and stepped out into the windy night.

"And I'll tell you something else," she said, holding the open door and leaning into the car. Her hair blew about her face and into her eyes, seeming to make them tear up. "I'm writing my story. I'm not waiting for the FBI or the SEC to do anything first about the Ponzi scheme. They probably never will. There's obviously corruption everywhere. This whole thing stinks, and the public needs to know. And I don't trust you anymore, either."

"Wait," Brock said, leaning over the passenger seat to talk to her.

He sucked in a breath, stunned at the radiance of her fury. Her cheeks were pink and flushed, and her eyes flashed brilliantly.

"Where will you go? Who will you call? It isn't safe out there," he said.

"Safer than it is here with a liar and a ch-cheat and a peeping, well, just a peeping liar," she said, straightening and slamming the door in his face.

He sat there watching her stomp down the sidewalk, swatting at her skirt, which had billowed up in the breeze, and wondering what to do next. The light turned green. He pulled forward and followed her down the street. She suddenly looked back over her shoulder at the car and sidestepped onto the glistening grass. When she ducked behind a tree, he shook his head in irritation and looked for a place to park. The car behind him pulled into the open spot he'd just passed, and he gritted his teeth in frustration. He had to go after her. She'd said she didn't have much money yet, having just graduated, and she probably wouldn't want to spring for an expensive hotel room. She also couldn't go back to her apartment — not yet, anyway. He couldn't let her spend another night in Washington hiding behind trees, especially if there was a killer after her. And he had to convince her not to write her story under her real name if she insisted on writing it. But he was near Capitol Hill, where parking spots were notoriously difficult to find. He circled the block and drove back down the slick street. A car fortuitously pulled out from a nearby spot, and he careened forward behind it, backing to the curb and parallel parking with the best of them. He hopped out and remotely locked the door before sprinting down the sidewalk toward the area where he'd lost her.

By the time he ran across the slippery grass and through the dripping trees into an open area, his hair was damp, and his feet were cold and wet. He didn't care. All he cared about was finding Tarryn. He looked around to get his bearings, then stood on his tiptoes to get a better view. But he couldn't see anything. It was too dark. Tarryn had disappeared into the outdoor National Mall and Memorial Parks. He headed toward the Washington Monument, which rose high into the night sky, bathed in white light and encircled by American flags. The glowing monument was about halfway to the Lincoln Memorial, which was fronted by the long reflecting pool he sometimes visited on the far side of the mall. He remembered talking to her about it. That could be where she was headed, knowing how water relaxed her. It was a long shot, but he had no other idea where she'd go. He fell into a swift stride and headed down the walkway next to a wide swath of grass, sidestepping tourists. He quickened his pace, straining to see her. It was no use in the dark. But she could be in danger if someone knew where she was. He thought again of the tailgater he'd avoided on the highway. Maybe it wasn't a tailgater. Maybe someone had been following them. He sprinted forward. He had to find Tarryn, and he had to find her now.

CHAPTER 15

Tarryn quickened her pace and darted around the circular, gray path surrounded by flags until she reached the other side of the lighted Washington Monument. She couldn't believe Brock was following her, but she'd seen him taking a call in the glow of his cell phone the last time she'd looked behind her. She had to stay out of the light to keep him from seeing her. He probably already had. And the last thing she needed was to get into an argument with a narcissistic jerk in front of a bunch of tourists. Some of them might recognize her from her photo in the newspaper and on social media, and she didn't want to risk losing her credibility by losing her cool in a public place. But how could she ditch him? If she stopped at the reflecting pool as she'd planned to think about Professor Hall and how she didn't have him to talk to anymore, Brock would almost certainly find her even in the dark. And she had no intention of going back to his place with him now that she knew what he was really like. He was untrustworthy, just like Todd.

She remembered coming to this same place with Todd not that long ago when things were still good between them. But that was before her time spent writing had altered their lives and led to their breakup. Now, she didn't have him to talk to anymore, either. She couldn't help thinking it was her fault that Todd had turned to someone else. But writing was her life. It was her identity. She couldn't change the fact that he couldn't accept that and accept her for who she was. Still, her life had changed so much in the last few days, and it was hard not to have anyone to lean on. But it was no use crying about that now, especially with Brock following her. What should she do? Maybe she'd text Carla and ask her to pick her up near the Lincoln Memorial. It shouldn't take more than twenty minutes to walk there from where she was, and that would give Carla time to get there.

She grabbed her phone out of her purse and texted as she walked, informing Carla of where she was and giving a short explanation of her situation. She sighed, feeling comforted to have such a good friend, when she texted back and told her she'd drive right over. But then she realized it would probably take Carla longer than she thought. She always got lost in traffic circles at night. Tarryn's phone rang just as she finished reading the text. She frowned when the U. S. News Chronicle popped up on the screen. Andy was the one who usually called her, but he used his own cell phone.

"Hello," she said, tentatively.

"Tarryn, it's me, Clark, from the mailroom. I'm working late tonight. You said to call if I got any more information about the blue envelope that was dropped off for you last week, remember?"

"Yes, of course. Hi Clark. What did you find out?"

"Well, it's not so much what I found out as what I'm writing about. I'm doing the obit for the professor that was murdered in Foggy Bottom last week, and it turns out he belonged to the economic club in town with a bunch of bigwigs."

She squinted her eyes shut. "Professor Hall's obituary? Really? I didn't know that was going to be publicized," she said, feeling a pang of sadness at the mention of his name.

"I'm sorry. Did you know him? It isn't going to press right away," he said.

"Well, I heard about what happened," she said, evasively.

"Yeah, it's sad. So, I got the go-ahead to write the obit and add a photo," he said.

"Okay," Tarryn said, dodging a tourist and hurrying in front of a large group of people.

"Anyway," Clark continued. "I went looking and found a photo in the newspaper library of the professor, and he was shown standing right next to a presidential economic advisor at an economic club meeting. Both of them were identified in the caption."

"Oh, well, that isn't so unusual, is it? I'm sure Professor Hall belonged to a lot of groups."

"Yeah? Well, what's even more amazing is that I found the same economic advisor in a private, recorded Zoom call that somehow got posted on social media. He was talking about running the Reardin Fund, which is an investment fund. Isn't that a conflict of interest? I was thinking I could incorporate that into the obituary as him being someone the professor knew and get a byline on a breaking story."

"Wait. What?" Tarryn asked. "The Reardin Fund? A byline for an obituary?" She took a deep breath as she processed what he said. The air smelled fresh and clean from the recent rain, and it calmed her, at least momentarily.

"Yeah, if I write it right, don't you think?" Clark asked. "It could be a career starter for me."

"Hmm. I don't know about a byline. But let's back up a little bit. Who was it that was talking about running the Reardin Fund?"

"The economic advisor. His name was Riley Keagan," Clark said.

"Oh my gosh," Tarryn said, gripping her phone. "Are you sure?"

"Yeah, why? Is it a conflict of interest?"

"I'm pretty sure it is. You can look into it," she said. "But are you sure that was his name?"

"Yeah. I'm looking at the caption on the newspaper photo right now."

"Well, if it is, that's the least of our worries," she said. If Professor Hall knew Riley Keagan in the economic club, it was possible he had talked to him about his concerns about the Reardin Fund without knowing that Keagan covertly ran it. He could have mentioned her name and her financial thesis, as well. Was Riley Keagan the person Professor Hall regretted confiding in?

"What do you mean that's the least of our worries?" Clark asked.

'Nothing. I'll tell you later. I'm glad you told me," she said. "But what's all this got to do with the blue envelope?" she asked, suddenly feeling unsafe. She glanced behind her, but she didn't see anything to base her fears on.

"Oh, I almost forgot to tell you," Clark said. "The guy Riley Keagan was talking to on the Zoom call was named Leo Harrington. He's the man that dropped the envelope off in the mailroom."

"No," Tarryn said, gasping.

"Yes. I'd bet my life on it," Clark said. "He had sunglasses on, but they weren't dark enough to really disguise him. It looked just like him."

"Oh no," Tarryn said under her breath, struggling to maintain her composure. She had to get off the phone to keep Clark from knowing how upset she was. She wanted to keep her own thoughts about Riley Keagan and Leo Harrington to herself for now. "Well, thanks for calling," she said as brightly as she could. "Talk to Andy about the byline if you want to write about Riley Keagan running the Reardin fund. He might give you space for a story on it next week separate from the obituary. I'll talk to him about it. Maybe it could expand on information from a story

I'm writing that incorporates the Reardin Fund."

"No kidding? My own article?"

"All I can do is mention it," she said. "He might ask you to use a pen name for now, given how controversial it could be. But it would be a start." Was there the shadow of a man behind the streetlamp, the trees, or was it her imagination? She narrowed her eyes and squinted. *Nothing.* It must have been her imagination.

"Okay. Thanks. I owe you one," Clark said.

"Sure," Tarryn said, hanging up. Harrington had a lot of gall delivering a note like that to a newspaper personally. He must not have trusted anyone else enough to do it for him. Maybe he was running solo more than she thought in covering up the fraud, picking and choosing who to trust. She shivered, thinking again of the message in the blue envelope that said, *"Be careful what you write. Be careful who you talk to. Ask the professor what this means."* It was etched in her mind. Had Harrington threatened Professor Hall, too, and that's why he wanted her to talk to him? Or even more disturbing was the thought that Harrington could have been the ringleader in the professor's impending murder and was warning her in advance that that could happen to her, as well. The more she thought about it, the more she wasn't sure what to think. She glanced behind her again as she slipped her phone back into her purse. Brock was nowhere to be seen, and he didn't appear to be on the walkway on the other side of the reflecting pool either. That was a relief. Maybe she'd lost him.

The distant roar of a rising jet rumbled through the dark, clouded sky. She caught a glimpse of it in a sliver of light from the moon until it climbed into obscurity high above the tall columns of the Lincoln Memorial. That's how she felt — obscured, hidden from the world with her dark memory of Professor Hall's murder. But she had to be alone. She couldn't trust anybody now except maybe Carla and her other friends from the lab. Brock wasn't on her trustworthy list anymore, and not just because he had lied to her about investigating her, which she was pretty sure he had. It was because he was friends with Riley Keagan, about whom she was beginning to have serious misgivings. Were there footsteps behind her? She turned and gasped. It was Brock.

"Man. How do you talk on the phone and walk so fast at the same time?" he asked, sidling up close beside her. "You're a tough lady to catch."

"I don't want to talk to you," she huffed, annoyed that he'd found her and determined to keep her distance even though she was somewhat reassured that she wasn't alone anymore. She tried not to notice how his casual nearness made her body tremble. "I thought I made myself clear."

"That doesn't matter," he said, brusquely. "You don't have to talk to me, but you do have to come with me. I can't leave you out here by yourself when you're in danger. You're not safe."

"I can take care of myself," she said, nipping her lip as she thought of the shadow she'd seen earlier behind the streetlamp.

"I don't think you can," he replied. "Not in the situation you're in. Let me help you."

"Help me? You've done quite enough already, I should think." She quickened her pace.

He kept up with her. "Come on. Cool it. I didn't do anything wrong," he said. "You need to listen to reason."

"Reason? Really. So, I can have some hotshot Lothario coming onto me all the time? I don't think so."

"Hotshot what?"

"Never mind," she said, hurrying up a mountainous tier of steps in front of the Lincoln Memorial. She heard him behind her. "Why are you still following me?" she called over her shoulder.

"Slow down," he said.

She could have headed for the street instead of climbing the stairs, but Brock's presence threw her. She didn't want him to see Carla picking her up, so she made a snap decision to leave him searching for her at the Lincoln Memorial. She jogged to the top of the slick steps and started up another tier of stairs. She kept going until she reached the top. The statuesque, seated figure glowing behind towering, fluted columns never failed to take her breath away, and tonight was no exception. She sighed and glanced around, checking behind her for Brock. He was halfway to the top, bent over. It was dark on the steps and hard to see, but it looked like he'd slipped and was recovering. She could lose him if she sneaked through the colonnade and back down the stairs before he made it to the top. There weren't as many people milling about near the statue as she thought there would be, but it was late and threatening to rain. Still, there were enough for Brock to possibly assume she was with the other tourists and check for her there, allowing her time to escape in the other direction.

She hastened forward between the marble columns, perusing the chamber and planning to make a quick exit. Her boots clicked on the floor and echoed. *Or was it something else?* She paused, listening. Were there footsteps near the columns on the right? Could be. She didn't see anyone. She hurried left instead, hoping Brock wouldn't suddenly appear and stop her. At the next column, she stopped and peered around to see where he was. He wasn't anywhere — not on the steps where only a few people remained, not in the chamber. Where could he be? She stood still, searching for a while, but to no avail. It was hard to see in the dark. He must be somewhere, and if she wasn't careful, he might see her. Maybe she'd walk all the way around the Memorial through the colonnade and leave down the right side of the front steps before Brock showed up and found her. That way, whoever it was whose footsteps she heard would probably be gone, too, and she could leave undetected. If she laid low and stayed away from the tourists, Brock would have no observer to ask about her whereabouts, either. He'd probably do that if he could, given how nosy he was. She'd been accused of being nosy before because of her investigative position, but it was nothing compared to him.

She walked quickly, hoping to turn the corner before Brock spotted her. Her boots clicked annoyingly, and she hoped he wouldn't recognize the sound and notice her. She reached the corner, turned, and walked down the side of the Memorial. It was quieter here except for the flutter of her skirt in the quickening breeze and the sound of her boots. No one was in front of her. She could probably make it all around in record time.

The car lights curving on the highway in the distance lit the dark night and made her wish she was traveling — escaping back to Michigan and the physical, if not emotional, safety of home. She was scared. There was no getting around it. Her article had started a maelstrom of problems she had no idea how to deal with. And now with Brock turning out to be an underhanded snoop, she didn't have him and the FBI to turn to anymore. She shook her head and hurried forward. The only solution was to lay low and write and publish another article. Only then would an informed public be able to protect themselves and take down the fraud, saving her and others from its evil tentacles.

Just as she turned the next corner, a shot cracked through the blustery night, muffled by the roar of another plane overhead. She ducked reflexively and jumped back a few feet behind the safety of the wall, terrified. That must have been what it was, but there was no one else around to confirm it. It seemed to have come from the colonnade on the back of the Memorial. What if Professor Hall's killer was there and after her? Had he heard her coming? Should she turn and run or stay and peer around the corner to see who it was? Her journalistic curiosity got the better of her. She took a tentative step forward.

Suddenly, footsteps pounded behind her. "Stay where you are," a voice commanded in a loud whisper. "I'll take it from here."

Brock raced past her, his gun drawn and his face taut. "Don't move," he said over his shoulder when he reached the corner. He braced his back against the wall and sidled toward the edge while holding his gun up in front of him with two hands.

"I w-won't," she said. She had no intention of moving. She was shaking too much. Instead, she froze in position and waited to see what Brock would do next.

CHAPTER 16

Brock gripped his gun with both hands, pressing his back against the wall as he prepared to storm the corner. He was glad he'd found Tarryn in time. He'd been tripped up on the stairs earlier from behind and hit the ground hard, banging his head and unable to see who had accosted him. When he'd eventually picked himself up, he'd groggily dodged a few concerned couples who hadn't seen who did it either and headed after Tarryn. Whoever had tripped him could have done so to get him out of the way and go after her. She was nowhere to be found. He'd finally spotted her turning the corner in the colonnade and, luckily, had almost reached her just as the shot clipped the air. Now, he was in a position to confront the shooter.

He paused for a few seconds, then glanced quickly down the back colonnade and, seeing no immediate danger, pivoted around the corner into a low stance with his gun pointed in front of him to scope things out. A dark figure ran down the back side of the columns and disappeared around the far corner. It must have been the gunman. He was too far away to shoot at, and Brock didn't want to do that anyway and risk scaring the tourists. Besides, it wouldn't accomplish anything to shoot someone for firing a shot without knowing why they did it or what their intentions were. He couldn't be sure it was someone after Tarryn, although it probably was. The movement of the runner seemed oddly familiar for some reason, but he couldn't pinpoint why in the dark. He stood and holstered his gun before walking back to assure Tarryn things were okay. The shot must have been cloaked enough by the sound of the plane to keep anyone else, including park security, from hearing it, as no one showed up to investigate — not yet, anyway. He would keep it that way. There was no need to escalate the incident and have Tarryn put in the position of needing to give a statement to the police. He wanted to keep her away from possible negative publicity and out of the turbulent political limelight.

She was crouched against the wall, staring blankly toward the back when he rounded the corner. Her eyes widened when she saw him.

"Who was it? What happened?" she asked.

"I couldn't make out who it was, but someone was there. He ran away down the other side. We have to get you out of here," he said. "I'll call a taxi to take us back to my car, and we'll go home."

"What do you mean home?" she asked.

"Back to my place," he said.

"I can't. I called Carla to pick me up. She'll probably call and tell me she's here any minute."

"Well, call her and tell her not to come."

"Why?"

"Because of what happened," he said, exasperated that she couldn't seem to accept or realize how much danger she was in. Or maybe she was just in denial so she could put it out of her mind and concentrate on her stories. "You're better off with me. That guy could be anywhere by now." He reached out to take her arm, but his head throbbed painfully, and he put his hand to it, feeling a bump. It was sticky and warm.

"Don't yell at me," she said, sounding hurt.

"I'm not yelling at you," he said, more loudly than he'd intended. He flinched at the pain in his head and pulled his hand down to look at his fingers. "I'm concerned about you."

Her expression softened. "You're bleeding," she said, reaching out. "Here, let me see."

She touched his hand, then reached up and shifted his hair, running her fingers over his head.

"Ouch," he said, pulling back. "What are you doing?"

"Sorry. That's quite a bump you have there. We should put ice on it right away."

"I'm fine," he said abruptly, "as long as you don't touch my head. Geez."

"You're not fine. What happened?" she asked.

"Someone tripped me on the steps earlier," he said.

"Tripped you? Was it the gunman?"

"I don't know. I didn't see who did it," he said.

"It probably was," she said. "We need to look out for you, too, to keep you from being hurt while you're around me. I'll call Carla and see where she is." Just then, her phone rang. "Carla? Yes, hi. You're parked where? The circle drive? Yes, I know you can't stay there very long. We're leaving the Memorial now. Maybe you can drive around and come back if you have to. Okay, we'll be right over. Yes, we. Brock's here, too. We made up." She paused. "I know. I know," she said after a moment in a placating manner.

He wondered what that meant. Was Carla putting her two cents in about their argument? He didn't like that very well.

Tarryn continued. "Can you take us back to his car near the Capitol? Good. We'll go back to his place from there. He's hurt." She paused. "Yes. He fell and bumped his head. Okay. See you soon." She hung up. "C'mon. We have to go. Carla's waiting for us."

"Okay, but stay close to me. I don't want you running off and getting shot at again." He firmly took her arm and walked with her back toward the front of the Memorial. "We'll leave this way and head down the front steps."

The view from the front of the Memorial looking out over the reflecting pool at the glowing Washington Monument was spectacular, and he paused to take it in. He'd been to the National Mall several times, but it never became commonplace. It always gave him chills and made him remember why he had become an FBI agent in the first place — to seek justice for everyone in this stunning democracy, including his late father and his family.

Tarryn looked up at him. "What are you thinking about?" she asked, quietly.

He looked down at her when she leaned in closer.

"How glad I am that I found you and that you're safe," he said, entranced. Her damp hair had tiny ringlets in it that sprung about her face and danced with her movements.

"Thank you," she said. "Maybe I didn't say it before, but I'm glad you found me, too. You saved my life again."

He nodded gingerly and didn't correct her. It was possible that he had. "We'd better get going," he said, gruffly, wresting his gaze away.

They continued on, walking in front of the Memorial, and Brock scanned the tiers of steps, looking for the gunman or any suspicious person. The area seemed secure, but it was too dark to be sure. He stayed close to her as they headed down the steps to make their way toward the street. They walked in silence for a while.

"That's her over there," Tarryn said, eventually.

Brock followed her to a running car and slid into the backseat as she got into the front. He leaned back, favoring his head.

"Thanks for doing this, Carla. You're a real friend," Tarryn said. "This is Brock. Brock, Carla."

The driver turned around, and Brock recognized her as the woman he'd seen at the research lab while the police were investigating Professor Hall's murder.

"Yes, hello," he said. "We crossed paths before under unfortunate circumstances. I hope you're doing okay."

"Of course. I remember seeing you," Carla said. "I'm coping as well as I can." She turned back around. "If you show me where his car is, I'll take you there." She pulled away from the curb. "I'll just go back home after that if that's okay. I got lost driving around Washington Circle on the way over and ended up on some street who knows where until I found a place to turn around. It scared me."

"I'm sorry. I know how you hate that," Tarryn said. "Sure. You don't have to come to Brock's place with me. We only need to get to his car."

When she left it at that, Brock realized she wasn't going to tell her friend about being shot at. Maybe Tarryn was beginning to come around to his way of thinking by keeping things private instead of telling everyone everything that happened all the time, which was her nature with her writing. They drove for a while before Carla started a conversation.

"Professor Hall's funeral has been postponed. In fact, it's probably not going to happen at all," Carla said. "I thought you'd want to know. The family is having a small memorial service for themselves and is asking people to give money to charities in lieu of flowers." She sniffled. "Jamie told me. Someone told her."

"Oh, thanks for telling me," Tarryn said. "I know this is really hard for you. It's hard for me, too, and for all of us. He was such a nice man."

"Yeah. I wish I knew who killed him," Carla said. "Whoever it was should go away for a long time."

"Yes. It's awful," Tarryn agreed just as they pulled up next to Brock's car. "Thanks for bringing us here," she said as she stepped out.

"Call me sometime, and we'll get Paul and Jamie together

and do something," Carla said.

"Sure," Tarryn answered before closing the door.

Brock got out behind her. Carla waved as she pulled away, and they waved back. Tarryn hurried forward and jumped into Brock's car just as the rain started again.

"Whew," he said, as he plopped into the driver's seat. "Looks like we barely avoided getting caught in a deluge."

Rain sprayed across the windshield as a sudden light flashed across the sky to a clap of thunder.

"Wow. Lightning, too. Looks like we're in for a real thunderstorm. I'll get us home as soon as possible," Brock said, as he navigated out of the parking space.

"Home. You keep saying that," Tarryn said.

"Well, my home," he said. "I only say that for lack of a better word. I don't mean anything by it."

"I know," she said. "But I miss my apartment. That's *my* home. All my things are there."

"We'll find a way to get you back there," he said. "Just not right now."

"Okay," she said.

He drove them back to his place without any further incidents, navigating through the storm as best he could. The rain let up just as he pulled into the parking lot of his building, and he hastened her inside and into his apartment, sighing with relief as he closed the door behind them. Safe. She was safe. He'd made it back with her.

She slipped off her soaked boots and left them by the door before heading toward the back.

"Would you like a glass of chardonnay?" he asked.

"Sure. Great," she said. "After I freshen up. I'll be right back. And we'll put ice on that bump."

He went to the kitchen and poured a couple glasses. As he brought them over to the coffee table, she returned and went into the kitchen.

"What are you doing?" he asked.

"Where are your Ziploc bags?" she asked back.

"In the drawer by the fridge," he said.

"Hang tight. I'll fill one with ice and bring it to you."

He sat on the sofa and waited until she came over with a bag of ice wrapped in a dish towel.

"Here. Put this on your head," she said, handing it to him. "It will help the swelling go down and make you feel better."

He took it from her and handed her a glass of wine.

"Thanks," she said. She took a sip and leaned back against the cushions. "I can't believe we're home safe. What a night."

"You said it," he said. He placed the ice on his head and leaned back against the cushions. It did make him feel better.

"You know you just said 'home,'" he said, eventually.

"What?"

"You just said, "We're home safe.""

"Oh. Well. Whatever." She took another sip of wine.

He smiled. "Yeah, whatever," he said. He liked hearing her call his place home.

They sat sipping their wine in companionable silence for a while. He didn't want to bring up the gunman again so soon. Maybe they'd talk more about what happened tomorrow when she'd had time to get over it. It seemed she had other things on her mind anyway. The tiny crease between her eyebrows returned.

"There's one other thing I should mention after thinking more about your grandmother's investments," Tarryn said.

"What?" Brock asked. "What more could there be?"

"If the Harrington Hedge Fund fraud goes public, it's possible the authorities will close it down due to public outcry. If that happens, investors still stand to lose a lot of money," she said.

"How does that work?" he asked.

She sat up and set her wine glasses on the coffee table before leaning back again. "If the fund is shut down and no new money is coming in from new investors, there won't be anything to pay the current investors with. And there's probably a lot of money on paper that isn't really there. Even if the SEC shores up the fund, there's no telling what they'll find when they delve deeper into it. If the whole truth comes out, I don't know what could happen. Well, actually, I do. The investments could tank really fast, probably down to zero." She placed her sock-covered feet on the coffee table and crossed them.

"Oh, man. I knew it. What about my grandma?" Brock asked. "She has a lot of money in the Reardin account that feeds into the Harrington Hedge Fund. Are you telling me she could lose it all?" He shifted the ice to the less tender side of the bump.

"Possibly," Tarryn said, slowly. "But if that happens, maybe investors could be reimbursed for their losses somehow."

"Like how? What are you thinking?" Brock asked, giving her a sideways glance.

"Give me a minute." She tapped her lips with her fingers. "What about the art collection?" she asked, after a moment.

"What about it?" Brock asked.

"Well, if Harrington has all that money tied up in an exclusive art collection, couldn't the art be sold and the revenue used to pay back the investors who stand to lose money when the fraud is exposed?"

He turned his head, flinching at the sharp pain the movement caused, and stared at her. He was mesmerized by the way her mind worked. "You're right. The collection has to be worth a lot. But he'd probably hide it if he knows someone's onto him and go into hiding himself." He thought for a moment. "We have to find the art collection and keep it available for possible sale. And we have to do it before the fraud is exposed to keep Harrington from hiding his assets. If he did, it could take a lot longer to locate them, if it were even possible. That means you can't make the Ponzi scheme public until the SEC comes down on him. You stomped away after our fight, saying you were going to write the story and not wait for the authorities to act, but you can't do that. I hope you've cooled off enough to realize that."

"Okay, but how are we going to find the art?" Tarryn asked.

"Well, we know Harrington's got this new place in Georgetown because he's running for office next term," Brock said. "I'll see if Abby can talk to her friends in town. Since she's connected politically, she might know someone who knows him and be able to find out more about him." He made a note to himself to talk to Mickey at the bar, too. He could have heard more rumors about Harrington.

"Good idea," Tarryn said. She paused. "How much you wanna bet he moved his art collection to his Georgetown residence or added to it at least?" she asked.

"Why do you think that?" Brock asked. He sat up, set the bag of ice on the coffee table and took a sip of wine.

"Is your head feeling better?" she asked before answering.

"Yes. Thanks. The ice is working."

"Good. Well, anyway, when I moved into my new place, the first thing I did was find pictures to hang on the walls, and you have paintings all over yours. He probably did the same thing, only on a much larger scale."

"Hmm. I hadn't thought of that. The half-mil painting he bought could be there." He contemplated the possibility.

"Half-mil?" Tarryn asked.

"Yeah, he bought a painting for a half-million dollars last week."

"That's incredible. You know what? If we could secure that painting along with others that he paid top dollar for, they could be sold, and the money could be used to pay investors back for losses."

"You're right. But we have to locate it first. Now that you mention it, the Georgetown mansion is where Harrington is holding the fundraising party that Abby's going to. She's getting an invitation for me. I'll see what I can find when I go there." He ran his hand lightly over the bump on his head. The swelling seemed to have receded somewhat.

Tarryn sat up and looked at him. "I want to go with you," she said.

"What? With me? No way. He could be the guy that's after you. That would put you in danger," he said, picking up his glass.

"I'm not going to hide out for the rest of my life," Tarryn said, putting her chin up. "I've come this far with my article and my writing. I want to take it to the next step. Maybe I could find out something more definitive that would lead to exposing Harrington and his hedge fund as a fraud and lead the SEC in the right direction toward closing it down." She paused. "I mean, after we find and secure the art wherever it is, of course. It's worth a shot."

"Are you kidding? Harrington could want you dead," Brock said, amazed at her audacity. "It'd be like a fly diving headfirst into a spiderweb. No way I'll let you do that."

"It wouldn't be that way if I went as your date," Tarryn said, "especially if we went with Abby. Harrington would see me as connected politically to people who could help him get elected. He wouldn't do anything to me, at least not while I was at the fundraiser at his house. You have to take me. It would be criminal not to."

"Criminal?" Brock said, abruptly. "What are you talking about?" The pain in his head had gone away, but she was giving him another one with her strange talk.

"Yes, criminal," Tarryn said, grinning. "I'd have to put you in relationship jail."

He scoffed. "Relationship jail? What the heck is that?" Were they in a relationship?

She grinned again.

"Never mind. I think I've already been there with you," he said. He set his wine down. "Come here." He pulled her to him and embraced her, reveling in the lavender scent of her hair and the lush softness of her body. She giggled when he nuzzled her neck, and he pulled her closer, kissing her solidly on the mouth. She yielded to him, kissing him back in a way that drove him wild. He held her, hoping the kiss would never end, but she pulled back.

"I'm not sure I'm ready for this yet," she said, breathlessly.

"Ready for what?" he asked, leaning in to kiss her again.

She put her hand on his chest. "Ready to have the feelings I'm feeling. I don't want to get hurt again."

"You won't," Brock said. "Trust me. You've trusted me so far, at least some of the time. I won't let anything happen to you. And I won't hurt you or let anyone else do that, either. You can let go of the past, Tarryn. You can feel what you're feeling. It's okay." He wondered at the intensity of his feelings for her. He wanted so much for her to continue to respond to him freely in the way that she just had.

"I don't know," she said. "I don't know what to think."

"Then don't."

"What?"

"Don't think," he said. "Feel."

He kissed her again, gratified that her body crumpled against his like a rag doll. She put her arms around his neck and kissed him with abandon and the strong response he had hoped for. After a while, he paused, intoxicated with her, and gazed into her half-lidded eyes.

"That's what I mean," he said. "Feel what you feel."

"I do," she said. "I really do."

He pressed his lips to hers again, addicted to the sharp surge of pleasure her lips engendered in him. He hoped beyond hope that things would stay this way and that nothing more would come between them. But even though that's what he wanted and what he hoped she wanted too, he wasn't going to bet on it.

CHAPTER 17

Tarryn stepped off the elevator into the U. S. News Chronicle offices the next morning after Brock dropped her off, excited to be back in DC. She was itching to get to her laptop and start writing even though she was still struggling with an undercurrent of fear. Professor Hall's murder and being shot at twice in less than a week had taken its toll on her, although she'd still been able to procure enough sleep to feel rested. She'd spent the night at Brock's place and had again worn the skirt and boots he'd bought her in Virginia. He'd told her to call him, and he'd pick her up after work and take her back to her apartment. She'd insisted that she wanted to go there, and he didn't want her to go alone.

"Tarryn. Glad you finally graced us with your presence," Andy said, walking toward her as he stuck a pencil behind his ear. "What's the deal?"

"No deal," Tarryn said, walking over to her desk with Andy close beside her. "I had a death in the family. I'll have my article on your desk by Friday."

"Oh, sorry to hear that. Make it sooner. Tomorrow would be good, or better yet, today. The paper's going to bed at 4:00. And make it 1000 words now. Almost gave this story to Stanford. He's been covering for you at the White House," he said. "This looming economic collapse is front page stuff."

"I'll get right on it," she said, feeling a rush of adrenaline along with her usual resignation to Andy's insensitivity. He was "all work" all the time, but his saving grace was that he did put out a good newspaper. She pulled out her chair and quickly sat down in front of her laptop to start writing. She didn't want someone else getting her story.

"Good. That's what I like to hear," he said, turning. "Hey, Radcliffe. Monitor the stock market channel. I want to know everything that happens when it happens," he called out, holding his arm up and signaling as he walked away.

She opened her laptop and, after checking a few things, got right to work. The notes she'd made at Abby's house came in handy, and the words flowed freely. Before long, she'd figured out her angle and had half the story written.

"Hey, Tarryn, do you want anything from the vending machine?" Clark asked as he rolled the mail cart past her.

"Sure. Thanks. How about a bag of Fritos and a Coke?" She bent down to pick up her purse.

"It's on me," he said.

"Thanks," she said, sitting back up.

He left and came back shortly with what she intended to be her lunch.

"Glad you're back," he said, handing her the items. "Guess what? Andy says he'll look at a story about Riley Keagan and the conflict of interest as long as I write it under a pen name. It could run later in the week."

"That's great, Clark. I'm really happy for you," she said. She hoped his story would run. That would give him the peer recognition at the newspaper that he craved, and it could be a career starter for him. He was a good friend and an ambitious writer, and he deserved a leg up.

"Well, anyway, see you," he said, leaving.

She waved and picked up the phone to make a few more calls in between scarfing down her makeshift lunch. Luckily, her press credentials and connections to people from Georgetown gave her quick access to the bank presidents and CEOs of the shuttered banks. And because the situation was so desperate, they were eager to talk. She got some great quotes. She looked up after adding a few more edits to see Paul and Jamie standing in front of her desk.

"Oh, my gosh. What are you doing here?" she asked, standing and going over and giving each of them a hug.

"We had to see you in person and not just talk on the phone," Jamie said. "It's been a terrible week, and we all miss Professor Hall so much."

"I know," Tarryn said. "Have you been safe?"

"Yeah," Paul said. "Although we're supposed to stay home. No one can go back to the research lab. The police have been keeping us updated on the investigation. It looks like they think whoever did it knew him."

"Knew him?" Tarryn asked.

"Yeah," Paul continued, and they don't think the gunman was a very good shot either because they found a nick on the railing that they determined was left by a stray bullet. So, he was probably an amateur."

"Really," Tarryn said, in a purposely measured voice to keep from letting on that she had her suspicions as to who might be involved, namely Riley Keagan.

"Yes, but who would want to shoot Professor Hall?" Jamie said, sniffling. "It doesn't make sense. Now, who am I going to talk to when I have a problem?"

"You can talk to me," Paul said, pulling her close. "I know, it's devastating. You did know the lab was secret and supposedly financially backed by a government agency, didn't you? He may have known about something dangerous to national security or something."

"I suppose so," Jamie said, leaning into him.

"It's possible," Tarryn said, quietly, thinking of her

financial thesis she'd entitled "The Blue Analysis" and hoping it didn't have anything to do with the motive for the murder. But what if it did? What if Professor Hall had mentioned his concerns about the Reardin feeder fund and shown her thesis to Riley Keagan who would then have known that Harrington's Ponzi scheme and his own complicitness in it was in danger of being uncovered? What if Keagan had murdered the professor to keep that from happening? And what if Professor Hall had realized his error in talking to Keagan and had told her to figure out what her thesis really said, knowing that he had put her and himself in danger? It seemed more and more possible that that was the case. She shook her head. She wouldn't think about that now, preferring instead to concentrate on her friends. It appeared from their physical closeness that Paul and Jamie were becoming more than friends because of the tragedy, something she understood given that the same kind of thing was happening between her and Brock. "I'm glad you two are taking care of each other," she said.

"We are," Paul said, smiling at Jamie.

"Did you figure out what was bothering you about the rate of return on the hedge fund?" Jamie asked.

"Yes," Tarryn replied. She lowered her voice. "You can read about it in the Chronicle tomorrow unless it's pulled at the last minute, which I don't think it will be. You'll know I wrote it by my writing style even if it isn't obvious."

"What does that mean?" Paul asked.

"You'll know when you see the article," she said. "And keep the fact that I wrote it to yourself for now, okay?"

"Okay," Paul said, sounding puzzled.

"Oh, and one other thing. If either of you has substantial investments in the funds mentioned or know someone who does, it would be a good idea to move them to another investment vehicle as soon as possible."

"Thanks for the tip," Jamie said.

"Yeah, thanks," Paul added. He looked around at the newsroom. "Well, we'll let you get back to work. Call us if you need us."

"Sure," she said, hugging them again. "See you later."

She watched them walk away and waved as they boarded the elevator. They waved back as the elevator doors closed, and she was left standing there looking after them with a lump in her throat. After a while, she sat down and got back to work, relishing the background buzz of the newsroom and the respite from her troubles her writing gave her.

As the afternoon drew to a close, she typed the last sentence of her article and held her finger over the send button on her computer to whisk it off to Andy. But before she did that, she gritted her teeth and did one more thing — something she'd grudgingly planned. She changed the name on the byline, then sent it and waited for Andy to call her and ask her why. Five minutes later, he did, and she gave him the pat answer she had ready. She breathed a sigh of relief when he agreed. Tomorrow, she'd check for the change in the paper. But for now, she had to call Brock and have him drive her back to her apartment.

He answered on the first ring, and she told him she'd meet him in the parking lot. He told her to wait inside until he pulled up to the curb. She agreed, and when he showed up twenty minutes later, she ran out to the car and hopped in.

"How'd it go?" he asked, pulling carefully into traffic.

"Good. I did some research and other things," she said, not mentioning that she'd written her article since she'd told him she wouldn't do that. She wasn't sure yet how to broach the subject with him. "It was good to be back in the office."

"I'm glad. Gabe and I went over the professor's case at the FBI office and talked to Kip about it. The consensus is that the gunman's an amateur because a professional wouldn't miss, and there's a notch in the upstairs railing at the research lab that is probably from a stray bullet."

"Makes sense," Tarryn replied, glad that the investigation was moving along and wondering how many people were involved in it. Paul and Jamie had already mentioned that fact, so someone must have told them. She leaned back and looked out the window while he drove to her apartment.

"Kip's also aware that you're back at work at the Chronicle, but he isn't aware that I'm staying at your apartment tonight. I thought we'd keep it that way. As far as he knows, I'm keeping tabs on you, but that's all. He doesn't know anything happened between us," he said.

"Oh, well, I didn't realize that was an issue," Tarryn said.

"Yeah, well, I guess it is with him. Don't worry, though. I can handle it. Here we are," he said eventually, parking at the curb down the street. "If I park here, it won't be so obvious that I stayed overnight when the car's still here in the morning," he said.

"Good thinking," she said.

They walked down the sidewalk toward her place. It seemed hot after sitting in the air-conditioned car, and she was glad when they reached the building because it would be cooler inside. She walked in first and said "hi" to Mrs. Griffith, who was coming out of her apartment. Mrs. Griffith said "hi" back and looked past her over her shoulder.

"You again?" she said, barely disguising her obvious disgust when Brock walked in next. She stepped past Tarryn to stand in front of him. "What are you pretending to be this time? A trapeze artist? Let's see, you've been a lawyer, an FBI agent, a do-it-yourself plumber who doesn't know what he's talking about — water in the pipes, my patooties," she said, clearly referring to Brock's explanation for the noises in Tarryn's apartment during the break-in — "and, oh yes, a fake fiancé." She stuck her chin out and looked down at him over the bridge of her nose.

"Now hold on, Mrs. Griffith," Brock said, holding his hands up, palms out. "You're obviously upset, and with good reason, but I can assure you I only have Tarryn's best interests at heart. And I am an FBI agent."

"Oh, really? Can I see a badge, or is it out of a cereal box?" she asked.

Tarryn put her hand to her mouth to stifle a giggle. Mrs. Griffith could really put Brock in his place, and it was amusing to see that he appeared to know it.

"No, here," he said, pulling it out and showing it to her. "See. It's the real deal."

"Hmm," she said, seeming to consider whether to believe him or not. "Well, alright. What's going on, anyway? Tarryn, are you back for good or what?"

"I just came back to get a few things. We may stay for a few days and then leave again. Things are up in the air for the moment. I can't be more specific right now. I hope you understand," she said.

"Hmm," Mrs. Griffith said again. "Well, I'm trying. It's your place. You can do what you want, but I have to say I'd reconsider who I let in if I were you." She gave Brock another once over.

"You're right, of course, but Brock and I will be fine," she said. "We'll see you later, okay?"

"Alright," Mrs. Griffith said, "but call me if you need anything."

"I will," Tarryn replied.

She and Brock spent the rest of the afternoon and evening talking and having dinner and wine. Brock took the sofa in his usual way for the night, and Tarryn retired to her bedroom. It was nice to finally be back at her apartment, where she could have her own things and access her own clothes. She slept fitfully until morning.

When she awoke, Brock was tiptoeing into the bathroom. He shut the door, and she jumped up, ran downstairs, and grabbed the newspaper off the stoop. Her story had made the front page in a column on the side. It looked good with a readable font and prominent placement, and, of course, the change to the byline. She read it as she moseyed back up the stairs and into her apartment. *What would the fallout from her article be this time?* She tossed the paper on the kitchen table just as Brock sauntered into the kitchen. His hair was wet and slicked back, and he smelled like her raspberry-scented shaving cream.

"Did you shave?" she asked.

"Yep. Hope that's okay. I found a pack of disposables."

"Sure. That's fine. You look good."

His phone rang, and he answered. "Hello? Gram? What's up?" He paused. "All of it? He's taking the rest of it out? Great. Where is he putting it? Oh good. Yes, that's a good investment vehicle. Oh, it has a lot of bonds?" He glanced at Tarryn, and she nodded. "Yes. That sounds good," he said. "I'm glad you're pulling out. We'll wait and see what happens. What made you do it? An article in the news? I'll check for it. Okay. Good to talk to you, too. What?" He paused for a moment and looked at Tarryn. "Yeah, sure. I'll tell her. Thanks. Bye." He hung up. "Abby's financial advisor is moving her money. She's in good shape, at least for now. The farm's safe."

"Well, that's a relief," Tarryn said. "But you looked at me for a moment while she was talking. What else did she want you to tell me?"

"Nothing. I'll tell you later. But it is a relief that her investments are safe," he said. "Although she does have other investments that we have to keep an eye on until the economy gets going again. If the economy tanks, I don't know what will happen with them. What's this?" He picked up the paper.

It seemed like he was changing the subject on purpose. What else could Abby have said to him that he didn't want to mention? "That's The U. S. News Chronicle. I have it delivered," she said.

He looked at it for a moment, then stiffened and looked up. "Somebody scooped you. The headline on the economic column reads, "It's a Fraud!" It's on the front page." He looked back down and narrowed his eyes, pulling the paper closer. He let out a breath. "Theodore Bearimore? That's the byline? You wrote it? You wrote the story after all?" he asked.

"Wait a minute," she said, surprised. "How did you know? I can explain."

His cheeks reddened. "What's there to say?" he asked, throwing the paper on the table, "That you did it to spite me? I thought you were going to wait for the SEC to investigate like we decided. What changed this time? Last time you decided to write it, even though you didn't go through with it, it was because we got into a fight."

Tarryn tensed and stood straight up. "No, I didn't do it to spite you. I did it to spite Harrington. I wanted the public to know what I found out so they could protect themselves and mitigate their losses if they could. It sounds like that's what Abby's financial advisor was able to accomplish for her. I hope others have the same experience. Waiting for the SEC or the FBI to look into it would have taken too long, given how quickly the economy is going downhill. You must know that. You're worried about the economy, too. And my editor knows how time-sensitive things are. He wanted to run it right away. Anyway, how'd you know I wrote the article?" she asked, abruptly.

"Oh, come on," he said. "Who else would write under the name Theodore Bearimore? You're the only one I know who named their teddy bear that."

Tarryn pulled back, nonplussed. "Oh, that's right. You

were in my apartment the night it was trashed, and I told you that. I was a mess then, and I don't remember much about it. Well, you're right. I wrote it," she said.

"Yeah. Well, here's what's going to happen next," he said. "Harrington's going to fly the coop now before the authorities can jail him and confiscate the art."

"Not necessarily. We don't know what he's going to do. It was important to get the story out," she said. "I hope you can understand that."

"Yeah. Well. It was a pretty crappy thing to do. I trusted you when you said you'd keep the Ponzi scheme a secret until the SEC looked into it," he said.

"You can still trust me," Tarryn said. "We're on the same side about stopping Harrington and ending the fraud, even if we disagree about how to do that."

"Maybe," Brock said. "At least you took my advice and used a pen name. That's some protection for you anyway."

The resigned look on his face made her reconsider her perception of him. "Yes. I compromised that much for you," she said, quietly, allowing herself to accept the possibility that he could have her best interests at heart and wasn't just being his usual overbearing self.

His gaze softened. "Thanks," he said. "I know how much your journalistic ethics and moral principles mean to you, as well as how much you didn't want to hide behind a pseudonym. You're definitely a fighter and a courageous one at that. You don't let people get away with things. I admire that."

"Well, thank you. And you don't always have to worry about keeping me safe, although I appreciate it up to a point. I can keep myself safe. I think you should know I used the pen name for my own reasons, too," she said, summoning her courage.

"Your own reasons? What do you mean?" he asked, frowning.

She paused, considering whether she should tell him or not. Her compromise on the byline wasn't only because she wanted to do as he had advised. And it wasn't just because she wanted to figure out a way to go to the fundraising party at Leo Harrington's mansion and spy on him, which was something she probably couldn't do if her name was on a story insinuating his hedge fund was a fraud. And it also wasn't because she thought Harrington was the man who killed Professor Hall and shot at her even though he'd threatened her in the message in the blue envelope not to write the story. It had to do with something else. She took a deep breath. "I think Riley Keagan is up to his ears in the Ponzi scheme, and it's possible he's the one that's after me," she blurted out. "I specifically didn't want *him* to know I wrote my second article." She cringed, anticipating Brock's reaction.

"Wait. What?" he asked loudly, crossing his arms and then pointedly uncrossing them in an umpire's "safe" gesture.

"Hear me out," she said. "I wrote about the Reardin Fund being part of the fraud in my second article, and I have it on good authority that Keagan is covertly running the fund. That's something he wouldn't want anyone to know, not only because it's part of the Ponzi scheme but because it's a conflict of interest with his advising position. Another ancillary story written by someone else could be coming out soon revealing that," she said, thinking of the story Clark wanted to write exposing Keagan.

"What do you mean?" he asked. "Are you telling me you think Riley Keagan is trying to kill you? That's absurd."

"I didn't say that," she said. "But the thought did enter my mind." She braced herself when his face turned red.

"This can't be true," he said. "Where are you getting your information? I need to know, and I think you should trust me enough by now to tell me. Or am I under the false impression that you care about me? Is what we have going on here just a passing thing, or what?"

Tarryn pressed her lips together and looked away. She hadn't expected him to be so direct. She did care about him. He was right about that. Her feelings for him had grown over their time together when he continually came to her aid. And the passionate way he kissed her drove her crazy. But that didn't mean she was obligated to tell him her sources or to give him Clark's name or Carla's or anyone else's name as a source. And she wasn't going to do that, no matter how much he pressured her. She had to remember that he was just doing his job in trying to find out her sources even though it directly contradicted her ethics as a professional journalist to not reveal them. Besides, her deductions about Keagan were based more on her internal investigative instincts than what she gleaned from other people.

"I'm not telling you my sources," she said, firmly. "But it's not just that. Other things have led me to conclude that Riley Keagan isn't on the up and up. I thought you should know, even though he's your friend."

"Other things? Like what?" he asked.

She paused. "Just things," she said after a moment. She was going to mention the chess set at Abby's and the king being tipped over in the same way it had been at the research lab where Professor Hall was murdered, but she didn't think he'd understand her concerns.

"Yeah, well. Whatever," Brock said. "You're not going to convince me that Riley's a crook."

"I won't try," she said. "We'll just see what happens."

"Yes, we just will," Brock said tersely, turning away.

Tarryn glared at his back, irritated that he was being so obstinate but not surprised. It was just Brock being Brock — something she was trying to get used to even though she wasn't faring very well. If he wasn't so good-looking and didn't have this hidden, vulnerable side she found so intriguing, she'd have a better chance of walking away from the whole relationship. But that and something else — she wasn't sure what — kept her there. She was going to say something more but decided not to. She didn't want to risk having another big argument with him when they were getting so close to taking out Harrington himself. Her energy was better spent coming up with a plan to find the art collection and writing about the Ponzi scheme than with making sharp retorts to Brock's exasperating statements.

He walked over and filled a glass with water from the tap. He stood still for a moment, then turned around, holding the Ziploc bag with the tin of peppermint chewing tobacco she'd left in the side sink. "What's this?" he asked.

"I found that on the floor the morning after the break-in. The intruder must have dropped it, and I saved it in case there were fingerprints, remember?" she said.

"Good idea," he said. He took a sip of water and set his glass down before opening the bag. "Wow, that's quite a strong smell of peppermint." He paused. "I think I've smelled this before."

"You have?" she asked, surprised. He'd said he hadn't noticed it before in her apartment when she had.

"Yeah. When I was chasing after the guy who threatened you in the park — the one who told you not to write any more articles about the economy. That's the smell that was wafting behind him."

"Really?" Tarryn said. "It must have been the same man that broke in here."

"Probably was," Brock said. "It could have been one of Harrington's men." He shook his head. "Harrington thinks he can terrorize and take advantage of everyone, including you and my grandmother. But that's going to end and soon. I'll take this to the office when I can, write up the break-in, and have the guys check on it. If they're his fingerprints and he's in our files, they'll more than likely arrest him, okay?"

"Okay," she said.

He closed the bag and put it back in the sink. When he turned around this time, he had a tense look on his face, and Tarryn didn't know what to think.

"By the way, Gram mentioned something else," he said after a moment.

"Oh, so you want to tell me now? What was it?" she asked, trying not to appear upset that he'd kept something from her. She'd thought they were closer than that.

"Harrington's fundraising party is Friday at 8:00 pm at his new mansion," he said.

"Well, that's good, isn't it?" she asked. "You can find out more about him."

"Yeah," he said, rubbing his hand over his face. "And one other thing if you're interested in fighting back."

"What?" she asked. "What does that mean?"

"We're both invited."

CHAPTER 18

She was stunning. That had been his first impression of her when Tarryn walked into the living room at her apartment in her black cocktail dress and strappy, black sandals. And it was definitely his impression now at the party in Georgetown. Her silky brown hair was pulled back into a loose, french twist, and she wore a simple diamond pendant with matching earrings that twinkled in the low light of the chandeliers. The overall effect was breathtaking. She blushed and looked down when she caught him looking at her in a surprisingly shy way he found enthralling.

They had toured the mansion with other guests and a guide after arriving at Harrington's estate earlier, and Brock had been amazed at its opulence and decor. Rooms below ground had been converted into museum-type areas, and their walls held a myriad of paintings. There weren't as many as he thought, though, and the selection wasn't as elite as he thought, either. Either Harrington had his expensive paintings elsewhere, or his collection wasn't as grand as he'd been led to believe. Somehow, Brock thought it was probably the former. He was pretty sure Harrington had a Munch and a Pollock from what Mickey at the bar had said, as well as a large collection of Impressionist and Post-Impressionist paintings, but he didn't see them. He could be keeping them at his home in New York, or he could have moved them somewhere else, especially since there were open areas on the walls where paintings seemed to be missing. And one of the converted rooms had no paintings at all. *That was odd.* Now, they were back upstairs in a large salon, having cocktails, champagne, and catered hors d'oeuvres.

Leo Harrington raised his glass. "Thank you to everyone who came tonight to help launch this humble art lover's political career," he said, after casually adjusting the tie on his tuxedo with his other hand. "I couldn't do it without you. It's good to know there are people who don't listen to idle gossip and the foolish ramblings of fake newspapers like the U. S. News Chronicle."

Brock glanced at Tarryn, who grimaced and shook her head. Was Harrington personally taunting her or just making political prattle? It was probably both.

"You're the best, Leo," an obviously slightly drunk man next to him said. "We're all rich because of you." He lifted his glass up to Harrington's.

"Hear, hear," another man said.

The crowd cheered and drank from their respective champagne glasses.

Brock deferred lifting his glass because of the probable snub to Tarryn about the newspaper, then suddenly, unintentionally slumped toward her. They were standing together not far from Harrington. She gasped and grasped his arm.

"What's wrong?" she whispered, balancing her glass precariously with her other hand. "Are you okay?"

He shook his head and remained silent, gathering his thoughts and squinting his eyes to keep them focused. She carefully led him away from the group nearer to the side wall as he tried to look as though everything was okay.

Riley Keagan raised his glass. "Here's to future Congressman Leo Harrington. We couldn't do it without *you*," he said, toasting in return.

The crowd laughed and cheered again.

"Are you sick, or is it the champagne? I mean, it's good,

but it's a little dry," Tarryn said.

"No. It's not the champagne. That's him," Brock choked out, holding onto her and struggling through the haze of denial that threatened to steal his memories away again.

"That's who?" she asked.

"Leo Harrington," he said, seeing Harrington again through the eyes of the eight-year-old boy who had watched a horror show play out in front of him. "That's the man who decked me when they beat my father to death — the man who shattered my life, who destroyed my family. It's him."

"What? How do you know?" she asked.

"The ring," he said, lowering his voice and leaning toward her. "See the ring? It's seared in my mind. I saw it when he raised his glass to give the toast. That's the same ring that split my chin and left the scar when he uppercutted me when I was a boy, the same ring that was on the hand that held me off when I tried to get to my father and save him from being killed by a gang of thugs, the same ring that taunted me in my memories and haunted me in my nightmares as a child." His voice crescendoed and cracked on the last word.

"Shh," Tarryn said, gripping his arm and looking around.

He followed her gaze. Everyone was looking at Harrington, who was giving another toast. It didn't seem as though anyone had noticed his outburst.

She turned back to him. "Oh, my gosh, really?" she asked under her breath. "I can't really see the ring from here."

"There's no question about it," he said, more quietly. "It has the raised horse head insignia on it with the pointed diamond eye. No other ring looks like that. He had a black beard back then, but I can tell, even without it, that it's definitely him. His eyes look the same as they did then — dark and menacing, almost black under his thick brows, piercing through me. It's all coming back to me."

"Oh, no," Tarryn whispered. We have to get out of here. We have to get out of here now. He could recognize you."

Brock shook his head again to clear it. He needed to keep his wits about him and not let the trauma of the memory fog his brain. And he needed to keep Tarryn and his grandmother safe. "We can't leave. We have to find out what's going on. He obviously read your second article, and even if he doesn't know you wrote it, he knows the Ponzi scheme has been exposed. He's probably going through with the party as a front to keep people from knowing it's all over."

"You could be right," Tarryn said a little more loudly, seemingly assured they weren't being overheard. "Or he could be trying to talk his way out of it. Maybe he thinks he can tell more lies and wait for this all to blow over, then run for office anyway."

"Wishful thinking on his part if that's what he's doing," Brock said. "I read the rest of your story. You nailed him. There's no way out for him. The SEC will be all over this right away."

"Do you think so?" Tarryn asked.

"Oh, yeah," Brock said. "And Harrington knows it," he said. "No way I'm leaving at this point. I want to see what he does."

The speech ended to polite applause, and a light jazz band in the corner struck up a tune. There were probably one hundred people gathered, but the large room wasn't crowded. Scalloped crown moldings and tiered silk valances delicately draped over tall windows added to the elegant atmosphere. Brock took note of Harrington's new location at the hors d'oeuvres table and led Tarryn in the other direction toward the small dance floor. Only one other couple had the same idea, so they had it to themselves for the most part.

"Would you care to dance?" he asked, holding his hand out to Tarryn after handing his glass to a circling waiter.

She handed her glass to the waiter as well. "I'd love to if you feel up to it," she said. "And if you think it's safe to stay here."

"I do," he said, taking her hand. Her simple touch sent a spark through him, and he marveled at her effect on him. "We might as well try to enjoy ourselves as long as we're here. I've never seen you look lovelier."

She smiled. "Thank you," she said, stepping forward into his arms.

She wore a soft, rose scent that made his head spin and reminded him of the day they met in the Rose Garden. He pulled her closer, enjoying the heady feeling. But this was no time for romance. He was there to scope out Harrington. They swayed together in time to the music.

"This gives us an opportunity to talk," he said after a while.

"What about?" she asked.

"Business, given what we're up against."

"Okay," she said.

"I have it on good authority that Harrington chartered a plane this afternoon to fly to his private island in the Atlantic tomorrow," Brock said. "He probably isn't taking his own plane because it's too big to land on a small island airstrip. And it wouldn't be that easy to hide the fact that he's leaving. Gabe's at the office calling around trying to locate a flight plan."

"What? He's leaving the country?" Tarryn asked.

"Looks that way if the feds don't stop him," Brock answered. "He must have gone ahead with the party as a front so that no one suspected he was taking off. Your second article obviously really rankled him."

"Who told you he was leaving the country?" she asked.

Brock paused. "I'll tell you, but you have to keep it to yourself, and I mean it this time."

"Okay, I promise," she said.

"Jackson, the groom at the farm, told me."

"Jackson?" she asked, dumbfounded. "How did he know?"

"He places bets for Harrington on the horse races, and he called him to see if he wanted to place a sure bet on a race down south. Harrington said 'no' because he was leaving the country. And Jackson knows he owns an island. By the way, Jackson's the one who told Harrington we were coming to the farm earlier this week. You were right. He did know you were going to be there."

"I knew it," Tarryn said. "I had a feeling. But why would Jackson do that?"

"Harrington was paying him for information. Mostly, he wanted to keep up on what horses Abby was racing and how good they were. Remember Millie told Abby Harrington bets at the track? That way, he could make more lucrative bets. Anyway, Jackson told Harrington about us, and Harrington could have told anyone. That could have led to someone following us home from the farm and trying to shoot you at the National Mall."

"You're right," she said. "That makes sense now. And I think I know who that was."

"Who?" Brock asked.

The song ended, and the band struck up another tune. A few more couples joined them on the dance floor.

"I'll tell you later," she said. "Let's find a quieter place to talk."

"Good idea," he said.

They walked toward the side of the room.

"How does Jackson know Harrington again?" Tarryn asked as they stood together near a landscape painting on the wall. Tarryn pretended to admire it.

Brock stared at her, trying to determine if he should press her for the name of who it was she thought shot at her. He decided not to and answered her instead while pretending to admire the painting as well.

"He knows him from the horse races. Jackson rides in them, and Harrington bets on them. They met at the track. Jackson puts down bets for him, too."

"So why did Jackson tell you all this if he's a lackey for Harrington?" Tarryn asked.

"Because he didn't want Abby to lose her investments and the farm. She told the staff that that was a possibility because of what was currently going on with the economy. It would have put him out of a job. He read your articles and found out Harrington was involved, so he called me and turned on him," Brock said. "When it came right down to it, he chose Abby over Harrington."

"Wow. That's something," Tarryn said.

"Yeah, but I don't know if we'll be able to trust him after this. We'll have to see how it goes," Brock said.

"I understand." She paused and pointed at the painting. "This is a nice shadowing effect here," she said, loudly enough for someone to hear and think she was critiquing it. She lowered her voice. "What about the paintings? Is he taking them with him?"

"Good question," Brock said. "I bet he is. That could be why one of the rooms downstairs was completely empty and why paintings were missing on the wall of the other one. They're probably already stowed on the plane and ready to go." He pointed at the painting, too, and raised his voice. "Yes, and the underpainting is an exquisite hue."

"I wonder where he'll keep them," she said.

He leaned in closer to her and whispered. "He has a guarded mansion on the island that evidently no one knows about. Gabe checked into it, but he didn't know exactly where it was or exactly where the island was. It's rumored to be protected by a small, guerilla-type army with machine guns and rifles.

Maybe he has a climate-controlled vault or something similar there for his paintings. If he takes the art collection with him, it'd be tough getting it back."

"Bingo," Tarryn said. "That must be where he's going. We have to stop him. We have to keep the art collection in the country so it can be sold to pay back the bilked investors."

"I know, but how? None of what's in your article has been proven by the SEC. And as far as Harrington goes, he's a free man. He can do whatever he wants."

"I don't know yet. I'll have to think about it," Tarryn said.

"No, *we'll* have to think about it," Brock said. He wasn't going to let her take over things again, which she'd do if she could. This investigation was his baby.

"Right," she said in the same way he usually did.

Brock glanced around the room, looking for Harrington. He was conversing with a group of people which included a senator on the far side of the room. It seemed he was already pretty well connected in town. Maybe he really was trying to bluff his way out of the Ponzi scheme, or maybe the senator was invested with Harrington and didn't believe Tarryn's article. He'd try to find out later. Abby was standing in a group near Harrington's, and she caught his eye, raising her hand in greeting and seeming to take her leave from the group.

"Looks like Abby's coming over," he said.

Tarryn turned. "Good. I haven't talked to her all night," she said. "I want to thank her for inviting me."

"Okay, but keep everything we talked about to yourself," Brock said.

"You got it," Tarryn said.

He hoped she would. Things were heating up in their race to end the Ponzi scheme, and they couldn't afford to have anything secret like Gabe's checking around or Jackson's sudden revelations about Harrington coming to light and messing things up.

CHAPTER 19

Abby walked over from where she'd been standing with a group of women, holding her champagne glass. She looked lovely in a long, silver gown with a plunge back. Tarryn was impressed with her elegant sense of style.

"Are you okay, dear?" Abby asked Brock. "Your face is ashen. I noticed it earlier."

"Yeah, I'm fine," he said, squeezing his eyes shut and pinching the bridge of his nose before looking at her. "What is it? You have your 'I have news' look."

"I came over to tell you that Riley wants you to introduce him to Tarryn," she said. "I talked to him earlier. He seems quite interested in the article she wrote last week." She turned to Tarryn. "He could give your career quite a boost, dear. Would you like me to do the honors or Brock?"

"Riley Keagan wants to meet me?" Tarryn asked, shaken.

"Yes. Is that surprising?" Abby asked.

"Maybe a little," she replied.

Brock sipped his champagne. "Go ahead. Go with her. I'll stay here and listen to the next speech," he said.

"Well, if you're sure," Tarryn said, hoping he'd come with her but realizing he didn't see Riley as a threat in the same way she did.

"I am," he said.

"Okay," she said, turning. "Thank you so much for inviting

me. This is a lovely party."

"You're more than welcome, my dear," Abby said.

She followed Abby to where Riley was standing near the salmon pate, and Abby introduced them.

"Well, if it isn't Tarryn Blue, journalist extraordinaire," Riley said, smirking. His thick lips glistened red under his mustache, and he patted them with a napkin. "So very nice to make your acquaintance."

Abby tilted her head and looked back and forth between them.

"Thank you. Lovely to meet you too, I'm sure," Tarryn replied, adopting a similar tone. She could give as good as she got.

"Forgive me. Am I missing something?" Abby asked.

"Not at all. I'm glad you brought her over," he said, keeping his gaze on Tarryn.

His eyes glinted wickedly, and Tarryn felt a shiver of fear. She glanced around for an exit. Abby didn't seem fearful at all, although perhaps a little confused. Maybe the tension was strictly between her and Riley. A woman nearby walked over and tapped Abby on the shoulder.

"Would you excuse me for a moment?" Abby asked.

"Of course," Tarryn said, swallowing as she walked away.

"Don't worry," Riley said. "There's nothing to be frightened of."

"I'm not frightened at all," she replied, hoping she sounded sure of herself. He'd clearly picked up on her trepidation.

"Good." He smiled.

"Did you have something you wanted to say?" Tarryn asked with distaste, not sure what he was up to.

"Now that you ask, I did want to mention that Professor Hall was a friend of mine, and I very much regret his demise. It was an unfortunate end for an eminent scholar," he said.

"Regret?" Tarryn asked. Had she heard him correctly? "As in, sorry you did it?"

"Yes, as a matter of fact," he said. "I only wanted to mention that so that you and I understand each other. I don't want to see any more articles in the paper relating to your ridiculous financial conclusions or "The Blue Analysis." Nobody messes with The Big Guy on this or my Reardin Fund. Would you care for some pate?"

Tarryn frowned and trained her eyes on him at the mention of her financial thesis following his nonchalant admission to killing Professor Hall. And why did he refer to himself as The Big Guy? Who did he think he was, anyway?

"No?" he asked rhetorically when she didn't respond to his question. He continued. "Your writing hits a little too close to home for my liking. I can't risk the exposure. And I'd hate to have the same thing that happened to the professor happen to you. Unfortunately, it's becoming inevitable."

She started. Did he really just confess to killing Professor Hall and threaten her directly with the same? It sounded that way. She stared at him, holding perfectly still.

"Oh, yes. You heard me correctly," he said, smiling again in a stone-faced way she found sickening. "I may have missed twice, but three times's a charm."

Tarryn had heard enough. She bolted backwards, almost tripping in her heels, and turned and ran toward Brock and safety. Riley Keagan was an evil man. He was clearly Professor Hall's murderer and the man who had shot at her. He must have heard from Harrington, who heard from Jackson that she was with Brock at Abby's farm and followed them to the National Mall when they left. She ran up to Brock, breathless.

"Is something wrong?" he asked.

"Kind of. I'll tell you later," she said. Harrington was in the middle of another speech, and she didn't want to talk over him.

"I hope you'll all visit my website and give generously to my campaign," Harrington said. "But when it comes right down to it, I'd be just as happy with your vote."

"You got it, Leo," a woman near him said, smiling.

"But for those of you who believe the papers and are thinking of voting for somebody else, just remember that I'm in charge of the real money, and Riley Keagan is the one they're writing about."

"You can't say that about me," a voice yelled from the back of the room. "I'm suing you for slander." It was Riley. He pushed his way through the crown toward Harrington's.

"You don't know anything about finance," Harrington said. "If you did, you never would have started that crummy Reardin investment firm. Now look what you got us all into."

"Me? You can't scapegoat me on this. I know exactly what you're up to, and I'm not taking the fall for anything. You're the head honcho of this sinking ship. Or maybe I should say this sinking house. What'd you fork over for this dump, anyway?"

"Dump? Get lost, loser. You don't have a clue what you're talking about," Harrington said.

"You can't talk to me like that," Riley said. "You wouldn't be anywhere if it wasn't for me."

"Back off Keagan. It's time you left. There's the door. Oh, and one other thing. Don't come back. Ever," Harrington said.

"What? No way. I'm not letting you run out and leave me holding the bag on this thing. You said you were taking me with you. Who do you think you are anyway?" Riley shouted.

"I don't know what you're talking about," Harrington said. "Get out, or I'll have my boys escort you. And let me warn you, they're not real polite."

"Is that right? Well, guess what, you backstabber, I'm not real polite either," Riley yelled. He pulled out a gun and shot Harrington, clearly missing him when a lamp behind him shattered.

"You traitor," Harrington yelled. He pulled out a gun and shot Riley, who lurched back and fell to the floor. Harrington turned and ran out of the room. Brock ran over to Riley and felt his neck for a pulse. The others stood frozen in place as though stunned by the sudden turn of events.

"He's dead," Brock said, after a moment. He looked up. "Get him."

The crowd gasped, along with Tarryn and Abby.

"Who are you?" someone yelled.

"FBI," Brock said, flashing his badge.

Two tuxedoed guests ran out the door after Harrington, one slipping in his shiny shoes.

"Stand back, everyone. I'm calling the police. Stay on the scene and stay away from the body." Brock pulled his cell phone out of his pocket. Tarryn ran over to him while he punched in numbers on his phone.

"We have to apprehend Harrington. Those guys won't catch him. Even if he claims it was self-defense, he can't leave the scene. I'm calling for backup," he said to her. "Harrington's not getting away with murder again like he and his thugs did with my dad. Not while I'm around."

She nodded.

"Are you in?" he asked.

"Yes, of course. Whatever you need me to do," she said.

"Good. Follow my lead." Brock made his phone call with his hand over his opposite ear amidst the loud murmurs and speculations of the guests, then grabbed her arm.

They took off running out the same door Harrington had escaped through. It led into the hall leading to the front door. They dodged a few servants with Brock flashing his badge and ran outside and down the stairs to the semi-circular drive. "Bring my car around," he yelled to the valet, who jumped to do as he asked when he flashed his badge again.

"Are you sure you want me to go with you?" Tarryn asked, as they waited for him to bring the car around.

"Yeah. I'm not leaving you there with Harrington's friends in case one of them is the person that's after you."

Tarryn remained silent. She was shocked at what happened to Riley, but she wasn't going to tell Brock what Riley said to her at the party. She wanted to focus on helping Brock stop Harrington from fleeing. With these new developments, Harrington could be leaving the country sooner than he'd planned and probably even taking his art collection with him. She couldn't let that happen, and she knew Brock wouldn't either.

"How do you know he left the estate?" she asked. "It seems like he would know someone would see him. The valet isn't letting on if he did."

"I don't. I'm making an educated guess," he said. "It wouldn't benefit him to stay here, and Harrington is all about what benefits him. He's on the run now, and I'll wager he's going to run all the way to his private island."

"Do you think so?" she asked.

"I'd bet on it," Brock said.

***

The valet showed up with the car, and Brock grabbed the keys, slipping him a five because he didn't have a ten. They jumped in, and he floored it, driving toward the street.

"Wait a minute," Tarryn said, glancing in the sideview mirror.

"Why?" Brock asked.

"There's a truck parked near the garage stalls in the back. I'm no expert, but that looks like an empty art transport crate next to it. There could be artwork in there."

"Maybe that's where his collection is while he's getting

ready to transport it to the plane when he leaves tomorrow. We might not have to chase him after all. The FBI can get him as long as we have his art collection here."

"True," Tarryn said. "If he left the premises. But would he really do that and leave his art collection behind?"

Brock braked. "What are you saying? Are you saying you think he's still here?"

"The thought had crossed my mind," Tarryn said.

"You could be right," Brock said. "Let's find out." He put the car in reverse and backed up all the way to the side of the truck. The valet kept up with them on a jog during the last half of the drive.

"What are you doing?" the valet asked when they exited the car.

"Just wanted to see what the deal was with the truck," Brock said.

"No deal," he said. "It's just a delivery truck. Nothing special."

"Really?" Brock said. "Mind if I take a look?"

"Actually, I do," the valet said.

"Well, that's kinda too bad," Brock said. "You don't get a say in this." He pushed past the rather perplexed young man and sidled up to the truck with Tarryn beside him.

"That does look like an art packing crate," Brock said. He walked forward and looked in the windows of the cab, but he didn't see anything.

"Who do I talk to about opening this up?" he asked the kid.

"Nobody. Guess you're out of luck," the valet answered, leaning against the truck and crossing his ankles.

"Right," Brock answered, annoyed to be dealing with a smart aleck.

"I'm calling Carla," Tarryn said.

"Why?" Brock asked.

"She'll know what to do. She always knows what to do. She's really smart," she said.

"Well, what am I? Chopped liver?" he asked rhetorically.

"No, you're smart too." She paused. "In your own way," she added.

"Gee, thanks," he said. Brock walked around the truck, checking out the area. He didn't see Harrington or anyone. When he passed the driver's side again, something glinted in the glow of the outside garage lights. "What's this?" he mumbled to himself, walking to the garage and stooping down. "Tarryn," he called after picking up an object.

"What is it?" She walked up to him, the phone to her ear.

"It's Harrington's ring," Brock said. "This is the horse head ring. We have to go. We have to find him. He must have lost it when he got in his car."

Tarryn held up her finger. "Let me ask Carla what she thinks about the ring. Paul and Jamie are at her place, and they're brainstorming ideas as to where we could look for Harrington. They all fly a lot, and they're coming up with places a chartered plane could leave from."

"No, we have to go. We have to find Harrington now that we know he drove his car off the estate."

"In a minute," she said, walking away from him.

"Geez," he said. He kicked the tire in frustration. She was again impossible to argue with.

"Hey, watch it," the valet said.

"No, you watch it," Brock said, exasperated.

After a moment, Tarryn came back, a puzzled look on her face. "Carla says the consensus is that Harrington can't castle in check."

"What?" Brock asked. "What the heck does that mean? We don't have time for riddles. Ask her what she means."

Tarryn held up a finger again. After a moment, she said, "Carla says to figure it out yourself. She doesn't want to be more direct and get involved in the investigation because she's upset that there wasn't a funeral for Professor Hall, and she blames the authorities."

"This is ridiculous," Brock said. "We're not playing games here. Hang up."

"No," Tarryn said. "Let's think about it. You can't castle in check essentially means the king can't make a fancy move to get out of a tough spot."

"Yeah, so?" Brock said.

Tarryn looked up and spoke into the phone. "I'll call you back later," she said, hanging up. "I know what they mean," she said.

"What?" Brock asked.

"Harrington's in the truck," she said. "If he leaves, he's in checkmate because we're here. He lost his ring while getting into the truck. That's what they mean."

Brock put his hand to his forehead.

The valet sneered at him. "What's the matter? Too intellectual for you, cheapskate? Are you sick or something?"

"Yeah, sick of you," Brock answered. "Get lost. Unless you've got a key to the truck."

"Not likely," he answered.

Just then, squad cars pulled in and surrounded the estate. Two officers ran up to the truck.

"FBI," Brock said, showing his badge when they reached him. "The perpetrator's in the truck. That's the consensus, anyway," he said, raising his eyebrow at Tarryn. "You guys will have to figure out how to get him out," he said. "Oh, and one more thing. He dropped this. I sure don't want it," he said, handing an officer the ring. "C'mon, Tarryn, let's go. She's with me." He took her arm to lead her back to the car. He'd make one more call in the car to Abby to make sure she was safe and had a ride back to Virginia. It was time to call it a night and go home.

CHAPTER 20

"It must feel good to know Harrington is finally behind bars after what he did to your father," Tarryn said as they walked down the path by the Potomac, holding hands.

Brock looked at her, gratified by her insight. "It does," he said. "Knowing Harrington will face the law for the harm he's done in the world gives me some solace, although, in some ways, it's not enough. It won't bring my father back. But at least I was instrumental in finding some justice for my dad."

"Yes. Yes, you were," Tarryn said, patting his arm. "It's a wonderful thing you did."

The stars were out, twinkling in the night sky and casting sparkles of silver on the black water below.

"There's something I need to tell you," Tarryn said, quietly.

"What? What is it?" Brock asked. She looked so downtrodden and vulnerable that he wondered if he'd inadvertently hurt her feelings again.

"I'm not sure how you'll take this, but before Riley was shot and killed at the party, he told me he murdered Professor Hall," she said.

His heart hit him hard in the chest. "He told you that?"

"Just listen for a minute," she said. "And not only that. He told me he was the one who shot at me at the research lab and at the Lincoln Memorial and that he read my articles and my financial thesis, "The Blue Analysis." He called himself The Big

Guy and threatened my life. And he was smiling when he said it."

"This is unreal," Brock said, shaking his head. He stood still for a moment, taking it in. If Riley was The Big Guy that was referred to in the note Laura had handed him at the off-the-record meeting they were in, that meant Riley had threatened him, too. And he remembered seeing the paper at the crime scene that Professor Hall was holding when he was murdered. It was entitled "The Blue Analysis." Tarryn was telling the truth. But he wasn't going to tell her he saw her paper in the professor's stiff hands and risk burdening her with guilt for a lifetime for no reason.

"Please say you believe me," she said. "You have to believe me. I was so scared, and I don't want to be the only one that knows this."

He gazed into her earnest eyes. There was no question in his mind anymore who to trust. "I do believe you. I'm sorry I didn't listen to you before. I didn't think it was possible that Riley was like that before, but now I do after he tried to shoot Harrington at the party. I'll have his gun checked at the FBI office. I'm sure they'll determine that the bullet they located that nicked the railing at the research lab was from that gun. They're going to have to revamp the vetting procedures for the White House after this. There's no way a guy like Riley should have been a presidential economic advisor. I'm glad you trusted me enough to tell me what he said."

"I'm so relieved," she said. "And I'm so glad you believe me."

He leaned forward and embraced her. "I do, and I want you to feel like you can tell me anything from now on, okay?" he said.

"Okay," she said, hugging him back.

He was glad his relationship with Tarryn was close enough

that she confided something like that in him, and it wasn't just because it gave him a warm feeling of being trusted and loved, although it did. It had to do with what he wanted to talk to her about later. But he had a few things to mention to her first.

"Abby called earlier. She's so glad she put her investments somewhere else before everything crashed. You saved her," Brock said. "You saved her and the horse farm from financial ruin. I guess you were right not to wait to publish the article until the SEC got involved like I wanted you to."

"I'm happy for Abby, but I didn't save the farm by myself," Tarryn said. "What's happening now is just part of the overall adjustments that are taking place because of the exposure of the Ponzi scheme. It's good that your grandmother's investments are safe. I hope other people were able to have the same experience."

"Yeah. It looks like a lot of people won't. It turns out Abby's friend, Millie, was invested with Harrington, too. She told my grandmother that after she found out she lost her investments. Abby's devastated about it. It's sad, and Millie doesn't know what she's going to do," Brock said.

"That's heart-wrenching," Tarryn said. "But at least Harrington's assets, including the art collection, can be confiscated and possibly sold to pay money back to those who lost everything like Millie."

"I'm sure that will happen in the future," Brock said. "At least the art collection is still in the country, and the authorities know it's at his estate. The FBI and the SEC are looking into everything, and it's possible a fund will be set up specifically to reimburse those who lost their investments in the Ponzi scheme."

"How wonderful," she said. "As far as the overall economy is concerned, it may take a while for things to get going again and for people to trust the banks and investment firms, but at least the underlying fraud has been uncovered and stopped, and recovery can begin. I'm looking forward to writing more articles about that since Andy wants to keep me covering the economic beat and the White House."

"That's great. You did it, Tarryn. You saved the world with your writing," Brock said.

"What? Don't be silly," Tarryn said. "The world saved the world. And Professor Hall was the first one to throw light on the Ponzi scheme. I only played a small part in illuminating the problem. And besides, it was Theodore Bearimore who wrote the second article and exposed the Ponzi scheme, not me."

"Oh, that's right," Brock said, grinning. "I'm glad you wrote under that name even though you didn't want to."

Tarryn nodded. "I'm glad I did, too, and I'm glad I listened to you and used a pseudonym even though I found it hard to change the byline. That keeps my name private and out of all the chaos that's happening now," she said. "It makes me feel safer. I'm glad my friend Clark's story ran, too, under a pen name. It shed more light on what Riley Keagan was involved in before he died."

"I'm happy you took my advice and realized that sometimes keeping things like your name out of the public eye is a good idea," Brock said. "But I know who really wrote the article. You did. I'm amazed at what you've accomplished, and I'm proud to know you."

***

Tarryn felt her cheeks get warm. "Thanks. It means a lot to hear you say that," she said. She looked down. "I wish my parents were around to say something like that."

He paused. "Someday, maybe," he said. "Things change. Maybe time will heal the wounds from their divorce, and you'll talk with them more often again."

"Do you think so?" she asked longingly, looking up at him and hoping beyond hope that that could be true.

He paused again before continuing. "I don't know," he

said, somberly. "But whatever happens, I'll be there for you."

He squeezed her hand, and she squeezed his back. It gave her a warm feeling to know he felt that way about her. "You know what? I'm proud to know you, too," she said. "You're a wonderful investigator and a stalwart protector. Being with you made discovering and publishing the truth for the public possible, and I couldn't have done it without you."

"Yeah, you could have," Brock said.

Tarryn glanced at him, surprised at his comment and even more surprised at his confident expression. "Do you mean that? Thanks. But I wouldn't have wanted it any other way but with you," she said. "You're the best."

"Thanks," he said.

She turned and sighed as she gazed out over the river. The Potomac shimmered in the moonlight, its black water rippling gently in the current. And the sky below the stars glowed dimly with the lights of Washington. Was it really over? Did they really have their lives back? It was hard to believe. For her, it would never really be over. The trauma over the loss of Professor Hall would be with her forever. The best she could hope for was to put everything behind her and move forward with her life and her career. They hadn't stopped her. Writing was a part of her. She would always write. And with Brock, maybe a safe future was possible. He had protected her and stayed with her through it all, whether she wanted him to at times or not. That was something Todd would never have done. She realized that now. Todd was her past. Brock was her future. She turned to Brock when he grasped her hand and held it in his warm grip.

"We made it," he said, quietly. "We got through everything together."

"Yes," she said. "We did."

He was silent for a moment. "I want things to stay this way. I want us to always be together," he said.

She didn't know what to say, so she just nodded and looked back over the water. When he moved and let go of her hand, she turned back. He was down on one knee.

"What are you doing?" she asked, perplexed.

"Haven't you figured that out by now?" he said. "You usually figure everything out."

"What do you mean?"

"I love you, Tarryn. I want to marry you."

She gasped when he held out a black velvet ring box and opened it in front of her. It held a beautiful ring with a large, sparkling diamond in silver facets and a diamond-encrusted band. It was the most beautiful ring she'd ever seen, more beautiful even than the one she had picked out with Todd months ago and never received.

"Are you serious? Already?"

"I've never been more serious in my life," he said. "Yes. Already. When I see something I want, I go after it. And I want you. Will you marry me and make me the happiest security guard in the world?"

She melted in spite of herself at his reference to their first meeting. "You're a wonderful security guard," she said. "And I love you for it. But this is so unexpected."

"Not really. Don't you believe in love at first sight? That's what we have, Tarryn. It just took us a while to realize it. I love you. I've loved you since the first moment I met you in the Rose Garden. What do you say?" he asked, holding the ring up.

She smiled and nodded. "I love you, too, very much. Yes, I'll marry you."

Brock stood and placed the ring on her finger. "What do you know? It fits," he said, chuckling.

She giggled, remembering how he had pretended to be her fiancé early on in their relationship and was having the ring sized to explain its absence on her finger. But she had a real ring now, and it fit perfectly.

He gazed deeply into her eyes. "Mrs. Tarryn Spencer," he said. "I like the sound of that."

"Me, too," she said.

He bent down to kiss her, and she shivered. His warm lips met hers, and she kissed him with all the passion that had built up since she first met him. And she felt something that she hadn't felt for a long time. Safe. She felt safe in her special agent's arms. And for the first time in a long time, even through all of her past relationships, that's where she wanted to stay.

Terri Greening is a creative writer in the Great Lakes region. She enjoys yoga, gardening, nature parks, walking, and biking. She has a B.A. in journalism from Central Michigan University and an M.B.A. from Grand Valley State University.

Other novels by Terri Greening:

The Lady of the Lighthouse

The Copper Isle Ghostslayer

www.ingramcontent.com/pod-product-compliance
Lightning Source LLC
Chambersburg PA
CBHW050740180626
46814CB00002B/840